Songs from the Deep

Also by Kelly Powell

Magic Dark and Strange

Songs
from
the
Deep

Kelly Powell

Margaret K. McElderry Books
New York London Toronto Sydney New Delhi

MARGARET K. McELDERRY BOOKS

An imprint of Simon & Schuster Children's Publishing Division

1230 Avenue of the Americas, New York, New York 10020

MARGARET K. McELDERRY BOOKS is a trademark of Simon & Schuster, Inc.

For information about special discounts for bulk purchases, please contact Simon &
Schuster Special Sales at 1-866-506-1949 or business@simonandschuster.com.

The Simon & Schuster Speakers Bureau can bring authors to your live event.

For more information or to book an event, contact the Simon & Schuster

Speakers Bureau at 1-866-248-3049 or visit our website at www.simonspeakers.com.

Also available in a Margaret K. McElderry Books hardcover edition

Book design by Tom Daly

The text for this book was set in Adobe Caslon Pro.

Manufactured in the United States of America

First Margaret K. McElderry Books paperback edition October 2020

10 9 8 7 6 5 4 3 2 1

The Library of Congress has cataloged the hardcover edition as follows:

Names: Powell, Kelly, 1991– author.

Title: Songs from the deep / Kelly Powell.

Description: New York : Margaret K. McElderry Books, 2019. | Summary:
Seventeen-year-old violinist Moira Alexander joins with an old friend, Jude Osric, in
seeking a killer after the sirens who live near their island are falsely accused of murder.

Identifiers: LCCN 2019005236 (print) | ISBN 9781534438071 (hardback) |
ISBN 9781534438088 (eBook) | ISBN 9781534438095 (pbk)

Subjects: | CYAC: Murder—Fiction. | Sirens (Mythology)—Fiction. |
Musicians—Fiction. | Violin—Fiction. | Friendship—Fiction. |
Mystery and detective stories.

Classification: LCC PZ7.1.P692 Son 2019 (print) | DDC [Fic]—dc23

LC record available at https://lccn.loc.gov/2019005236

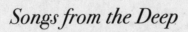

Songs from the Deep

CHAPTER ONE

THERE ARE THREE SIRENS on the beach today.

I watch them, rosining my bow slowly as I do. The tide comes in, restless and white-capped, pushing at the shoreline. The cliff grass pricks at the thin cotton of my dress as I stand, keeping my eyes trained on the beach below.

They are distant and impassive, marble statues staring out to sea.

Movement is rarely what catches their attention. Sound is how they hunt, what they wait for. Any noise is tenfold more interesting to them than a wave of fingers or shuffle of feet.

I slide my bow across the violin in an open note. The song becomes slower, softer, as I dip into a lower pitch. When I quicken my pace, the violin's sound vibrates through the air, and I feel it humming in my chest, in the soles of my feet. The music is sharp against the noonday stillness, the only sound in my ears.

It is a cool afternoon at that. My breath mists in front of me, my fingers holding stiff to the bow's polished wood. The sirens do not seem to mind the chill. They are folded between a bramble of large rocks, their backs to me—long stretches of pale white skin, dark tangled hair—and one of them leans over, resting her head upon the shoulder of another.

I play by the cliff's edge, allowing music to tumble over rocks and into sea. It's the closest I dare play to the beach, as the melodies may well turn siren ears and eyes in my direction. Nothing wrong with a bit of danger though, when it polishes the notes. I play best on days like this, with the sirens near, before the unending sea.

Perhaps they talk to one another. Yet it's the songs they sing that lure anyone within earshot and without protection. I've seen those rescued taken to the hospital: bloodied from teeth and claws, delirious, all too keen to return to the sea, to the creatures in the depths below. Terrible business for the tourists in the end, and still they come. Every summer. For the scenery or for the sirens, perhaps hoping this year shall be the year when Twillengyle Council finally lifts the ban on siren hunting.

That is the year I dread.

I curl my fingers tighter around the violin to get some life back in them. A few minutes more and I'll pack up. Feels lonely, playing for only three sirens, when I've seen groups of ten or fifteen together on the sand at one time. The wind picks up, biting at my cheeks until I know they're rosy with cold, and the sea's string of whitecaps blacken the rocks with their spray. I skip from one tune to the next in an attempt to find a rhythm.

Each note flies off on the wind—toward sirens who do not even turn an ear in acknowledgment. I touch bow to strings a little more firmly.

When the music falters, I stop. A breeze catches the hem of my dress, flicking it this way and that, while I place my violin into its case. It's a battered little thing, black leather faded and scuffed. My father gave it to me years ago, with my initials stamped along the side.

> *M. A.*
>
> *The music of my heart.*

Not a very good turn of phrase, as his heart ceased beating only two weeks after. *Or not very good music*, I think, loosening the hair of my bow before setting it inside.

I gather up the violin case and take one last glance down the cliff. The sirens have barely moved. One has twisted around slightly, so I can see the knife edge of her cheekbone. Not enough to see her eyes properly. Before, I have—at the right angle and with enough light—and their wide, dark eyes seem to mirror the deepest parts of the sea.

It was my father who first brought me to them, taught me how to clean salt from violin strings, where to watch sirens without being seen, how to protect myself with cold iron and charms. He showed me an island smeared in blood, and I fell in love with it.

On those days, when the sky was still pink with dawn, my father told me the island's folktales. He brought me to the beach and spoke of the creatures the sea sheltered, of the magic that dwelt on Twillengyle's shores. And when the moon shone overhead, full and bright as a coin, ghost stories were told—the souls of those killed by sirens said to wander the cliffs evermore.

But today is windblown and damp, fog misting around me,

clinging to my dress. These are the days for ballads and sorrow, remembrances of widows standing in my place, waiting on the cliffs, not knowing their husbands had already been swept out to sea. The beach gives way to rocks that rise above the waves like chipped grave markers. It's scenery the tourists adore: dark-green swaths of moss and red-brown grass, the sheer face of the crag stained salt white.

I don't know whether the sirens watch me as I leave, or if the cliff's edge holds a pull of its own. Whichever way, my heart feels leaden as I head for home.

But I have long realized a piece of it will always belong to the sea.

CHAPTER TWO

"THE SALT WATER will ruin it."

My mother shuffles around our tiny kitchen, making cakes, and still finds time to pause to lecture me. Often when she begins to repeat herself, I pay her no mind—but the changing weather puts me in an argumentative spirit.

"Evidently not, as it still sings."

She looks at me, disapproving that I've spoken out of turn. The lamplight makes her look more weary than usual. Or rather, my presence has. Her hands are covered in flour, and whatever storm is brewing outside, the smell of baking suffocates it inside. The air is made sickly sweet by the scent of honey and melted butter left to congeal in one of the bowls on the counter. Opening the stove, my mother scrapes another full pan across the grills, before saying,

"Then it would make no difference for you to play at the dance hall."

It would make a world of difference. As she well knows.

"I like playing by the cliff."

"I would much prefer you didn't, Moira. It's dangerous. Not to mention foolish besides." She gives a small shake of her head. "Playing music for sirens—even your father wasn't so senseless."

The cunning retort I was set to offer sticks in my throat. Playing for the sirens fills a dark and hollow yearning, a cavernous desire I've no other way to appease.

My mother's eyes fix on the stove, shining with the knowledge that she has said something insightful. My gaze shifts to the one window in the room. Its lace curtains are drawn back, showing rain clouds heavy on the horizon. The gale will turn the island bleak and wild, the light already failing as darkness settles over us like a nightmare cloak.

My mother says, "We'll need to prepare for the storm tonight."

I don't reply. Her words, like needle and thread, have stitched my lips shut. I stand there, feeling as foolish as she called me, as proud as I know myself to be, until an adequate amount of time has passed to leave with my dignity still intact. I walk down the hall to my bedroom, and in the small space, my mother's words liken to an echo. They scratch themselves into the desk chair, curl against the floral wallpaper, slip between the pages of my books. *Even your father wasn't so senseless.* The walls seem to press close, almost to the point of suffocation, and I need to get out—if only for a little while. I button my coat, take hold of my violin case. Then I'm unlocking my window latch and climbing over the paint-flecked ledge.

As soon as I step away from the overhang, the first drops of rain land in my hair. I start back in the direction of the cliffs, the heels of my boots sinking into the mud as though the island wishes to claim them for itself.

My father used to carry me along this path—when I was little and ankle deep in puddles—on his shoulders where I had a clear view of the horizon, sea and sky coming together to form a blurred line in the distance. My mother was softer then as well. I'd wave a clumsy goodbye toward the house with my handkerchief, while she stood by the door, sending kisses into the air as we set off.

Admiration of the island, of the dangers it held, was always there in my father's stories.

Twillengyle is a place to be embraced with one arm, with a dagger ready in the other hand. To be charmed by its magic is not the same as becoming its fool, Moira. Remember that.

As I turn the final corner, the pathway opens up to the great expanse of the moors. To my left is the lighthouse, a blue-and-white tower clinging to the rocks, and the keeper's cottage attached to it, a modest structure of clapboard siding. The beacon light above circles in a bright arc out to sea, making the sky appear darker overhead. The wind brings with it the clean, cold tang of salt water. My fingers become numb around the handle of my violin case, and it'd be rather pointless to take it out now. I can't even separate the music in my mind from the oncoming gale.

It's not a waste though. I needed the walk more than the music, I think. Fresh air to clear my head. From above, I hear the first rumblings of thunder, and I wonder where the sirens have sheltered, whether they'll take to the storm-ravaged beach come morning. Dawn will be quiet, pale and colorless, after a night streaked with thunder and lightning. September has turned cruel quickly, leaves already beginning to change color and litter the ground.

As I near the cliff's edge, I catch movement in the corner of my eye. Coming up the path from the beach is Jude Osric, his shoulders hunched against the wind, eyes cast down. His red-brown curls poke out beneath his cloth cap, windblown and tangled. I look to the lighthouse before returning my attention to him. Jude is its sole keeper, and at nineteen, he is two years my elder. Before I can decide whether to call out or take off into the shadows, he glances in my direction. "Moira," he says, breathless.

I jam my free hand into the pocket of my coat. Wind howls across the moors, and I narrow my eyes against it. "Shouldn't you be up at the light?"

He makes his way toward me. As he does, I realize Jude looks truly terrified. His eyes are shiny and rimmed with red, his already pale face drained of color.

"You can't be here," he says. "Moira, listen, you need to go *right now.*"

This is quite the opposite thing to tell me if he has any real hope of making me leave. I grab hold of his coat sleeve, and for a moment I see the little boy I used to play with, the one who ran after me on the moors.

"Jude." I swallow hard. "What is it?"

He closes his eyes. Bowing his head, he whispers, so quiet it almost gets lost in the wind: "There's a body." He looks up and gestures back toward the path, hand trembling. "Sirens—the sirens must've . . ."

I try to recall if anyone I know planned to go down to the beach today. I think of the fishermen at the harbor, their families . . .

My fingers dig into the sleeve of Jude's coat. "Who is it?"

"I think it's Connor," he says. "Connor Sheahan."

I look out at the cliff's edge. Dread settles deep inside me, clawing its way from the inside out, pulling me into the black. It can't be Connor—I saw Connor just last week. I was teaching him to play his first reel.

He was twelve years old.

"I'm sorry," Jude continues. "I know—I know you were tutoring him."

I meet his gaze. "Show me."

Jude stares as though I've gone mad. "What?"

"I want to see the body." I grab his collar, yanking him close. "Where is he?"

"I really don't think that's wise, Moira. We need to tell the police. I'll wire them from the watch room and . . ."

Adrenaline shoots through my veins like quicksilver. Before Jude can finish his sentence, I tear away from him.

"Wait—*Moira!*"

Jude makes to stop me, but I'm already racing for the pathway. Below the crag, I pinpoint what I'm looking for fast enough. A smear of red—a color that has no place among the dark waters and wet sand. It's a thin ribbon I track along the beach, a crimson that mixes with the edge of the sea in wavering bands. Then I see a patch of black hair, a white shirt soaked through, pale skin cut and bleeding. The body lies near the path, half buried in blood-drenched sand.

My feet slow as I approach. The smell is almost worse than the sight itself. A harsh, metallic odor burns in my nose, fills my throat until I'm close to gagging.

"Oh God."

It's Connor. Connor as he never should've been—left discarded, a deep slash across his neck. The blood is everywhere, a pool of red, staining the tide.

Nothing makes sense.

Behind me, Jude makes a sound quickly covered by a cough. "Moira," he whispers, and it sounds desperate. "Please, Moira, we oughtn't be here."

The words are a plea, but I can't move. I'm frozen in place, my eyes fixed on the boy I once knew, the boy I'd been teaching. Sickness washes over me, making me light-headed, and I dig my nails into my palm to ground myself against it.

I close my eyes. "This was sirens?"

A gust of wind comes to rip the words from the air. I repeat myself and turn to find Jude standing beside me. "Yes," he says. "I believe so."

I shake my head, whether in denial or anger or some combination of the two. "Can't be."

"We need to tell the police," Jude says again.

"Jude, this—this is *wrong*. What was he even doing here? How did he . . . ?"

I look to the boy at our feet. There are things children are taught on this island so they might survive. Connor knew how to listen, how to be careful, to keep still when it was needed.

He'd been a fine student. Sometimes he'd press on the strings too hard, or his posture got lazy—but he was willing to learn and practiced often. He kept track of his mistakes.

Now I'll have his blood on the soles of my boots.

"Sirens wouldn't have left him here," I mutter. "Why didn't they take him out to sea? Why is his neck cut like that? I don't . . ." A lump forms in my throat, and I stop speaking before the weight of everything crushes me.

Jude pinches the bridge of his nose between forefinger and

thumb. I wonder if the memory of his own family has managed to slip into his thoughts.

"Do you not think it at all strange?"

I force the words out, but it isn't the real question I want answered. What I want is to know why Connor was down here in the first place. My heartbeat is rapid as whatever bravery I had leaches into the sand like the blood at our feet.

Jude's too-pale countenance makes it clear he doesn't have much bravery left either. "A strangeness," he says, "I'm sure the police and the *Twillengyle Gazette* will be most concerned with."

I swallow. "Of course," I reply, yet I can't shake off the sense of *wrongness*. I've seen siren deaths before, read about them in the paper, and this isn't like any of them.

Jude doesn't look back as we travel up the cliff, but I do exactly that. I study the crimson stains in the sand, the small and crumpled form of Connor's body. I've no idea what the police will do with him, but I know this is the last time I'll be able to see him as he was. Only then do I turn away and follow in Jude's footsteps to the lighthouse.

The rain and wind pick up, rendering conversation impossible. My violin case bumps against my leg, a small comfort, as I try not to let my mind wander back to the body we've left behind, to the Sheahan family, who'll soon find out their youngest son was taken from them.

The stone path to the keeper's cottage is cracked through, grass and moss softening the edges. We duck under the narrow overhang, and Jude takes a skeleton key from his coat pocket. The door is bright blue, but chipped in places, paint peeling back from the wood. I wonder when he last painted it. He fiddles with the lock, leaning upon the door before twisting the brass knob. We hurry over the threshold, and Jude swings the door closed, shutting out the force of the gale. My ears ring in the sudden silence.

He leads the way through the cottage, past a heavy oak door, and up the winding staircase to the watch room. Most of its small space is occupied by a desk covered in papers, journals, nautical instruments. A map of Twillengyle hangs from one wall, while another has a window overlooking the nearby harbor. There's no bed, but the room looks lived in, like Jude has taken to sleeping at his desk.

He settles into the chair, shifts a stack of documents to reveal a metal instrument fitted with all sorts of dials and screws. Jude touches a hand to the paddle at one end, clicking it to produce a long series of *dah* sounds. Morse code, I realize belatedly.

In a moment his hand is still. "They'll be on their way," he says, looking out the window instead of at me.

"I suppose we need to wait for them?"

He turns back around, and I see something like relief in his expression. "Yes," he says. "I'd like that—you staying here, that is. If you want."

I smile as best I can. "Thank you."

"I'll make tea, shall I?" The way he says it, I can tell he's grasping for some purchase on routine. I nod all the same, and together we go down into the kitchen.

CHAPTER THREE

I'VE BEEN IN THE OSRICS' LIGHTHOUSE many times in my life. I'd come with my father, eager for adventure, listening to tales of shipwrecks in the night. It was only after his death that my visits tapered off. To be back here now, as blood reddens the shoreline below, seems grimly fitting.

In the few years since, the place looks little different. Cracks run through the white walls from salt air and humidity. My father used to say that each crack in the lighthouse held a secret. There are even more cracks now, jagged and spreading like vines. I wonder how many more secrets are hiding in the dark. I wonder if my own are counted among them.

The kitchen is situated on the first floor of the cottage. It's uncluttered and well kept, with a washstand near the window, an oil lamp lit at the table. I take a seat on one of the crooked chairs, setting my violin case on the tabletop. From here, the storm is a low rumble, the steady rain like a distant thread of music. Yet I find myself listing from the present moment like an unbalanced ship—and each time I drift, I'm back on the beach, standing over Connor's body, watching the rain wash his blood into the sea.

Jude stands at the counter, filling the kettle and lighting the stove. He looks more disheveled without his coat and hat. He is a lean figure in the dim, his face tinged pink from the cold, exhaustion darkening his eyes. Since coming down from the watch room, he hasn't said a word. Over the years, I've found Jude predisposed to such behavior. The death of both his parents made him grow up cautious. Though as the kettle boils, he offers me a small smile and says, "I'm afraid I don't remember how you take your tea."

I exhale slowly. "Just black, please."

"Right." He turns to the stove, only to look back a second later. "Moira—"

I interrupt. "I'm sorry you had to be the one to find him."

Jude pauses, lips pressed thin. "Can't be helped, I suppose."

I rub my thumb over the newest scuff on my violin case and push back another image of Connor—smiling at our last lesson, pleased when I complimented him.

This island would eat you alive, if you let it.

Jude pours the kettle's contents into a teapot, steam rising in gray coils before disappearing in the light. He tugs at the cuff of his sweater, staring out at the rain. "I saw you playing on the cliff earlier."

I swallow. My mother's words over the matter still shine slick as tar, coating my thoughts. Jude brings the teapot to the table and continues. "Is that why you haven't been at the hall?"

I haven't played at our local dance hall for two summers now. At the moment the only thing I'm missing is the pay, though my tutoring has done a fair job of shelling out coins to warm my palm. Stiffly I say, "I can play where I like."

Sitting down across from me, Jude looks a touch uncomfortable. "Of course," he says. "I meant no ill by it."

I doubt Jude Osric would wish ill on even his worst enemy. I curl both hands around my steaming teacup and say, "I find it difficult to believe you've attended many dances in my absence."

I mean to be lighthearted, but Jude says, "To quite a few I've been," and sounds almost defensive.

I raise a brow. "I hope you're not waiting on me. I hear Peter and Flint are managing rather poorly."

He ducks his head to stare into his teacup. Silence settles between us, but there's an edge to it, as though we are both skirting around the real topic at hand. Jude's gaze soon returns to the window. Rain lashes the glass, dim light yellowing the sill.

"A bad one tonight," he murmurs. "Storm to drown the sirens."

It's just a saying, an adage as old as the island, but the comment twists my stomach. Connor's death isn't all that's left unsaid between us. Jude is likely too gracious to ask outright, but he must wonder why I've not visited the lighthouse these past four years, why I've ignored every invitation offered. Our interactions have narrowed to greeting each other in town, smiling at one another across the street. We are little more than strangers when we were once the best of friends, and I feel the ache of those lost years now, sitting in his company, as keenly as a missing limb. Jude, I realize, must be worse off. I know our separation is by design, but that design is my own doing. Or, perhaps, undoing. I've kept secrets from him, secrets I'm too cowardly to share, too self-serving to face directly. If he ever found out—

A knock sounds at the door. Jude flinches, sloshing tea onto the table. "That'll be them," he says, adding, "You needn't accompany me," when I move to get up.

I ignore this. Together we head for the entrance, and Jude unlocks the door, pulling it open to reveal two policemen on his doorstep. I recognize them both, though I can't recall the taller one's name. The pair have donned heavy tweed overcoats against the rain, their shoulder capes dark with damp. The shorter man, Inspector Dale, doffs his hat. "Afternoon, Mr. Osric," he says. "Miss Alexander."

"Afternoon," says Jude. "Did you, ah, receive my wire?"

"It's the reason we're standing here," the taller one says. Thackery, I remember. That's his name. "You found the boy on the beach?"

"Yes. I—I saw him from the gallery deck. I was doing observations." Jude swallows. "Do you need me to come along?"

"That's quite all right," says Inspector Dale. "If you'll point us in the right direction, we'll take it from here."

Jude gestures to the cliff's edge as a thin bolt of lightning streaks the sky. "About half a mile down the beach. Near the path."

Dale replaces his hat, touching the brim. "Much obliged. And were you there as well, Miss Alexander?"

"I'm just visiting." Irrespective of seeing Connor, I'm not a witness by any means.

"We'll need a proper statement later, Mr. Osric, you understand," says Thackery.

Jude nods. "Certainly."

The two gentlemen step away from the overhang, trudging off toward the cliff path. Jude closes the door and turns to me. "They'll have it sorted," he says, like I haven't been standing here the whole time. A low echo of thunder rumbles through the lighthouse walls.

"Are you all right?" I ask.

"Are you?" He regards me, expression somber. "Connor—he was your student."

My heart clenches. "Yes," I say quietly.

Jude rakes a hand through his hair. The action only succeeds in making the curls less tidy. He says, "There's not been a siren attack around these parts since last summer."

I bite my lip. Jude's expression is shuttered, his gaze stripped bare. I know he'll be recalling the worst, and more than anything, I wish to spare him from it.

We return to the kitchen and sit down at the table, both of us watching the rain outside, sounding as if the sea herself is pressed against the cottage. I wonder if the beacon light still cuts through the blackness.

"I need to check the lantern room," Jude says, echoing my thoughts.

And as he takes his leave, I look to my violin case. The thought of playing something for him comes to mind unbidden. When we were children, I'd play whatever song I'd learned most recently, and Jude would collect coins for me in his flat cap. It's a memory that sinks into my heart like a hook. I wonder if he even remembers.

By the time he comes back downstairs, I've found a tin of biscuits and eaten three. Jude has soot across his forehead, a pink flush to his cheeks, but he looks better for it, less shaken. I feel he's glad for having something to do.

"All's well?" I ask.

"Well enough." He takes a drink of cold tea, grimacing at the taste. "I really ought to be staying up there, what with this gale, but not—not tonight, I think."

I picture Jude within the glass lookout of the lantern room, performing that solitary vigil, while Connor's body lies on the beach below. It's something he'll have to write up in his logbook, an inked record of the event, as he would a shipwreck or a drowning.

I swallow. "The police are taking a good while."

Jude looks toward the doorway, as if he might find the pair waiting in the hall.

"Considering how he was killed, it's not surprising." I take a breath in the hopes of keeping my voice level. "Sirens leaving him on the beach, slicing him open—I've never seen anything like it."

At that there's another knock on the door. Jude goes to open it, revealing Dale and Thackery standing once more beneath the overhang.

"Mr. Osric," says Inspector Dale, "we've just come to get your statement down."

Detective Thackery glances at me and back to Jude. "If we might speak to you alone."

Jude meets my gaze. I give a small nod. "In the watch room," he says. "Can I get you anything else? Tea?"

"Just the statement, please," Dale says.

Jude nods, brisk, before leading them through the door into the tower.

I've nothing to do while I wait. My fingers trace over the knots on the kitchen table as Connor Sheahan slips into the forefront of my thoughts, and I wonder what would've drawn him to the shore in this sort of weather.

Sirens lure people with music that can make one's ears and nose bleed from the sound. They call their victims to the ocean, dragging them into the depths. They wouldn't leave a boy like waste on the shore. They wouldn't cut his throat. Enchantment is enough to silence anyone. Connor's wounds were clean, sharp, dissimilar from the jagged scrape of teeth and claws.

The sound of a door opening pulls me from my thoughts. Jude appears in the hallway, alongside Dale and Thackery. He says, "Moira," and I wish I could somehow alleviate the sadness clouding his features.

The police give their farewells. Jude begins clearing the table, gathering our cups and mopping up tea. Outside, it's black as pitch, the sky only outlined by the occasional streak of lightning.

"Would you like to spend the night?"

I can't tell whether he asks for my sake or his own. "That's very kind," I say, but the words don't sound as grateful as I feel. I've kept myself from the lighthouse for years, and now that I've broken the spell, I've little desire to return home so soon after.

"I made up the bed in the guest room just this morning."

"Oh." I clasp my hands together. "You had company?"

"My uncle," Jude says shortly.

I raise my eyebrows at that. The last I'd heard of Jude's uncle, he'd boarded a tender ship to help manage the offshore lighthouse around the other side of the island. For a moment I think of asking after him, before deciding otherwise. It's been a long while since there was any fondness between the two—indeed, I find it curious his uncle came to visit at all.

We finish setting the kitchen to rights. Or rather, Jude does, waving off every attempt I make to help. He washes tea stains from the cups, places them side by side in a cabinet, and fetches a candlestick holder, striking a match to light the half-melted candle. I gather my violin case and lean against the wall. I trace a thin crack in the plaster—but it does not whisper its secrets to me.

"Moira?"

I look over. Jude stands at the doorway, waiting for me. He holds the candle aloft, his other hand knotted around the fraying cuff of his wool sweater. Together we head into the hall, and he starts up the stairs to the second floor. I'm about to follow when a dull *thump* echoes from the far end of the cottage. I pause with one foot on the step, eyeing the door, the last before the entrance into the lighthouse.

"That'll be the pipes," says Jude quickly. "They creak something fierce when the weather turns." He takes the stairs two at a time then, and there's nothing for it but to go up after him.

Four bedrooms occupy most of the space on this floor. Jude opens the door to the guest room, letting me pass, and I see it's just as orderly as the rest of the cottage. There's a single bed, a writing desk, and a mirror adjacent to a lace-curtained window overlooking the cliff. Rain strikes the blackened glass in an unremitting patter.

Lonely. If feelings may be used in that way, that is how the room appears. A deep-seated loneliness that has forgotten any other state.

Jude lights an oil lamp left on the bedside table. After, he runs a quick finger over the table's surface, nervously wiping the dust off on his trousers as he straightens up. "I do hope it's all right," he says, glancing in my direction. Though no sooner have I met his gaze than his brown eyes cut away from mine, looking black as midnight in the low light.

"It's fine," I say, voice curt. There was a time when softening my words didn't present such a challenge. "Thank you."

Jude smiles, close-lipped. He still looks as tired and nervous as before, but he stops destroying the cuff of his sweater, so that's something. "Right," he says. "Well, good night, then."

"Good night, Jude."

I close the door in his wake, listening as he continues farther down the hall to his own room. Not long after, there's the soft click of a door opening, then silence. Shutting my eyes, I take a breath, my insides coiled tight in a way that cannot be undone by music.

I wander over to sit on the bed. The sheets are tucked into the mattress in hospital corners, white and neatly pressed. The tidiness is made disconcerting by the storm's darkness, by the thought of blood staining the shoreline below.

In past times, the lighthouse had been a home. Old books were left open on the counter, children's toys on the steps. These walls had echoed with my father's laugh; the floorboards knew his footsteps. He and Llyr Osric, Jude's father, would sit for hours in the kitchen, studying charts and old bound books I could not yet read.

Rowan sticks were hung above the kitchen window, sea-pink flowers in a vase on the sill. Now it appears Jude Osric is not at all concerned about keeping good luck. The herbs he has are common ones, the rooms smelling only of salt air and wood smoke and floor polish.

Hospital corners—I tug the sheets back and they come free. I set down my coat at the foot of the bed, my violin case on the floor just below. Often, when a storm like this batters the cliffs, I'll wake during the night to play something low and soft at the window. Not tonight, I think. However much he likes my playing,

I don't believe Jude Osric, with his quiet disposition, would look favorably on violin music conducted at this hour.

I'm staring up at the cracked white ceiling when my eyes begin to slip closed. The events of this afternoon swirl around me like a fog: Jude walking along the cliff, shoulders hunched against the rain; dread like a weight in my stomach, boots slipping on mud as I hurried down to the beach; Connor lying still and cold, buried in wet sand and blood. A shiver creeps over my spine.

Sleep does not come easy. Each crack of thunder booms like a drum. I hear the wind whistling through the night and imagine it sweeping through the moors as a living creature—a wolf howling at the moon.

I've no idea of the time; perhaps it's near morning already. Perhaps my mother is worried sick over my whereabouts, but that's a slim possibility. She may well pretend, but that's all it would be: a feigned sort of affection, attempting to play the part of concerned mother. I'm careful to tuck that thought into memory as I turn over on the bed; could be good fodder for a row.

And as I fall farther into sleep, there are footsteps, Jude's familiar tread on the stairs, and I'm almost certain I hear him talking.

Murmured whispers coming from the room below.

CHAPTER FOUR

SUNLIGHT PAINTS RED ACROSS my closed eyelids. I open them—blinking at white sheets, dust motes drifting above the floorboards—feeling lost and bewildered until my mind snaps to waking as well. I remember the storm and Jude Osric, a bloodstained beach and Connor left to the mercy of the elements.

My heart feels heavy with a grief I've no real claim to.

I turn over the affairs of last night once more before getting up out of bed. The sheets are a twisted mess, and I try to put them in some semblance of order. I don't have Jude's talent for folding something within an inch of its life, but I feel it's a good attempt. Outside, pink tints the early-morning sky. The window's angle makes it difficult to gauge signs of the storm's passing, but I know the marks it will have yielded—grass flattened by wind, uneven shifts of sand on the beach, clumps of seaweed strewn about, cliff sides gritty with salt.

There will be no sirens, not so soon after such a tempest. I imagine them sheltering in the rocky crevices, in the darkest places of the sea. Turning back to the bed, I fetch my things and consider the possibility of Jude being awake at this hour. Quite likely, as I find a note written in his hand slipped beneath the door's edge.

> Morning, Moira.
> You'll find me in the lantern room or up on the gallery deck.
>   —J

I fold the note with care, tucking it into the safety of my coat pocket.

At the washstand on the first floor, I splash my face with cold water, pin my brown hair into a tidy chignon, and wrinkle my nose at the mud-spattered hem of my dress. My long coat fares even worse, but I shrug it on nonetheless.

Making my way toward the tower, I pause near the end of the hall. I stare at the closed door of the last room, beyond which I heard voices in the night. It's a storeroom, I think, or it used to be, before the death of Jude's parents. I'm unsure of what he could be keeping in here now. I try the knob and find it locked. When I put my ear to the wood, I'm met with only silence.

Perhaps it's nothing. The cottage is an old structure, after all, afflicted by frequent creaks and groans, as Jude said. I turn away, open the oak door, and head up the iron stairwell that spirals up, up, up, along the sides of the lighthouse. When I reach the gallery deck, a rush of cold air cuts through my coat.

Yet the view is well worth the chill. A panorama of sea and sky and sunlight greets me, the cliff below a sharp black drop, bestowing a scattering of rocks to the sea. The sight is wondrous in a way that makes me want to play something entirely new just for this moment and never again. I grip the rusted railing and feel like shouting for the sake of it, but I swallow the feeling when my eyes find Jude Osric.

He leans back fast asleep in his chair. Without his cap, his curls tangle in the wind, ash and oil staining his hands. He must've already visited the lantern room. I take a step toward him and he starts awake, his eyes glassy and unseeing. Half a second later, recognition sets in. Jude blinks, rubs a hand over his face, and gets soot in one eyebrow. He says, "I didn't mean to fall asleep."

"I wouldn't think so."

Reaching into his coat, he pulls out a pocket watch. The glass over the clock face is scratched and clouded with age, but the hands still keep time. It's just gone seven o'clock. Jude brushes his thumb over the face, and I turn my gaze on him.

"You look filthy."

He yawns and says, "Thank you," so he might still be half-asleep. It's not hard to guess he's been up all night, seeing how bloodshot his eyes are. Though whether it was because of his duties as keeper or by choice alone is another matter.

I want to ask after his night terrors. Seeing Connor down on the beach, it would be of little surprise if Jude's nightmares return full force. What actually comes out of my mouth, however, is quite another thing. "I just wanted to say goodbye,"

I tell him. "Thank you again for letting me spend the night. It was more than generous of you."

That seems to wake him up. "You're leaving already?"

"I'm sure I've kept you long enough."

"Not at all." He leans forward, holding my gaze. "Really, Moira, having you—having someone here—it's a welcome change of pace." His eyes look honest as he says it. "At least stay for breakfast."

My guilt, deep-rooted as it is, branches in two directions. On one dark bough, I curse my efforts to drain our friendship bloodless, when neither of us desired the ax. On the other, I find myself reluctant to take advantage of Jude's hospitality, fully aware he wouldn't want me at his table if he knew what truths I've buried.

"All right," I say. "Tea would be lovely."

God, I am such a wretched creature.

Jude's smile lights up his whole face. He wipes his palms on his trouser knees and gets to his feet, running a hand through his hair. It hurts to think of him spending night after night in this tower without another soul, taking meals and working the light with only himself to talk to.

What befell the Osrics is common knowledge on the island. It's a history most prefer to forget, violent and horrifying in its suddenness. Seven summers ago, Llyr Osric went out on his boat, accompanied by Jude's mother and older sister. Jude was left behind to watch the lighthouse—but ended up watching sirens drag his family into the sea.

Pieces of the boat washed ashore the following day, cracked and splintered, the bodies found later, just as broken. Jude's uncle manned the lighthouse for a time, but Jude now manages on his own.

I watch him prepare breakfast in the sunlit kitchen. He has changed and washed up for the day, his shirtsleeves pushed to his elbows as he digs out bread from a yellow bread bin and sets the kettle to boil. I breathe in the smell of wood smoke from the stove, the warm, floral fragrance of dry tea leaves. It's worlds away from the wickedness of last night, yet I can't help but notice the repetition. My thoughts wheel back to the whispers I heard in the dark, and I ask him, "Who were you talking to last night? Did the police come back?"

Jude turns to meet my scrutiny. "I wasn't talking to anyone."

"I heard something—like voices. It was coming from that storeroom."

Uncertainty sparks deep in his bright eyes. He laughs, high and light, so unlike his normal laugh it gives me pause. "I think you might've been dreaming, Moira." The kettle sings for his attention, and he makes a fuss over taking it off the burner.

He carries the teapot to the table, sitting in the chair across from me. I stare at the coils of heat, thinking. It sounds like I'm not the only one with secrets, but as I'm in no mood to turn out my own, it's only fair to let Jude fold his away.

His eyes shift to where my violin case rests near my elbow. "Will you be playing out on the cliff again?"

"Why? Do you wish to come along?"

I want to bite back the words the moment they pass my lips.

Jude looks taken aback by the question. He drops his eyes to the table and presses his knuckles to his mouth. I imagine his thoughts, like mine, have circled back around to Connor Sheahan.

The rest of the Sheahan family must know by now. They'll be grieving, cursing the sirens for their loss, cursing the entire island perhaps. In the wake of Connor's death, people might well be arguing for revocation of the hunting ban before the month is out.

Jude says, "I'd love to, Moira."

His sincerity is almost too much to bear. He takes up the teapot, pouring tea into my cup, and I do my best to ignore the lump at the back of my throat.

When we journey out onto the moors, we head for the cliff's edge. A quick glimpse over the crag confirms a beach empty of sirens—leaving Jude as my sole audience. He follows my gaze and turns back, offering up a smile. "None of the sirens."

Well, I can't blame him for being happy because of it. Especially after last night. Sirens are the cause of many wounds in Twillengyle, and few of them are deeper than Jude Osric's. "The storm," I mutter, certain he can draw his own conclusions.

"Where are we going?"

A good question. It doesn't make much difference, really, without the sirens as my compass. Moor grass borders the entire island, a vast sweep of red and green falling away to dark rock and sand.

On impulse, I stop. "Here."

He watches as I kneel, releasing the clasps on my case. I hold the violin gently in my lap, checking its strings before loosening the bow.

"Do you think you'll ever go back to playing at the dances?"

"Heartsick without my music, are you?"

I glance up at him, and he doesn't look away. Slipping his hands into his trouser pockets, he says, "I've missed it quite a lot, yes," and I have the distinct feeling we are no longer talking about music.

Still, there is no part of me that yearns to return to the dance hall. After last time, I swore I wouldn't. Let Peter and Flint manage the sets; let them deal with the swarms of tourists—I won't lift a finger to help.

Standing up, I tuck the violin under my chin. I touch bow to strings in the opening chords of "Over the Moor and Heather," closing my eyes in concentration, my fingers firm against the strings.

The song shifts, growing and changing out of the chorus, until it's no longer "Over the Moor," but the murmur of waves against the shore, cold wind at my fingertips, cliff grass beneath my feet. The music is in my breath and sings through my blood. I near the end and everything in me is still as I slide my bow across the strings in one long note. I exhale, open my eyes, and bring the violin to rest at my side.

I look up to find Jude standing as he was, albeit a little slack-jawed. It seems to take him a moment to realize I've stopped playing. "Moira," he says, and his voice does not sound like his own.

I grin at him. "Liked it, did you?"

He rubs the back of his neck. "It was lovely."

The words make me feel warm and agreeable. I'm reminded once more of when we were children, when I played music on the moors with the wind and the sea and Jude Osric for company. These past few years have put a distance between us that was never there before. We used to explore the tide pools together, run around barefoot, take up sticks in imaginary sword fights. Jude was loud and lively and quick to grab my hand. *Come, Moira, I need to show you something* . . .

Now he considers the horizon, solemn. "I ought to get going," he says in a mournful tone.

"Yes." I shift my grip on the neck of my violin. The cold has turned my fingers stiff. "If the police do come back . . ."

Jude smiles. "I'll let you know."

He starts back toward the lighthouse, and I look along the beach to the patch of sand where Connor was found. Nothing remains of the incident, the shore washed clean.

I still think it's peculiar that sirens left him there. Closing my eyes, I call up the memory of Connor as I last saw him. The slice across his neck was knife-sharp, and it's quite possible sirens were not the ones to take his life. After all, there are plenty of other ways to die.

It's quite possible he was murdered.

CHAPTER FIVE

It turns out I do not need Jude Osric as my informant in police matters. I find what I'm looking for in the next morning's *Gazette*, typed neatly into a narrow column.

> *A SAD TALE.*—*Connor Sheahan, aged twelve, was attacked and killed by sirens the day before last, on Dunmore Beach, as confirmed by police. Funeral services will be performed by Father Teague at St. Cecilia's churchyard this evening at five o'clock.*

Scowling, I toss the paper back onto our kitchen table. The more I thought about this yesterday, the more convinced I became that sirens weren't responsible. Surely it can't be that difficult to ascertain the true cause of death. The police ought to be looking for evidence of Connor's killer this very instant.

Murder. It has to be.

My mother—sitting across from me—looks up to study my face. "Don't let it wind you up, Moira."

The words irritate me to an extent. I don't like the idea of my expressions being so easily read. "I'm not wound up."

"Yes, you are," she replies. "And perhaps you wouldn't be if you weren't looking at the sirens through rose-colored glasses all the time."

I press my lips together, staring down into my teacup. Whatever fondness I have for the sirens has nothing to do with this. This is ignorance in its highest form.

I look back at the *Twillengyle Gazette*, taking the page and folding it up into smaller and smaller sections. The words "killed by sirens" fill my mind, black as the printer's ink. Connor Sheahan's death had been printed like a well-worn formality, fit into a corner of the page. A local boy—the son of a fisherman no less—would know better than to wander so close to the shore without iron. Connor knew the hazards. The storm alone should've kept him away from the beach.

Clenching my jaw, I slip the article into my dress pocket. Perhaps they're trying to keep murder out of the papers— wouldn't want to scare off the tourists. The danger of sirens is one thing, but the idea of human violence? Best swept under the carpet with no one the wiser. Perhaps Twillengyle Council hopes ignorance will lead to bliss.

My silent rage is jarred as my mother scrapes back her chair. She crosses over to the counter, gathering two wicker baskets in her arms. They're filled with the cakes she baked earlier, each wrapped tidily in cloth, ready to be sold at the market in Dunmore. When she drops one of the baskets in front of me, I give her a dark look.

"Take it, Moira," she says. "I won't have you sitting around here being morbid. You can help me at the stall today."

"I'd rather not."

"It wasn't a suggestion, dear." She touches her fingertips to the closed basket. "You spent all night at that lighthouse the other day. It's time you did a few errands."

"Jude needed me there," I press. "The police . . ."

She doesn't wait for the rest of the excuse but goes to stand in the entryway. I grit my teeth, snatch up the basket, and follow.

With her hand on the doorknob, she says, "It was good of you to visit Mr. Osric. It's a terrible affair, Moira, but you should know better than to go off in a storm like that. What was I supposed to think happened to you?"

"I can take care of myself."

My mother's expression is pinched—because she knows it's true. Pity the same couldn't be said for Connor Sheahan. *Terrible affair* indeed.

She opens the door, and I duck my head as I step out onto the walkway. My thoughts are crowded with awful things, my fingers curled around a wicker handle rather than the worn leather of my violin case. Connor's curt obituary burns in my pocket. It's a counterfeit tale, the easiest to tell because everyone already believes it.

I will prove them all wrong.

Dunmore is one of two towns on the island, on the east side, with the other, Lochlan, located to the southwest. They are small, concentrated places from which the houses of Twillengyle circle around and scatter out toward the coast. Lochlan is the busier of the two, with a harbor that parallels the mainland. Dunmore is nearer to the coast and its cluttered appearance is something tourists would call quaint and the townsfolk would call shameful. In the summer, its streets are crowded with tourists having travel-worn clothes repaired at the tailor's and gathering outside the dance hall in the evenings. It feels exhausting just to look at them.

With autumn leaves littering the cobbles, Dunmore is empty of everyone but the locals I know by face, if not all by name. I walk alongside my mother through the winding streets, stopping every so often to chat with this person or that.

Old women with pearl earrings pat my cheek, tell me how they've missed hearing my violin; won't I come play at the hall this weekend? I smile, close-lipped, and bear it, making hollow promises through gritted teeth.

Soon enough a pupil of mine will play finely at the hall. I clutch my basket tighter, remembering how I'd once thought Connor might fill my place, and my stomach pinches at the realization that I'll have to find someone to fill his spot instead. Without him I'm down to but a handful of students.

We're next snagged by my mother's friends. They call out to her—*how are you, Lenore? I see you've Moira lending a hand today*—and become benevolent shadows as they follow us to the market that curves along the main road. The air here is filled with the smell of fresh fish and salted butter. Stalls line both sides of the street, selling everything from trinkets and fishing tackle to baked goods and protection charms. Our own stall is slight and exposed, a plain cloth arranged over the counter. I smooth down the fabric and set my basket atop it.

I've already heard half a dozen whispers of Connor's name. Rumors and curiosities alike.

What was he even doing down there?

A good family, but they've always been soft on those boys, you see.

Without any iron, it's bound to happen.

I feel nauseous as I handle coins and pass over cakes. Any mention of the Sheahans cuts into me like wire, while every muttered oath for the sirens turns my stomach. Tourist deaths are to be expected, their blood darkening Twillengyle waters almost every summer. The death of an islander is different. When the sirens take one of our own, it leaves people shaky and nervous, spitting curses as we are reminded once more how closely we flirt with mortality.

There must be some way to set the police straight. If I can lay out enough evidence, they'll have to admit sirens didn't play a factor in Connor's death. I straighten the assortment of cakes in front of me, biting my lip. The cool air nips at my fingers, but it helps numb my anger as well. I wonder if Jude has seen this morning's article, what he thinks of the shoddy police work.

When I look up from the stall, I see the boy in question crossing the street toward me. He looks very fine in his town clothes: his wool sack coat buttoned at the top, his matching brown waistcoat, and dark trousers. He smiles, doffing his cap. "Good morning, Moira. I didn't think you'd be at market today."

"Nor did I." I glance over at my mother—occupied with a customer—before returning my attention to Jude. "What are you doing here?"

"Just wanted to say hello." He kneads his cap, a flush rising in his cheeks. "I've some things to get at the hardware shop."

"Have you read the paper yet?"

A crease appears between his brows. "I have," he says. "What of it?"

I press my palms flat against the counter. Anger returns in a wave, rolling through me like the nausea I felt moments ago. "Sirens didn't kill Connor Sheahan."

Jude frowns. He says, "Of course they did."

"No, Jude. Think on it." I lower my voice. "Sirens wouldn't have cut his throat so clean. They wouldn't have left him on the beach."

He stares at me, lips parted. "I don't understand," he says softly.

"I think—" I start, but cut myself off as my mother comes to stand at my elbow.

Glancing between the two of us, she smiles at Jude. "Hello there, Mr. Osric."

"Morning, Mrs. Alexander." His eyes slide away from mine to meet hers. "How are you today?"

"Fine, thank you. I'm much obliged to you—giving Moira a place to stay in that storm the other night."

"Oh." Jude's earlier blush returns in an instant. "It was no trouble at all, ma'am. I was glad of the company." He swallows visibly, looks to me, and adds, "I wish only that it were under better circumstances."

I drop my gaze to the countertop. Jude sounds wistful, kind, but the words drive through me like a hot poker. My mother clucks her tongue in sympathy, pushing one of her cakes into his hand. When he tries to pay for it, she waves him off, and I fume silently at the whole exchange. My mother can be wonderful at public niceties when she chooses.

I tell her, "Jude was on his way to the hardware shop. May I go with him?"

She runs her fingers through her hair, seeming to consider the idea. "Very well," she says. "But be back within the hour, Moira. I need you here."

She doesn't, really. Most days she manages selling pastries on her own. She only wants to keep me from doing anything useful with my time. I slip out from behind the counter, joining Jude on the cracked sidewalk.

Around the corner, I pull him to a stop. He looks back at me, and his eyes are troubled, nearly black. I take note of the dark circles beneath them, pressed into his skin like bruises. Keeping my voice quiet, I say, "I think someone murdered him, Jude. I think someone led him down to the sand and took a knife to him."

Jude casts his eyes heavenward. "You're not making any sense."

"I'm making *perfect* sense."

He lets out a little off-key laugh and looks in the direction of the street. "Someone murdered him. Right. Yes. Whatever were the police thinking? Of course he was—"

I give his sleeve a sharp tug, lifting my chin. "Are you going to help me or not?"

"Help you?"

I swallow. My resolve crystalizes the longer I hold the image in my mind: Connor lying on the beach, blood seeping from the slash at his throat. "I'm going to find out what happened to him," I say. "I'm going to find the killer."

"Moira . . ."

"Don't *Moira* me, Jude Osric. In fact, forget what I just said.

I'll manage fine on my own." I turn back in the direction of the market, but Jude steps into my path.

"Wait." He raises his hands, palms out. "You can't say something like that and expect me to . . . I mean, you can't really think—"

"Yes," I say. "I do."

Lowering his hands, Jude bites his lip. He ducks his head to study the ground, and I cross my arms, waiting for his answer.

It comes out as a question. "You really believe he was murdered?"

Disquiet makes a home inside my heart. Connor's obituary was written like so many other attacks, but I know—*I know*—it doesn't belong among them.

"He was, Jude. I know it."

His mouth thins, but he nods. "All right," he says, voice quiet. "I'll help."

I sigh in genuine relief. Jude believes me, and it feels like the world will follow. It makes the task ahead seem possible, manageable, whatever the danger.

"Thank you," I say.

Tucking his hands into his pockets, he starts down the cobbles toward the hardware shop on the opposite corner. I keep in step with him, eyeing him as we walk. He looks so tired, so pale. I wonder what it is that keeps him up at night, to put such shadows under his eyes.

I realize it's perhaps ill-advised to enlist his help. I'm in no position to ask anything of Jude Osric. Truly, he would be better off staying away from me altogether. It's selfish, cruel even, but I've not the time nor inclination to seek out anyone else. Jude is one of the few on this island I trust, one of the few I still hold in high regard.

The front windows of the hardware shop are large, clouded panes mirroring our reflections. Jude looks colorless within the glass, and for one vicious moment I want to know what his face looked like when he first found Connor.

Inside, he heads down one of the narrow aisles. I look about the space, at the dusty shelves, the boxes of nails, locks, door hinges. My nose wrinkles at the sharp odor of paint and varnish. Jude picks through the boxes before taking up a small bronze hinge. He inspects it as he says, "This isn't just about Connor, is it?"

I hesitate. "Does it matter?"

"Yes." He nods. "Yes, I think it does. The Sheahans are a good family—they deserve closure." The light in the shop glints off the surface of the hinge, shining copper like the color of Jude's hair.

"And that's what we'll give them," I say.

A pause. He turns the hinge around in his hands, not looking at me. "You care for the sirens, also," he murmurs.

I stare at the shelves. Jude once cared for them, too, but I dare not mention so. That was another Jude, a younger Jude—one who skipped stones alongside me on the beach, who listened to the tales our fathers told with rapt attention. We'd sit on the lighthouse steps together, or take to the gallery deck, looking out to sea, watching for sirens.

Little is known about the sirens beyond the means of keeping them away, but during their lifetimes, Gavin Alexander and Llyr Osric set themselves to the task of learning. It was, by and large, my father's idea. In the same way Jude became fearful of sirens after his father's passing, my father became fascinated after sirens took his own when he was just a boy.

It was his efforts that led to the establishment of the hunting ban ten years ago.

Facing Jude, I say, "I can't watch them be hunted down. I can't. My father—" I stop short, lest the words unravel me. My heart hammers inside my rib cage.

Sunlight flashes across the sea the first time Jude clambers into my father's rowboat. I am eight, he is ten, and he plunks down gracelessly beside me, rocking the boat as he does.

"Steady," says my father. "Unless you fancy going overboard."

Jude grins as if the notion entertains him. "No, sir."

My father rows out until we are quite a ways from shore. It's been a full week since a siren was last spotted around Dunmore, so this trip is likely to indulge us, but I dutifully survey the horizon, gripping an iron charm in a closed fist.

Jude looks back at the island, to his lighthouse perched at the edge. He shifts, turns to me, and lets out a gasp. "There!" he says, jumping to his feet.

"Jude," my father snaps.

But it's too late. The boat tips, unbalancing him. Jude yelps and goes straight over the side. I scramble to peer down into the water, even as my father catches hold of him, hauling him back in. Jude sprawls on the bottom of the boat, coughing and sputtering, soaked to the skin. I pat him soundly on the back, while my father says, "At least you managed to keep your boots on."

Jude laughs, none the worse for wear. "Saw her just past the breakers. She's watching us."

I look up. The siren remains, only a few boat lengths away. Her dark hair is slicked back from her salt-white face, her mouth a thin slash of red. She did not touch Jude. Indeed, she makes no move toward us. I'm fixed in place, breathless at the sight of her.

My grasp on the iron tightens until it cuts into my palm.

When she disappears beneath the waves, I feel pinned to the moment. I replay it like a song, over and over, until it's familiar as a heartbeat.

In the dusty hardware shop, there is little of Jude that reminds me of the boy who went overboard that day. He is silent and still, his head bowed in consternation. "I understand," he says, but I wonder if he truly does.

We find Mr. Bradshaw toward the back of the shop. He wears a heavy knit sweater, his brown hands folded atop the shop counter. He and Jude talk about how dreadful the weather's been lately and that dear poor boy on the beach; his father's a fisherman and works hard, don't know what that family's going through now, and are you all right up at that lighthouse? Yes, sir. Fine, sir.

Mr. Bradshaw looks satisfied with this. He calls Jude "Wick"—an old nickname for lighthouse keepers—and Jude smiles as he passes over a few coins, pleased to go by the same name as his father.

Back outside, Jude pulls his cap on, shadowing his eyes. "How are we to go about this, then?" he asks.

I set my gaze on the street ahead of us. Faded shop awnings cast long shadows across the cobbles, making the way appear more dark and narrow than it really is. Chairs sit next to doors with peeling paint, dried leaves tossed up against the thresholds.

"I'd like to speak with the police first," I say.

Jude nods. "You think they'll listen?"

"It's worth a try."

He puts his hands in his pockets and scuffs his heel against the sidewalk. "Mr. Daugherty always looks like he's got murder in his eyes whenever I'm late with the monthly report. If we're to make a suspect list, I'd jot him down."

I grin despite myself. "You're not the murder victim."

"No, but see here . . . If I ever am, you know just where to start."

"I'll keep that in mind."

Sunlight peeks between the row of shops and marks the street in a patchwork pattern of light and shadow. We head for the market, walking beside each other, and I feel glad in a way I haven't for a long time. I keep the feeling close to my heart, safe and hidden from the world. Like a secret.

CHAPTER SIX

THE EVENING OF CONNOR'S FUNERAL is chilly and damp, everything gray with fog. Grave markers form dark outlines, the taller stone crosses looming out of the mist. Though the churchyard is small, dozens of people have congregated for the service.

I make my way past the gates, into the little field. Beside me on the path is my mother, and together we are cloaked in black. I wear a necklace of jet beads, the same I wore at my father's funeral. He is buried in this churchyard too, and as we pass his grave, I let my gloved fingertips rest on the stone. "Hello, Da."

There are those who believe the nature of this island is so awful, so wicked, sometimes it must steal away the best of us to keep its equilibrium. If it didn't, squalor and malice would overwhelm it, and the ocean would rise up, drowning us, in order to cleanse our sins. I think I believe it too. It explains why I am still here and Connor is not. Why my father is not.

I have countless memories intertwined with this churchyard, and none of them are good. They are thick with sadness, muddled in grief. I catch the familiar scent of salt water and brine, but I've never felt farther from the cliffs, from the sirens who glide through our waters, taking shelter between jagged rocks.

As we reach the gathering of mourners, I search the dark suits and bowed heads for Jude Osric, but I can't find him. Instead, I see the remaining members of the Sheahan family, standing at the mouth of Connor's open grave. His coffin has already been lowered, out of view, tucked into the earth, closer now with his ancestors than any of us. It makes my heart ache, being here, where I am forced to remember all my past sorrows. Knowing this will not be the last funeral I attend.

You had so many songs yet to play, Connor.

I would have taught you all of them.

My mother tries to place a hand on my shoulder, to whisper in my ear, but I shrug her off. I want silence, for the ground to swallow me. I study the faces of those gathered, wondering if the murderer has come to see the consequences of their handiwork. To my left, a young girl with dark ribbons in her hair, hands clasped, whispers to herself. Whether it's a prayer or a blessing, I can't tell.

By the grave, the Sheahans take turns kneeling, tossing handfuls of salt down onto Connor's coffin. Another image pulls at my mind—of a younger Moira, dropping salt into her father's grave. I can almost feel the grit on my palm.

Father Teague brings the service to an end, and the tide of

funeral-goers begins to shift. Most depart once he's finished, resuming their lives, the death of Connor Sheahan a cautionary tale to tell their own children. Some stay, offering condolences, asking if there's anything they can do.

I edge closer, catching the eye of Mrs. Sheahan. She tugs me into a fierce embrace, and I try to return it the best I can. "Oh, Moira," she says.

With her arms still wrapped around me, I say, "I'm so sorry, Mrs. Sheahan." My voice comes out soft, surprisingly hoarse. I step back and clear my throat. "He was a good student."

She wipes at the tear stains on her cheeks, but her eyes have dried. I recognize the look of someone who's already cried to the point of exhaustion—it's an activity I'm well versed in. "Thank you, dear."

My mother joins us, saying, "It was a lovely service," and I watch the two of them embrace as well. They murmur to each other, quiet and sad; a mother who's lost a son, a wife who's lost a husband. Both circumstances far from unique on Twillengyle.

I look back in the direction of my father's grave. *I miss you, Da. God, I miss you, I miss—*

"Moira."

I turn at the sound of my mother's voice. She holds out her hand, beckoning me.

I am wound tight enough to shatter.

"Come along," she says.

We walk away from the churchyard, soon on the trail back home. Houses grow from the moor grass in uneven rows, made up of brightly colored siding. Laundry hangs from several clotheslines: white sheets, frayed work trousers, floral-printed dresses. A trio of little girls plays in a wilted garden. One of them stands in the center—singing a melancholy tune and biting back a smile—while the other two inch toward her, closer, closer, until the girl stops singing. They scatter with gleeful screeches as the singer springs into action, trying to catch them.

I know it, the siren game. Jude and I used to play it out on the cliffs. We worked valiantly to convince his older sister to be the siren.

Emmeline Osric was a lovely singer.

"I didn't notice Mr. Osric at the funeral," says my mother.

I drop my gaze to the path. "He wouldn't miss it."

She says, "Your father and Llyr Osric were always close," as if I weren't already aware of the fact.

"Yes, I remember."

"And I remember it's been quite some time since you went visiting the lighthouse. You mustn't keep him from his job, Moira."

"I'm not." Kicking a pebble ahead of me, I add, "He gets lonely is all."

And it feels better having Jude Osric by my side again. We'll solve Connor's murder together—bring real closure to the Sheahans, keep the sirens safe.

We'll be unstoppable.

That night I write *Connor Sheahan* on a blank sheet of paper.

Downstairs, I hear my mother cleaning. Cabinet doors squeak open and shut and glasses clink together. Each small sound cracks through my concentration like a shot. I hold my pen a little tighter, pressing down, and ink blots the page. I watch, unfocused, as the liquid blackness spreads, gleaming under the light of my lamp.

I write *knife*, adding a question mark and circling it.

It's little to go on. Plenty of people on this island know their way around a blade, myself included. Jude Osric included. Fishermen, dock workers, butchers. I set my fingertips to my temples and close my eyes.

There was blood in the water, pooled around Connor's body in the dark. Had someone forced him down to the beach? Someone he knew, someone he trusted?

My father's hand holds tight to my own. It hurts my fingers a little, but I don't say anything. I stare into his eyes, unblinking. They are blue, dark blue like mine, like the ocean at twilight. Today, he says, we'll go down to the beach, to watch the sirens come ashore. Do you trust me, Moira? Do you trust me?

Brushing the memory aside, I write *suspects* near the bottom half of the page.

Connor must've been murdered just before the storm. It was perfect timing, the harbor emptying out as everyone headed home. The killer could've discarded the body at sea with no one the wiser.

Did they want him found? Did they realize the police would lay blame on the sirens?

If that's the case, they must hate them well enough to frame them.

Below *suspects*, I write *Jude Osric*.

But I've hardly finished before I'm crossing it out. An ill sense of dread floods through me, leaching into the very tips of my fingers. I take up the paper and crumple it, smears of ink staining my hands. Crossing the room to my bed, I burrow under the blankets, blocking out the world. Sleep tugs at my eyes, and I gratefully surrender to it.

CHAPTER SEVEN

I DON'T LEAVE FOR THE LIGHTHOUSE until noon the next day. Before I go I sit on my bed, trying not to catch my eye in the mirror above my vanity. I pick every stray piece of lint from my dress, my hands much steadier than how I feel inside. The words I wrote last night bleed into my mind like poison.

Jude Osric, Jude Osric, Jude Osric.

I shake my head like I can dispel the memory.

Lifting my gaze to the mirror, I pinch my cheeks to get some color in them. Sleep hasn't done me any favors in terms of making me look well rested. I sweep up my long hair into a chignon and take a deep breath.

Once I'm out of the house, I allow myself to turn over the possibility. That Jude Osric—a boy I've known my whole life, someone I've always called a friend—might be a killer. He likely expected me to come knocking at the crack of dawn, and I likely would have—but now I've no idea what to say.

Around the side of the tower, I spot him at work in the vegetable garden. On his knees in the dirt, he wears overalls, his shirtsleeves rolled up, and digs into the soil with trowel in hand. As I walk over, he lifts his head, catching sight of me.

His teeth flash white in a smile. "Moira." Getting to his feet, he wipes the hand not holding the trowel on his clothes. "Good morning."

I clasp my hands in front of me. "Afternoon now."

"Is it?" Shading his eyes, he looks out to sea. Dirt smears the underside of his jaw. He turns back, and there's a softness to the curve of his mouth, the tired lines around his eyes smoothed over. "Shall I make tea?"

I say nothing. I try to picture him taking Connor by the shoulder and slitting him open, his hand clutching a bloodied knife in place of his trowel. The image frays my nerves, quickens my pulse, until all I can hear is the shallow thud of my heartbeat.

It can't be him. It just can't.

He was the one to find the body. The thought is a low and lethal whisper. *You saw him coming up from the beach.*

Jude had been swift to fault the sirens, keen to have me think the same.

"Moira?"

I take a step back. "May we speak inside?"

"Yes, of course." He glances down at his trowel before shoving the tool in a deep pocket. "I suppose you're still set on visiting the police station?"

"That's the plan."

We walk from the garden to the front of the cottage, and Jude takes off his boots at the threshold so as not to track mud inside. It's such a habitual gesture, such a simple one, my treacherous heart tries to win out over reason.

In the kitchen, I press my fingertips to the table's edge. "I didn't see you at Connor's funeral."

His brow creases. "I was there."

I nod, looking away. I feel the weight of his gaze as he waits for me to say something. A chill brushes over my spine, my vision turning watery at the edges. And I can't stop myself.

"Did you kill him?"

For the space of a breath, there is nothing between us but silence.

Jude opens his mouth. "Pardon?"

I glare back, teeth bared, my voice as fierce as I can make it. "Did you murder Connor?"

A light goes out in his eyes—one I didn't realize was there until I no longer see the spark. His face drains of color until it is tinged gray. "Moira," he says, "what are you talking about?"

My heart threatens to beat out of my chest. The world tilts beneath me, like the deck of a ship in the midst of a squall. It's all I can do to stay on my feet.

"You're the one who found him," I say.

His face reddens. "Well, someone had to!"

I dig my nails into my palms, hard enough to know they'll leave half-moon crescents in their wake.

"You know me," says Jude, almost pleading. "How could you even . . . ? I thought we were—" His voice becomes choked, and he takes a deep, shuddering breath. "You really think that of me? That I could do something so monstrous?"

"No."

The word is hollow—too little, too late. I've ignored what my heart already knew, and the cost is more awful than I could've imagined. Jude looks like he can't stand the sight of me. It's made worse by the fact that I deserve it. I shouldn't be accorded Jude's kindness or his understanding or his friendship. He has given so freely, and I have taken it all for granted.

He says, "And yet you accuse me of it."

My skin feels flushed and uncomfortable, stretched too tight over my bones. "It was my mistake. I'm sorry."

He laughs in disbelief. "A grand mistake to make. I saw *you* there on the cliffs, but you don't see me accusing . . ." He brings a hand to his chest, across his heart, fingers curling inward. "I would never, in all my life, think so poorly of you."

Shame heats my face. "Jude—" I start, but I pause when something sounds from down the hall. I turn toward it. The noise is like scraping on wood, repetitive. Jude follows my gaze, his tear-filled eyes widening.

And without looking back at me, he says, "I think it's best you leave now, Moira."

I open my mouth, then shut it. His hurt expression scatters my thoughts, the ache in his voice pressing upon my heart. Turning away, I head for the door before he can show me out. I close my eyes as I step onto the path, taking a deep breath.

Alone, I start across the moors in the direction of town.

The police station is a narrow brick building on Dunmore's main road. Its lobby is stuffy, smelling of must and wood polish. A secretary sits behind an oak counter, her fingers tapping at a typewriter. My heels click against the floorboards as I walk over, but she doesn't look up.

"Pardon me," I say. "I'd like to speak with Inspector Dale."

She stops typing. I know her as everyone knows one another on this island. A familiar face with an even more familiar family name. Catriona Finley is pale-skinned, freckled, and only a couple of years older than Jude. Over her shirtwaist blouse, she wears a silver locket. The teardrop shape of it is one I've seen before, a gift from sailors to their sweethearts prior to long voyages. Meeting my eye, she tells me, "He isn't in today."

"Well," I reply, a little clipped, "is there someone else in?"

"Detective Thackery." She gestures down the hall, doors to sectioned offices lining both sides of the dimly lit corridor. "If you'd like to speak with him instead."

"Which office is his?"

"Second door on the left."

I nod my thanks. As I cross the lobby, Thackery's door seems an ominous thing. I knock thrice on the polished wood, and a muffled voice calls, "Come in."

I open the door to find Thackery sitting at his desk, pen in hand. His head is bent over a slip of paper, and there's a certain urgency to the speed of his writing, the page marked in quick, pointed scrawls.

"Miss Alexander." He offers me a fleeting glance and continues with his letter. "How may I be of service to you?"

The indirect attention is somewhat off-putting. Folding my hands in front of me, I say, "I was hoping to have a word with Inspector Dale—"

"Who is currently away," interrupts Thackery. "So I say again, how may I be of service to you?"

"It's about Connor Sheahan, sir. About his death."

Thackery leans back in his chair to appraise me, setting down his pen in the same motion. "Oh? And what about it troubles you?"

Every single thing about it troubles me. The memory of that day returns to the forefront of my thoughts again and again, like a flame I can't extinguish.

"I read the article in the *Gazette*. They say you're not investigating, that you've closed the case."

Thackery's mouth is a thin, tight line. "Not much of an investigation," he says. "Poor boy killed by sirens like that. Not the first nor last, unfortunately." Compared to his appearance on Jude's doorstep, he looks less striking holed up in this cluttered office. His face is pale and drawn, and his hair is not as neat, dark strands falling into his eyes.

I bite the inside of my cheek. "Are you positive it was sirens, sir?"

The lines across his forehead deepen. "What do you mean by that, Miss Alexander?"

"His wounds seem to suggest another cause."

"Do they, now?" Thackery leans forward, hands clasped atop his desk. "I'm curious how you came to that conclusion. I was under the impression you were visiting Mr. Osric—and when we asked, you said you hadn't been down to the beach. Has that fact changed? Should I be taking another look at Mr. Osric's statement?"

I swallow hard, caught in the lie. "No, sir. I perhaps misspoke earlier. Mr. Osric took me down to see the body. I asked it of him."

"I see."

Undeterred, I say, "Connor's injuries were much too clean for a siren's claws, sir. I've seen survivors of their attacks—the cuts are ragged and not quite so deep."

Thackery raises his eyebrows. "Do you consider us incompetent, Miss Alexander?" Without waiting for my answer, he goes on. "I know your late father was viewed as a fount of knowledge in regard to the sirens, but we're all accustomed to their methods. I'm sure Mr. Osric can attest to that."

My stomach churns. Thackery wields his words like he means to draw blood, and I feel the sting of every cut. "Sir," I say, "I think you would do well to listen to me. You ought to be looking for a killer. A human one."

He heaves a sigh. When he stands, making his way around the desk, I realize he's about to see me out. "I assure you," he says, opening the door, "we have considered Connor Sheahan's death with as much thoroughness as any of our other cases. Now, if you please, I've a lot of work to be getting on with."

"Detective," I persist, "if you'll just—"

"Good afternoon, Miss Alexander."

I feel Catriona's eyes on me as I head across the lobby. My jaw tightens, my hands turn to fists in my pockets, and I want to push my way back into Thackery's office and shout at him that yes, I do think the whole lot of them are incompetent.

Rather than the usual path back home, I take the roundabout way along the cliffs. I see the lighthouse in the distance, and scuff at the damp grass with the toe of my boot. When my eyes shift to the beach, I catch sight of a pale figure at the shoreline.

A solitary siren rests in the shallows, her dark hair knotted, sleek with salt water, each wave rushing over the fold of her legs before retreating into the ocean. My pulse flutters as adrenaline floods my veins. I feel the all-too-familiar tug at my heart, the song of the whispering sea. She clutches a dying fish in her hands; its blood and oil trail over her skin as she tears into it, sharp teeth stained red.

It's been said just the sight of a siren is enough to drag men into a watery grave. Children's stories, for the most part. But in this moment I have little trouble believing them. I imagine her gaze flitting up the cliff—watchful and hungry and dark as the deep—to find me staring back.

I won't let them blame you, I tell her silently.

Whoever killed Connor, for whatever purpose, I'll track them down myself.

CHAPTER EIGHT

I TAKE COVER IN THE CLIFF'S CREVICE, hidden among the shadows. The cliff itself is a black looming wall in the twilight, and the sand shifts beneath my bare feet, the sea whispering music in my ears— but it's not for the sea I wait.

My father's hand on my arm. *You must be patient*, he says.

I make myself completely still. I feel the hard grit of the crag against my back, the taste of salt bitter on my tongue. My heart beats loud in the silence, a steady rhythm, and I wonder if that's what calls the sirens to shore. A living composition, heartstrings sounding a promise of blood.

In the encroaching darkness, she rises from the water like a ghost. My father's voice is a quiet breath at my ear.

See her there, my dear. She has come.

Her face is white as chalk, sharp as a knife. Her eyes are deep blue like the sky in the final hour of evening. She moves as though she's still under the waves, a smooth dance over rocks and sand. She is stark and dangerous—and she is absolutely lovely.

Pacing along the beach's edge, she keeps her feet in shallow tide. I do not dare blink while I watch her. We wait in the shadows, hidden, long after she passes over the mouth of the crevice.

Beside me, my father lets out a quiet sigh. I turn to see his smile outlined by the fading sun. His eyes glitter and I feel the grin that spreads across my face. Adrenaline hums through my veins, blood singing in my ears, as the last streaks of sunlight disappear into the sea.

I wake gasping, jolted by the sudden scrape of branches outside my window. I stare into the darkness of my bedroom, breathing hard, waiting for my heart rate to slow. Just a dream. A memory—woven into the fabric of nightscape, timeworn and dusty.

I lie back on thin sheets that feel cold against my skin. As my eyes close, the tears come, unrelenting.

I do not try to stop them.

CHAPTER NINE

I STAND ON THE DOORSTEP to the keeper's cottage, my knuckles touching the wood without knocking. From below, I make out the low rush of the sea, waves surging and breaking against the shore. I close my eyes.

Just leave. Go on. He doesn't want you here.

I won't ask his forgiveness, but I must do my best to apologize. Jude is owed that. If he wishes to rake me over the coals, to never have me set foot here again, I've brought it upon myself.

I breathe in, breathe out, attuning my heart to the ebb and flow of the tide. I pull my hand back to knock, but the door swings open the next instant.

Jude stands before me, dressed in his wool coat and cap. His eyes alight on mine, and he removes his cap, holding it to his chest. I suspect he does so unthinking—I don't imagine Jude feels obligated to extend me any sort of courtesy.

"Moira." He says it similar to how he did that storm-dark afternoon. Startled, a little breathless, as though I'm one of the apparitions thought to haunt the moors. He squints. "How long have you been out here?"

"It's no matter. I see I've caught you on your way out." I back up, stepping down onto the path. "I'll come back later. Or not at all, if you prefer."

For a moment he looks pained. Moving aside, he opens the door wider. "Please, come in." As I step over the threshold, he sets his cap on an empty hook. He holds out a hand, and when I simply stare at it, he murmurs, "I'll take your coat, Moira."

"I don't mean to keep you."

His dark eyes shine. He doesn't draw his hand back, so I surrender my coat to him. I watch as he places it on the hook next to his cap, something raw and tender about his expression.

"Jude," I begin, "I'm here to say how truly sorry I am for the other day. I regret it more than anything."

He ducks his head. "There's no need . . ."

"I never believed it was you. I let logic sway me when I oughtn't have. You're not a killer—and I had no reason to accuse you of something so foul."

Jude leans back against the wall opposite me. Narrow as the hall is, we remain close. Light from the doorway threads gold into his hair, catching in his brown eyes. His mouth curves. "Thank you," he says, sounding somewhat wry.

I swallow. "What I did was unforgivable. I'll understand if you don't . . ."

"I forgive you, Moira. Gladly I do." He passes a hand through his curls. "I shouldn't have acted the way I did."

"You had every right."

He straightens up. "Well, we'll agree to disagree on that."

I falter, muddled by uncertainty despite his words. I stare down at my boots, black and scuffed around the edges, and say, "I'd still like your help."

Jude takes off his coat and hangs it up, whatever errand he meant to run forgotten. He wears his brown waistcoat, a white collared shirt, and a tie, so likely he'd planned to visit Mr. Daugherty. "I thought you might." He gives me an easy smile. "Have you already spoken to the police?"

"Yes." I scowl, recalling my exchange with Thackery. "They were quite useless."

We head into the kitchen. Jude prepares the stove for tea, putting fresh kindling into the firebox. He lights a match, nearly dropping it, as someone hammers at his front door.

Frowning, he shakes out the tiny flame.

I look to the hall. "Do you know who that is?"

He fidgets with his shirt cuff, rubbing the fabric between forefinger and thumb. "Someone from the harbor, probably."

I take a seat at the table as he disappears down the hall. Skimming over the knots in the wood, I listen as he lifts the latch, opens the door. I expect him to greet whoever's out there, but what I hear next is dead silence.

A voice—distinctly male but not Jude's—says something too muffled for me to interpret. Though I hear Jude quite clearly when he says, "You have *what*?"

I'm out of my chair in a flash.

At the entrance, Jude stands with one hand clutching the

frame, like he'll fall without the support. I peer around him, and my heart begins to race rabbit-fast.

Two young officers stand beneath the overhang.

"What's all this?" I come up beside Jude, narrowing my eyes.

The officers seem unsettled by my appearance. It's obvious they thought Jude was here alone. They doff their hats upon seeing me, and one of them folds a piece of paper, tucking it away in his coat. He says, "We have an arrest warrant for him, miss."

I turn to Jude. He continues to lean against the doorframe, his face sheet white, his eyes staring out at nothing. I've no doubt what the warrant is for, but I ask anyway.

The officer scratches the back of his neck. "He's a suspect in the death of Connor Sheahan."

At this Jude squeezes his eyes shut. Facing the officers, I say, "Your lot already deemed sirens responsible."

"There's been a recent development," replies the other officer. "They're reopening the case, having another look at things."

"And what part of that warrant says you can take Jude Osric in without proof?"

"We have probable cause, miss. You'll have to speak to our superiors."

Rage coats my throat like bile. "I was just there yesterday," I snarl, "and I'll tell you what you're doing is ridiculous."

Eyes still shut, Jude whispers, "I can't leave." It comes out low enough he might very well be talking to himself. "I can't."

The first officer clucks his tongue. "Come now, Wick."

Jude looks up, eyes hazy. He stares off into the middle distance as though seeing something different than the rest of us. He says, "Who will keep the light?"

"We've sent word to your uncle. He ought to be here before dark."

Jude presses the back of one hand to his mouth. He exhales shakily.

"Jude," I say. "Jude, don't you dare go with them. This isn't right."

"We're following the letter of the law, Miss Alexander." The officer sets his sights on Jude. "Your uncle is on his way over from the offshore light. Mr. Daugherty cleared his transfer this morning. If you don't come willingly, we'll have to cuff you, and for your sake I'd rather not."

I grab Jude by the back of his waistcoat. I'm desperate for him to hold his ground, to argue, to *stay*. All too well, I can see my part in this. Would these officers be here to collect Jude if I hadn't visited Thackery? Had I persuaded him to reopen Connor's case?

I put my finger on the trigger, but the shot was poorly aimed.

"Moira," says Jude, voice flat. "Let me go."

He won't meet my eyes. His gaze is far away, expression vacant. I fear he's torn the heart from his sleeve and buried it somewhere too deep for me to find. I release him, feeling like I've pushed him off the cliff to drown.

One officer actually has the boldness to offer to walk me home.

I present the full force of my glare in return. "I'll be at that station of yours first thing tomorrow," I tell him. "If I pass you there, you best cast your eyes down in shame."

Snatching my coat from the wall, I shove between the pair. On the path, I look over my shoulder to rest my gaze once more on Jude Osric. He hasn't moved. His shadow falls upon the open door, dark and rough as a sketch.

Sickness twists my stomach. It's doubled when I remember my thoughts from yesterday, minding that siren in the shallows.

I won't let them blame you.

Wrapping my coat around myself, I walk quickly away. These are the consequences of my actions—and I can't bear to watch.

Throughout the rest of the day, I'm unable to ease the distraction of my mind. I've a tutoring session—my first since Connor's death—but the memory of Jude standing before the officers, the shock writ so clearly on his face, leaves me faint and fractured. I cut the lesson short, only to feel guilty for doing so, and return home to write up a flyer to place in the schoolhouse.

Adjoining St. Cecilia's, it's a squat one-room building of white siding. The students have been let out; I worry momentarily the school is locked up for the day. I try the door, reassured when it swings open. Closing it behind me, I glance around to find my former teacher, Nell Bracken, still seated at her desk in front of the empty class.

"Oh, Moira," she says, looking up. "Is there something I can do for you?"

I make my way over to her, passing the neat rows of desks. Tall windows let in the pale afternoon light, accentuating scuff marks across the floorboards from countless shoes. Here, children are taught reading, writing, and arithmetic until they're thirteen. That is the principle, at least. Quite a number leave early: if they're needed at home, needed to work. Jude did not return after his family died. An ache would bloom in my chest afterward, whenever I'd look toward his desk across the room and remember anew that he wasn't there, *why* he wasn't there.

Gripping the flyer, I say, "Yes, only . . . Do you mind if I pin this up?" I hand Nell the slip of paper, an advertisement of my violin lessons.

She reads through it. She has changed little since my school days, dressed in her practical shirtwaist and skirt, her chestnut hair done up tightly. Her expression softens upon meeting my gaze. "Of course, dear." As I turn to hang it on the wall, she continues. "You must be terribly cut up about it, losing one of your students."

I pause. "He was your student too." And because my back is to her, because there is no one to see my face, I close my eyes, biting my lip, as her words coil tight around my heart.

"Yes," says Nell. "Not the first I've lost, but I find that does not lessen the pain of it."

I set a hand on the wall, needing something solid to lean against. I wonder what Nell might say if I told her Connor was murdered, that he was taken by one of our own. Word of Jude's arrest has yet to spread. The gossip will be passed around tonight, in casual conversation over tea. And all the while Jude . . .

Jude will be . . .

I hear rather than see Nell get up from her desk. I hurriedly pin my flyer, blinking back tears. When she looks into my face, I cut my eyes away from hers. She *tut*s. "My dear, you're quite undone. You ought to rest."

Undone. Yes, I suppose that's the word for it. I feel cut loose, set adrift on uncertain waters, without the means to chart my way back. Clasping my hands in front of me, I gaze out one of the windows.

Jude and I heading out the door, falling into step beside each other. Jude taking my bookstrap onto his shoulder, Jude walking me home.

I shouldn't have come here.

With a nod at Nell I say, "Thank you kindly, Miss Bracken. I fear you're right. I've been rather out of sorts."

"You get on home and have your mother make you a cup of tea."

She ushers me toward the door. When I'm alone on the sidewalk, I flex the fingers of my bowing hand. Playing now, in this temper, is likely to yield only a broken string. Clouds have settled over the slate roofs, a cold drizzle speckling the cobbles. Starting for home, I duck my head against the rain.

The chill still manages to work its way into my bones.

CHAPTER TEN

THERE ARE FIVE SEPARATE LOCKUPS in Dunmore's police station. The cells run along a corridor of white tile and metal piping, toward the back end of the building. I smooth down the buttons of my coat as I enter the hall. My eyes go to the ceiling, and I spot mold flourishing in patches.

Jude spent a night in this place.

Did they leave him in the dark?

So many pressing thoughts, yet that one—that one unnerves me at my core. The corridor is empty, quiet, and it soon becomes evident Jude is the lone occupant. I come to a stop outside his cell. It has a small, barred window, a wooden bed against the wall, and a pail tucked beneath it. In the dim, it takes me a moment to locate Jude Osric. He sits on the floor, wedged into a corner. His eyes are closed, and he clutches one knee to his chest.

The police have taken his boots. His waistcoat and tie are folded neatly on the bed. He wears only shirt and suspenders, trousers and socks. It makes him look younger, apart from the sleepless smudges marking his eyes. My chest tightens.

"Jude," I murmur. "Please, look at me."

He presses his forehead against his knee, hiding his face from view. In a rasp, he says, "I believe I told Miss Finley not to let you down here."

"She knows which of us not to cross."

Jude raises his head. His lips quirk in a humorless smile. "She might be remiss in that regard. I'm the one behind bars."

I curl a hand around one of said bars, the metal cold against my palm. The morning sun emerges from cloud cover, its light shining sheer through the window to dash upon the floor. Jude picks at his shirt cuff, eyes lowered to the task.

"Tell me what they did to you," I say.

He continues to fidget with his cuff. I worry, for a moment, he won't say anything at all. He swallows, and softly he asks, "Do you think I did it? Truly?"

"I've already told you I don't." My grip on the bar is white-knuckled. I wish he'd get up and walk over to me, so I might bring a hand to his cheek and look into his eyes proper.

Instead, Jude rests his head back against the wall. He is a shadow cloaked in shadows. He hasn't once met my gaze. "Well, that's a comfort," he says, and I hate how unfeeling he sounds, when it's plain he must be feeling a great deal. "I think the police mean to keep me here a while longer."

"I'll talk to them. I'm going to get you out."

"Fine." At last his eyes settle on mine. "Let's say you do.

What of Daugherty? Do you think he'll permit my return to the lighthouse?"

Now I realize: This is the root of what really plagues him.

"That's your post, Jude." I falter, unsure. "Once your name is clear, he'll have no choice . . ."

"It's been my family and no other working that light for generations. My ancestors walked that staircase. They trimmed the wicks and stood on the gallery deck just as I do." He scrubs a hand over his eyes. "I felt the press of those years—felt them watching over me. I was meant to add my page to that book, but now I—I've broken the line. I've ruined it."

"Jude, stop." My voice is thick, my heart aching like his words have run me through. "You haven't ruined anything. You've done nothing wrong."

He sets a hand on the floor, fingers splayed. "I must ask something of you, Moira."

I nod. "Anything at all."

"However long I'm in here"—he pauses, biting his lip—"don't visit the lighthouse. Don't speak with my uncle." He rubs his palm against his trouser knee, dark eyes gleaming. "Stay away altogether. Promise me, please."

"I promise." I believe it would hurt too much, anyway—going back when Jude himself isn't free to do so.

He bows his head. "Thank you."

After I leave him, the storm inside me seethes. I'm awash in it, rage boiling over until I'm shaking. If Jude were not here and I was given a match, I think perhaps I'd burn the whole place to the ground. I march down the hall to Thackery's office, banging my fist against the door.

"Yes, Miss Alexander, do come in."

I bring the tempest to him. My hands slam down on his desk, hard as a wave smashing up against the island. "I'll grant you the generosity of thinking you've made a mistake," I tell him, "but you've imprisoned a good man, and I demand you release him at once."

Detective Thackery considers me with disinterest. "Your idea of what constitutes good in a man is too broad, Miss Alexander. We've a suspected murderer behind bars."

"You suspect Jude Osric because he found Connor on the beach? Because he reported it? You're punishing him for doing what he's tasked as keeper."

There is little in Jude's power to alleviate disaster, when it comes. A fishing boat might run aground on the rocks, some iron-less sailor might be charmed overboard by sirens, but Jude can't save everyone from the perils of the sea. Nor is he expected to. He is meant only to report the occurrences.

He is meant to keep the light.

"I'm not required to present our findings to you." Thackery folds his hands over his lacquered desk. "Miss Alexander, you reminded me that I ought to investigate every avenue. You directed us to look for a human killer. At the moment Mr. Osric is our prime suspect."

"You can't keep him in that cell forever. You can't."

Thackery hums. Looking elsewhere, he says, "It's true we can't hold him indefinitely. Not without solid evidence." He unfolds his clasped hands to tap twice against the edge of his desk. "We'll be releasing Mr. Osric no later than tomorrow."

Relief rushes over me, cold and clean. I draw back, straightening up. "And what of his position? I do hope unfounded suspicion won't deprive him of his livelihood."

Thackery's gaze swings back around. A muscle twitches in his jaw. "I'll speak with Mr. Daugherty," he says cautiously. "I'm sure he'll reinstate Mr. Osric as keeper. Provided he's innocent, he won't be removed from his posting."

"Very good." I head for the door, but as I reach it, I turn back. "Sir, why did you do it? Why reopen the case?" Hope flutters in my rib cage, but fear stills it in one fell swoop. Even if the police no longer fault the sirens, they have a poor handle on things going by their first arrest. "Do you not think sirens attacked Connor after all?"

"My thoughts haven't changed, Miss Alexander. You'd do well to remember that."

"Right." I grind my teeth. "Well, sir, I'd say good day, but it'd be quite the lie with Jude Osric sitting in jail."

"I don't see how it's any of your concern," he says, eyeing me. "This is police business—something I suggest you keep in mind."

I stare back at him. "Mr. Osric is my friend. Connor Sheahan was a student of mine. Perhaps you ought to keep that in mind, sir."

"Take care, Miss Alexander."

Out on the cobblestones, I push my hands deep into the pockets of my coat. I make my way toward the moors, toward home, but I feel directionless even as my feet set me on the path. I've no idea how to solve a murder. I've no idea how to set things right. A killer walks free, going about their day, while Jude Osric is under lock and key for their crimes.

Frustration grips me. If the murderer did mean to frame the sirens, what purpose did it serve?

In Lochlan, I know, records of siren attacks are kept in the library. If indeed Connor's death was made to mirror them, perhaps they're worth a look.

It's not much. But it's a start.

CHAPTER ELEVEN

I survey the harbor from beneath the curve of my umbrella. It's been raining on and off all morning, making the docks slick underfoot. There's a chill in the air, and my breath escapes in a mist. I dig my free hand into the pocket of my long coat. For God's sake, September is not meant to be this cold.

I stare down at the vacant boats, all of them with flaked paint, tangled knots, unclean sails. More than a dozen masts pierce the gray sky. Of the several faces I recognize, it's Gabriel Flint who's first to notice me. From the boathouse, he grins wide enough to reveal his chipped incisor. He wears no hat, and the dampness has given his blond hair a cowlick that curls back from his forehead. Driving his fillet knife into the cutting table, he heads over to where I stand.

"Moira Alexander," he says. "A pleasure to have you here on such a foul day."

"Keep away from me, Flint."

He does quite the opposite, offering his arm as if I'm fool enough to take it. I skirt around him. He's quick to follow after, saying, "You're not still angry with me, are you? My, you know how to hold a grudge, girl."

Inside my coat pocket, my fingers twitch with the desire to seize him by the collar and pitch him over the side of the dock.

"Is that why you stopped playing at the hall?" he asks. "Just to spite me?"

Ignoring him, I continue down the pier, passing rowboats and fishing trawlers. Warren Knox straightens up after securing one of the trawlers and makes his way toward us. It seems I'm not the only one wanting to take Flint by the collar—Warren does so as he passes us, pulling him to a stop. "Where do you think you're rushing off to?" he growls. "There's still work to be done."

Flint pats him on the shoulder. "I'm doing a simple kindness, is all. Our Moira is looking to go somewhere, and I've offered to take her." He glances at me, eyebrows raised. "Isn't that so, Moira?"

"Hardly the weather for it," says Warren.

"Why, this?" Flint gestures to the storm clouds overhead. "It'll blow itself out before evening."

Warren grunts and releases him with a shove. I watch him walk off toward the boathouse, until Flint draws my attention back, saying, "You are looking to go somewhere, then."

I pause. I'd come here with a mind set on taking the ferry, but that's time and money I'd rather not spend. Snapping my umbrella shut, I jab him with the pointed end. "I'm not paying you."

A corner of his mouth lifts. "I don't want your coins, Moira."

I didn't expect so. Flint is always asking something of me, but it's never in the form of silver. He presses me to read his compositions, to join him in a duet at the dances. It's ironic, really. He's the main reason I cut ties with the hall.

"You oughtn't ask anything of me," I tell him. "Where's your boat?"

Flint jerks his chin toward it. Terry Young is there on the dock, tightening knots against rough tide. Waves lash the harbor posts, choppy and white-capped.

The stormy weather isn't fierce enough to trouble the sirens. I imagine looking over the edge of the pier to find one there: a silvery flash emerging from the dark waters, smiling up with sharp teeth. Most times their dislike of iron—an essential part of many fishing vessels—is a good enough deterrent to keep them from the harbor.

Most times.

Terry glances around at the sound of our footsteps. Like his name, he's young—fourteen at the most. He's also excitable and kind, which makes me worry over him. I know what this island does to softhearted boys, how much it takes from them, wearing them down just as the wind and sea erode our cliffs. Removing his cap, he waves to us. "Hello, Miss Alexander. You picked a fine day to come out."

Flint claps him on the shoulder. "Get these knots untied, Terry. Miss Alexander has business"—he looks to me—"where?"

"Lochlan," I answer.

"Lochlan. Right."

Terry grumbles, but crouches down to do as he's told. Flint's boat rocks to and fro with the current, the blue paint on the hull peeling and cracked through. Flint jumps aboard and holds out a hand. Ignoring it, I step down after him.

There's a bundle of tangled line on deck and, beneath it, a box of fishhooks and a slim knife. I sit and take up the knife to study it. It's stained and well rusted for something that ought to be used only for cutting line.

"Mind," says Flint. "I'm not answering to your mother if you slice your finger off."

I scowl at him and drop the knife back into the heap of fishing line.

The storm seems to worsen once we're underway. Each wave threatens to spill over the hull, and Flint curses, grip tight on the tiller, as he concentrates on steering into the wind. I pull my coat close, blinking against the rain.

"What are you needing in Lochlan?"

I hadn't thought he'd start a conversation, with the wind roaring in our ears, but he manages. I've not even answered before he's asking, "How's Wick faring these days?" And the way he says it, I can tell he knows Jude's whereabouts. Gossip is second only to siren song in enchanting the island, spreading like wildfire in the daylight hours. News of Jude's arrest and subsequent imprisonment would've struck like lightning.

"They're going to release him," I say shortly.

"He's off his head." Flint's tone is wicked. "Sitting up at that lighthouse all by his lonesome. Matter of time, if you ask me."

I glare back at him. "I haven't asked you anything."

He smiles just enough to show his teeth. "You think he's innocent."

"Of course he's innocent," I snap. "He's Jude Osric."

Flint groans. "There you go sounding like everyone else at the harbor." He takes a moment to tighten the sails, then touches the back of his hand to his forehead like some fainting maiden. "Our Wick? Accused of *murder*? It's them sirens who took dear Connor!"

I cut my eyes away. The island's cliffs loom over us, tall and ethereal in the mist. "The sirens are still suspect," I say.

"Aye." Flint shifts our angle. The boat pitches up and down on the growing swells. "That must tear into you, eh?"

I don't speak. Curling my fingers around the gunwale, I gaze over the side to watch the hull cut through strings of kelp. The sirens will be in the depths below, waiting, swimming in the silent blackness. Sometimes, in the back corner of my mind, I think I wish to hear them sing. I want it with a desire that is nameless and cares not if my ears bleed from the sound.

Sometimes the things I desire terrify me.

Flint calls, "Nearly there," and adjusts the sails to keep us parallel to the shore. I stare across the expanse of water until Lochlan's harbor appears out of the fog. It's larger than Dunmore's, with several ferries anchored at port. Men in wool sweaters and trousers stuffed into heavy boots walk up and down the docks, checking lines, logging the arrival of each ship. They remind me of Jude, in some way, and I shake my head to dispel the image.

Flint passes the boat's line over to one of the men at the edge of the dock. He has a shock of ginger hair and a quick smile, his hands tying the fishing boat in place with smooth efficiency. We step onto the pier, and he takes down our names.

"Awful weather to sail in," he says. "Do you know when you'll be casting off?"

"Before evening," I reply. "We'll not be staying long."

We walk away from the harbor, up the wooden staircase set

into the side of the cliff. Every step is slick with rainwater, and Flint is thoroughly irritated after almost slipping twice. A tourist ship has disembarked its passengers, probably the last of the season, and a trail of people follow behind us. Their voices are loud and accented, rising easily over the noise of the harbor.

Neither Flint, nor I, nor any other islander I know holds much fondness in their heart for tourists. Even Jude's goodwill— seemingly limitless—begins to chafe after long exposure.

I hazard a glance over my shoulder to catch a few of the newcomers leaning forward at the dock's edge, peering into the water. I'll be surprised if any one of them had the foresight to carry iron on their person.

Flint looks around, spots the group, and lets out a single bark of laughter. "Don't even need singing to," he says. "They'll just fall right in."

Every summer tourists come to call as though the sirens have sung them to our shore. It's little wonder their self-absorbed selves account for most of the siren death tally. They see Twillengyle's sirens as charming curios rather than creatures who could charm them into a sea grave.

Above the harbor, the smart cobbled streets of Lochlan stretch out before us. Shoving both hands in his pockets, Flint asks, "Where to?"

"Well, *I'm* off to the library," I tell him. "You're free to do what you like."

"The library? Oh, I see. Real important business, that."

"Yes," I say. "Though not any real business of yours."

He scuffs the toe of his boot on the pavement. "So what am I meant to do?" His voice sounds a little accusing.

"Explore, Mr. Flint," I say, leaning into our island accent.

"May you discover all the truths and treasures of Twillengyle." I curtsy to him.

"Clear off," he says. "And be quick about it."

"A good day to you, also!" I call back, grinning, already heading into town.

I haven't been to Lochlan since last summer, yet not much has changed since. Twillengyle Council sees the town as the island's gateway to tourism, and it shows in the even cobblestones, the curbs swept clean of dead leaves and debris. The shops are neat as chocolate boxes, the public houses freshly painted. It's a world away from Dunmore, made pretty for the sightseers, so they might overlook the unsightly.

Blood billowing up around the harbor isn't illustrated in the brochures.

I make my way through the downtown to the library. It's relatively new, this library—only fifty years old or so. It takes up the space of two terraced houses, the first floor for literature and nonfiction from the mainland, the second floor for old documents concerning the island.

I sign in at the front desk and head up the stairwell. Weak light filters past the cloud cover and through the windows, streaking across the steps. I've always thought it a sort of magic—dust suspended in the sunlight, the creak of floorboards, the smell of leather polish and yellowing book pages—and I guess it rather is.

In the archive, there are shelves upon shelves of historical documents: Council rulings, old diaries, lighthouse logbooks. The siren records crowd several bookcases, detailing when islanders and tourists alike strayed too close and were taken in by their song.

There are also records of the hunts. Conducted for sport or for

vengeance, they cast a long and bloody mark upon our island. The
hunting ban is what brought it to a stop. Sirens made their home
here just as we did, and by killing them we were only killing a part
of the island, a part of ourselves.

It was not a decision made without consequences.

The death records are categorized by year. Out of some
perverse sense of curiosity—for I've never looked before—I pull
free the book documenting victims from seven years ago. Flipping
to the month of June, I stare down at the names printed there.

Llyr Osric, aged 38

Pearl Osric, aged 38

Emmeline Osric, aged 16

*The three were taken from their boat off the coast of Dunmore. They
are survived by twelve-year-old Jude Osric, who reported the incident.*

I trace over the letters, a lump forming in my throat. Three
islanders taken in one fell swoop is nigh on unheard of. We're
raised on cautionary tales, given cold iron to keep in our pockets.
We take heed because we know the hazards. Plenty around
Dunmore were aware of the work my father conducted, Llyr
Osric alongside him. They supposed it was inevitable one of them
should meet their fate in this manner.

My insides pinch. I set the book back on its shelf, reaching
for the most current records. Last year two tourists were dragged
from Lochlan Harbor, and Iona Knox, who I'd seen quite
regularly at the dance hall, was lost to siren song while offshore,
north of Dunmore. I call to mind Warren Knox as I saw him
at the harbor. Iona had been his younger sister. She was taken
in much the same manner as the Osrics, stolen away into the
depths. None of the reports I come across mention anyone left
on the shore with their throat cut like Connor Sheahan.

In the current book, his entry is only a handwritten slip of paper, attached to the page, waiting to be added to the list. I've half a mind to tear it out.

Few islanders have fallen prey to sirens in recent years. Yet Connor's death was made to reflect their attacks—surely his killer must resent them for some past sorrow?

I close the book, abruptly unsettled. I'd yet to give much regard to the closeness of this murder. Whoever committed the act, that person is out there now, walking the very streets of Dunmore—a familiar face, someone I may well have spoken to.

A shiver creeps over my spine.

With great haste, I leave the library, seized by a desperate need to be back in Dunmore. I step out onto the rain-dappled street, not bothering to open my umbrella. A gaggle of tourists jostle me, and I bare my teeth in a snarl, my pulse tripping even as they flinch away. I find Flint conversing with a girl on the steps to the hotel. Whatever he sees on my face has him cutting the conversation short, and in the next breath he's at my side.

"Time to leave," I tell him.

Only once I reach the harbor and am clambering into his boat do I look back at Lochlan, allowing my mind to wonder just what I've gotten Jude and myself into.

CHAPTER TWELVE

THE NEXT MORNING I walk across the moors to find Jude Osric standing near the cliff's edge. His cloth cap casts a shadow over his eyes, his head bent as he stares down the crag as though contemplating the long drop into the sea. He clutches a little slip of paper, and as I watch him, his lips move, mouthing words I cannot hear.

In Twillengyle, they say the sea can grant wishes. If you want something desperately enough. If you turn out your secrets in a whisper.

Jude tosses the paper over the cliff, and I wonder what secrets he has to give.

My boots sink into the damp grass, and Jude turns, taking his cap in hand. All the things I thought to say in this moment vanish as we regard each other. The wind tangles his hair, tugs at his wool sweater, and I wish I could wipe clean the memory of that cold and darkened cell, of the bars that kept him from the world.

He says, "Hello, Moira."

"You should've told me." I swallow. "You should've knocked on my door as soon as you were out of there."

His mouth curves in a half smile. "You're glad to see me, then?"

"Very much so."

He looks away, cheeks pink. Below us, the sea is restless and alive, churning against the weather-beaten rocks. I study the froth and spray of the waves, hesitant to speak of my visit to Lochlan. Now is the time to step back, to keep myself from Jude Osric as I've kept myself from the dance hall—lest I bring about more damage, lest guilt shred me to pieces.

I've already withheld plenty from him.

The wind pushes at my back, daring me forward.

I can't do this alone.

"Jude," I say, "I have something to tell you."

Jude listens as I recount my afternoon in Lochlan Library. He leans back against the kitchen counter, rubbing a hand over the nape of his neck. "You've made a suspect list?"

I set my hand atop a chair back. Looking down, I grimace upon noticing an ink spot on the cuff of my printed dress. "One name is not a list," I say, raising my eyes to Jude's.

"Warren Knox." His brow creases as he shifts his gaze. "I've gutted fish next to him. I can't imagine he'd kill anyone, much less Connor."

"Well," I reply, a little snappish, "my apologies, if it's not to your liking—"

A sudden ringing pierces the air, and the two of us freeze. We both recognize the sound. The alarm bells go off only when sirens are spotted near the harbor. I dash over to the window, but at ground level, the cliff is too sheer to see what's going on. When I turn around, Jude is right behind me, biting his lip as he tries to peer down to the docks.

The ringing continues, over and over, terrifically loud. I meet Jude's eye. "I need to see what's happening."

He doesn't argue. Perhaps he realizes it would be pointless.

We hurry outside, and beyond the walls of the keeper's cottage, the alarm sounds a clear warning. *Keep away. Leave the area. Danger.* I carry on despite it, approaching the cliff's edge. By the beach, the harbor front is a blur of movement, but when I scour the water, there's no flash of silvery-white skin, no shadows circling beneath the waves. I make a start for the pathway.

"Moira," Jude says, "don't. They know what they're doing. The sirens . . ."

"They've gone," I say shortly.

"How do you know?"

"I just do."

He's silent at that. Like so many islanders, Jude thinks all he need ever know is to keep charms of protection on his person and a safe distance if he could help it.

The alarm cuts off as suddenly as it began. I give Jude a wry grin. "Come on."

We head down the crag's winding path toward the harbor. It's silent apart from the soft hush of waves, my breath fogging the air, Jude's footsteps behind me. There's a group of men huddled together, their expressions sharp and furious, but their voices are too low for me to catch any of the conversation. I frown at the sight of several rusted cans along one pier.

Grabbing one of the nearest dock workers, I ask, "What's happened? Was someone attacked?"

The boy grins. He's young, fifteen or sixteen, his waistcoat unbuttoned and frayed over a rumpled shirt. "Shouldn't be down here, miss. Didn't you hear the alarms?"

I glance again at the huddled crowd, before leveling the boy with my best glare. "Answer me."

He leans over and spits onto the dock. "Nah, no attacks," he says. "They didn't get a chance, you see. With the stuff Russell poured into the water—I think he killed a couple."

My fingers slacken on his shirt collar. "What?"

"Someone gave him cans of the old poison. When the sirens showed up, he tipped it right over the pier. Look . . ." He points to the group, and this time, when I really look at them, I see they're not gathered together, but gathered *around* something. I let my hand fall from the boy's collar, and Jude catches hold of my wrist.

"Moira." His voice is tentative, almost a whisper. He doesn't know which is the better option—to pull me back or to let me step into the dark. I wrench away from him.

My legs feel unsteady, pins-and-needles numb, and the crash of my heartbeat is louder than any alarm as I push through the mass of people. *It's a lie*, I think wildly, because killing sirens is forbidden; there's a ban in place. They're meant to be *protected*.

I find them laid out on the dock.

Two of them, still and white, their limbs splayed over the wood. A greasy sheen stains the water lapping at the edge of the pier. All the pieces are there, but my mind can't make sense of it. I'm shaking so badly; I wrap my arms around my waist, hoping to keep myself together. This isn't right. This isn't supposed to happen.

"Where's Russell?" I ask. Then again, "Where's *Russell*?"

He's easy to spot in the end, because he's the one being scolded. One of the older fishermen has a firm grip on his arm, but that doesn't stop me from going over and slapping him.

"What have you done?" I snarl.

He bares his teeth. He isn't much older than me—but he looks it now. There's a red mark forming on his cheek where I hit him, and veins trace the whites of his eyes. Prison will age him further.

"You care about a couple of monsters, Miss Alexander?"

"You've just made yourself a criminal." Rage burns in my chest, enough to make me want to smack him a second time. "Seems to me you're the only monster here."

"They killed Connor Sheahan," says Russell. He shrugs one shoulder, careless, like this is a victory. "Would've taken one of us here probably. I was getting back our own."

"Where did you get the cans?"

Siren poison is tricky to come by these days. Most of the cans were disposed of after the hunting ban was enacted, the remainder kept in police possession. Yet some, I know, are still tucked away in households. *Just in case*, they say. *Just a precaution*.

Russell's smile is despicable. "Wouldn't you like to know?"

Thoughts of Connor's murderer bleed into the moment. If they wish to blame the sirens, this is just the way to do it. Even when the police took it upon themselves to reopen the case, to arrest Jude Osric—no one at the harbor believes Connor was killed by human hands.

My pulse jumps, and I ask, "Who gave them to you, Russell?"

Still smiling, he shakes his head. "None of your business."

I'm cut off from questioning him further by the arrival of Detective Thackery and two officers. The officers handle Russell roughly, handcuffing him, while Thackery surveys the docks as if he's taking a count of everyone present. His eyes meet mine, and I try to make my gaze as fierce as possible. The police should've been able to stop this. This is their job. Enforce the ban, protect the sirens—that's what they're meant to do.

Thackery and his men lead Russell from the harbor, and the fishermen begin discussing how they'll clean the polluted water. I turn to see where Jude has disappeared to. He's still standing by the dead sirens, his skin nearly as pale as theirs. As I head toward him, he stumbles a little, catching his heel on an upturned slant of wood. Then he kneels and retches over the side of the pier. Warren Knox leans down, asking if he's all right.

A part of me wonders at it, the intensity of this reaction—the same part that knows of Jude's dislike for the sirens. Russell is not the only person who considers them monsters. I wouldn't have guessed Jude Osric would be sick upon seeing their corpses. Perhaps it's more the violence of the situation that churns his stomach.

He rests his forehead on his knees. "I'm fine," he says quietly.

Warren shakes his head. "It's a terrible bit of business." His voice is rough, his eyes fixed on the harbor steps where the police and Russell are making their way up. When he catches sight of me, he touches his cap, before starting back toward the other fishermen.

I feel numb even as cold wind blows in off the sea. I can't think of anything other than Russell tipping poison into the water, alarm bells ringing, sirens choking, dying, their bodies dragged up from the waves. Jude straightens and lays a hand flat over his sweater.

"We need to visit the Sheahans," I tell him.

If Russell killed those sirens on Connor's behalf, it's high time we pay them a visit.

So close to the beach, everything looks colorless and damp. The cliff rises above us, a wall of jutting rock and mossy outcrops. There are crevices as well, good for hiding, for watching the sirens unseen. Russell's impetuosity reminds me how humans can be just as dangerous.

Sometimes I imagine Twillengyle as the ebb and flow of the sea. Kept in a pattern of bloodshed and carrying on despite it, cleaning its wounds with each coming tide. Not all the wounds are neatly mended, or ever heal completely, but the traditions carry on and the islanders carry on and Twillengyle survives.

Jude says, "Right now?"

I stare out at the sea, a gray expanse stretching toward the horizon. "Get yourself cleaned up," I tell him. "Then we're going."

CHAPTER THIRTEEN

THE SHEAHANS ARE one of the families who live on the far side of Dunmore, a ways from the harbor and the cliffs, so it's a bit of a walk to get there. We're silent for most of the way, the both of us still fixated on the events of this morning. I can see it in Jude's expression, ragged and gaunt, and I find it strangely reassuring. I don't think I could bear it if Jude approved of Russell's actions. He concentrates on the trail, humming an old island tune. The rhythm of it sticks in my head, until he steps into a puddle and the hum breaks off. He says, "I don't recall their house being this far off."

"It's just up here."

"And what are we to say to them, Moira? You want to tell them about Russell?"

"They're bound to hear it from someone, if not us."

Jude frowns, casting his eyes down. "I can't believe he did it," he whispers.

In my mind I see Russell's vicious grin once more.

I can't remember the last time someone violated the ban. It's a guaranteed prison sentence; as long as there are witnesses, the guilty party is nearly always convicted. Killing two sirens—alongside his possession of siren poison—will put Russell behind bars for quite some time.

You care about a couple of monsters, Miss Alexander?

The important question is: How long will the Council care? If a dock worker with no close ties to the Sheahans felt the need to attack the sirens, what's the rest of the island thinking? I used to have such faith in the ban. It was my father's endeavor, and once in place, I thought it unshakable.

Now I fear even those hard-won promises might fall to ruin.

I say, "What if whoever killed Connor gave Russell those cans?"

Jude scratches an eyebrow, looking puzzled. "Why would they do that? Russell could've gotten that stuff anywhere."

"Not anywhere." I bite my bottom lip. "That poison should be locked away in police stations, town hall, buried under floorboards. There's no reason for people to have it with the ban."

"There's cans in the lighthouse," says Jude. When I look over, he hastens to add, "I haven't had a chance to get rid of them. My uncle—"

I scowl. "Those sirens paid for a death they had no part in."

"I know." He sounds honest, but exhausted, and I recall the way he looked down at the dead sirens, shaky and pale-faced.

The dirt path curves ahead of us, flickers of sunlight catching on the fallen leaves at our feet. With a sigh, I say, "We'll have to ask Mr. Sheahan about that day."

"Moira." Jude hesitates, before continuing. "Remember to be kind to them. They're still under the impression Connor was lost to sirens."

"Except he wasn't."

"Think of me, then," he says, meeting my eye. His jaw tightens, until he drops his gaze, rubbing the back of his neck, and I hate how his sadness spelled out in so few words can dig in and cut out my heart.

The path leads us to the Sheahans' house of pale-yellow siding. In their window boxes, bluebells have dried up and browned, curling in on themselves. The shutters above are latched shut, and I think of one of the rooms beyond lying empty, collecting dust year after year. The room of a ghost.

Jude pulls off his cap and steps up to knock on the door. I stand a little straighter, smooth a hand over my coat. He gives me a sideways glance, looking as if he's about to say something, when the door opens.

Mr. Sheahan stands before us, blinking in the sunlight. He wears only a cotton shirt and trousers, his eyes red-rimmed and tired. He looks at Jude, perplexed. "Wick?" And then, "Moira?" Our names are questions in his mouth, like he's wondering if we're real.

I nod at him. "Afternoon, Mr. Sheahan."

"What are you doing here?"

It seems he might just fall to pieces where he stands, so I rush to get my words out. "Something's happened down the harbor. With Russell Hendry. We were wondering if you could—"

"That is to say," Jude interjects gently, "Moira and I have come to express our condolences. I understand how hard it must be for you at the moment."

Sheahan mumbles something like an affirmative. He looks a bit lost, clenching his hands before shoving them into his pockets. "Would you . . . like to come in? I can put the kettle on."

"Thank you kindly," Jude replies. "We don't mean to trouble you."

Sheahan steps aside, and we move into the entryway. I let him take my coat, studying him as he does so: the heavy shine to his eyes, that of a person who has spent several hours crying and is planning to go another round later in the evening.

Remember to be kind to them.

We follow him into the drawing room. The curtains are drawn like the latched front shutters, a sofa and mismatched armchairs turned toward the fireplace. In the grate, a fire burns low, giving the furniture pieces long shadows, darkening Sheahan's expression. I sit on the sofa, Jude taking a seat on the cushion next to me. Thoughts of tea are forgotten as Sheahan settles into an armchair, considering Jude.

"A great disservice they did you, Wick," he says with a grimace. "Arresting you of all people for a siren's doing. They ought to know better."

Jude ducks his head, saying nothing.

"Must've been difficult for you," Sheahan continues. "Finding him."

My eyes flit to Jude, but his expression doesn't change. He rubs his palms together, his voice soft as he replies, "I only wish I'd found him sooner."

Sheahan drags a hand across his face. "Don't think on it, Wick. I've done so myself enough times these past few days." He clears his throat. "I know you did all you could."

"We've just come from the harbor," I tell him. "Russell Hendry—he poisoned two sirens this morning."

Sheahan makes a sound of disappointment rather than surprise. "Shouldn't have done that." He moves his gaze to the floor. "Suppose the lad's in custody now?"

"He said he did it for Connor. To protect everyone else on the docks."

I was getting back our own, he'd said. Russell grinned while siren corpses lay just a few feet away. He called them monsters, like he wasn't one himself.

Mr. Sheahan only stares at me. His eyes look hollow, and I see no answers in them.

"Do you have any idea why Connor was on the beach that day?" I ask.

"No." He shrugs. "I don't know."

"Bit strange, isn't it? What with the storm."

"What about George and Brendan?" asks Jude, referring to the Sheahans' older sons. "Perhaps they could've been with Connor?"

Slowly, Mr. Sheahan shakes his head. "No. No, they were at the harbor with me. Securing boats for the weather, you see."

Jude meets my eye, and the expression he wears reflects my own thoughts. We aren't getting anywhere. Leaning forward, I say, "Was Connor at the harbor as well? Do you remember who saw him last?"

"He was." Sheahan swallows. "He was helping me strip sails. I—I told him to get home before the storm hit. Warren Knox offered to walk him back. A bit odd, that, actually. He'd never offered before, but you know he's awful careful now since Iona passed, God rest her. I told him Connor knew the way, can get there on his own." Regret weighs down each word, the sound of it worse than any possibility of seeing him cry.

I say quietly, "So Connor went back alone?"

He looks to the ceiling, closes his eyes. "Warren left a little while after him, but we all headed home soon enough. Thought we'd meet Connor on the path." He pauses, exhaling. "God, I was sure he had iron on him that morning. I was *sure* of it."

"Who else was by the harbor that afternoon?"

The question seems to sharpen Sheahan's confusion. His brow furrows. "Why do you ask?"

From down the hall, there's a soft shuffling. The three of us look over as Mrs. Sheahan appears in the doorway. She wears a dark dressing gown, her hair falling loose over her shoulders. She smiles upon seeing us, saying, "I thought I heard company. I'll make tea, shall I?"

Jude, having stood at her arrival, takes a step forward. "If you'll show me where everything is, Mrs. Sheahan, I'd be happy to help."

My lips thin. I try wordlessly to order him to stay put as he crosses the room. At the doorway, he glances around, and my irritation tapers off. His hands are shaking, just slightly, but it makes me think he might need the escape. I nod at him and he's gone.

Mr. Sheahan says, "We still have his violin."

I look back. "Sorry?"

"Connor's violin. Still packed away in his room."

"He was a quick learner." A smile tugs at my mouth. "Had a good ear for music. He would've been playing at the hall soon enough."

"You were his favorite at the dances." Sheahan rubs his eyes, but not before I see the wistfulness in them. "Always. Never had to drag him along when he knew you were playing."

"I remember." I clasp my hands together, anchoring myself. "Mr. Sheahan, you said Warren offered to walk Connor home? Can you think of any others who were there? On the path? Perhaps heading toward the beach?"

He heaves a sigh, grief outweighing any lingering curiosity.

"I don't know," he says again. "There was a lot of rushing around. Saw the Bracken sisters on their way home. Dylan Osric was at the harbor. Trying to get back to the offshore light before the storm hit, I reckon."

I swallow. I'd seen Nell Bracken just the other day. She'd mentioned losing students to sirens, but would she murder one of her own pupils? Perhaps her sister, Imogen, could be involved.

And Dylan Osric.

That very afternoon Jude had told me of his uncle's visit. I realize only now the timing makes him a suspect. His ill will toward sirens is also something I'm well accustomed to. In the years between Llyr's death and my father's, when Dylan Osric acted as Jude's guardian, there were many times he gave voice to his grievances. He'd hated my father, and my father had hated him in turn.

Bringing my attention back to Mr. Sheahan, I find him staring down at his hands. "If you don't mind my asking, Moira," he says softly, "none of this matters, does it?"

I've no desire to burden him with the knowledge of our investigation. I look toward the fireplace, but the fire has burned down, reddened coals and ashy-white wood left to grow cold in the grate. Already, the room feels colder.

And where is Jude? He and Mrs. Sheahan can't still be making tea, can they?

Standing up, I walk over to where Mr. Sheahan sits in his armchair. I take one of his hands in both of mine. "It may not," I tell him, "but thank you for telling me, all the same."

I head out of the drawing room, making my way toward the kitchen. Mrs. Sheahan must hear my footsteps. She leans out from the doorway, and I work to frame my expression into something pleasant.

"Looking for Wick?" she asks.

I nod. "Yes. Where is he?"

"He went out into the back garden. Poor dear. I think he was wanting some fresh air; he was looking so pale-like."

"I'm sure he's quite all right."

Rosy light warms the scuffed kitchen table and chairs. Through the lace-curtained window, I note the faded touch of evening in the sky.

"I'll just go and fetch him," I say, starting for the door.

Outside, two white sheets flutter on the clothesline. Across the way, Jude sits hunched over on a garden bench, his head in his hands. Though as I near, he rallies quickly, taking his pocket watch from his waistcoat to study its face. "My," he says, "is that the time?"

I take a seat beside him. "It's getting late," I agree.

His eyes slide toward me and away. "Did you get much else from Mr. Sheahan?"

"He mentioned some people near the harbor, yes." My thoughts are so full of names and possibilities I fear they'll all tumble out with the slightest sound.

"You're not still set on Warren Knox, are you? You think Connor's death has something to do with Iona?"

"There's also the Brackens to keep in mind—Mr. Sheahan said

he saw them heading home just before the storm. He brought up your uncle, too."

I hadn't seen Dylan Osric those few days Jude was behind bars. I'd kept my distance just as promised, but now I wonder why Jude asked it of me.

He makes a noncommittal sound, twisting the cuff of his shirt between his fingers.

I chew my bottom lip. "Perhaps Warren—perhaps he took Iona's death out on Connor."

He'd left the harbor soon after him that day, and his sister's demise gave him motive enough to frame the sirens. It could've been Warren who gave Russell Hendry those cans of poison.

Jude doesn't look convinced. "The Sheahans seem friendly with him."

"I suppose."

"And her death was more than a year ago. Why kill Connor now? Why kill him at all? He wasn't the one responsible."

I know this. I know all of this already. Staring up at the sky, I watch the clouds begin to thin over the horizon. "You think there's no association between the two," I say, without voicing it as a question. It's obvious from the way he disputes each piece of information.

"Well, it's a bit of a puzzle why a girl taken by sirens would relate to a boy murdered on the beach a year later."

"It's our best lead," I reply.

Jude looks away. He surveys the patchy grass, the rusted bicycle leaning up against the house. I fist my hands in my lap. I ask him, "Why did you leave?"

He swallows. "It's been a long day is all."

As we sit there, the sun dips below the fence. The moment

feels similar to when we stood over Connor's body—afterward, a silent walk along the cliff and up the spiral staircase of the lighthouse. Things left unsaid.

Turning toward him, I ask, in a softer voice, "Are you all right?"

I likely should've asked this earlier. Jude has been suspected of murder, taken from the lighthouse, put in jail. And I've yet to ask after his welfare.

He stands up. "It's late," he says. "We'd best be on our way."

We take our leave, and Jude is a paragon of politeness, straight-backed and smiling. Setting ourselves on the path, I let my thoughts turn over recent events. Not too far from the house, we come across Brendan Sheahan. Jude spies him first, saying, "Brendan," which makes me look up as well.

He raises a hand to touch the brim of his cap. "Hallo, Wick. You doing all right? I heard what happened down the docks. Some fellows said you were sick over it."

Jude flushes. "I'm well, thank you."

"Now you've come to convey your condolences, eh?" Brendan looks over at the house. "You and the rest of the island."

"We came to talk about Connor, yes," I say, stepping forward. I study him, wondering if he knows anything more than his father. "Russell Hendry killed those sirens on his behalf."

"I know." He makes a start for the house, but he half turns, letting me see the edge of his smile. "I only wish I were there to thank him." He touches his cap again, about to move on, when I grab hold of his sleeve.

"Can you meet me tomorrow morning?" I ask.

"What if I've got things to do?"

"You don't."

A grin cuts across his expression. "All right, Moira. Where?"

I tell him to meet me at the old church in Dunmore, and he promises to be there. Jude watches this exchange in silence, biting his lip. I think he'll question me about it, but once Brendan leaves, Jude doesn't say a word.

My hand catches at leafless branches as we continue on the trail. I smell wood smoke in the air, wet leaves, pine needles. It all seems magnified by the night, the wind whistling through the trees, the snapping of twigs underfoot. Neither one of us has a lantern, but it's odd when Jude ventures onto the wrong path. From here, the lighthouse is still visible, the white tower standing stark over the moors.

"Jude." I raise a brow, gesturing in the direction of the cliffs. "Your lighthouse is this way."

He puts his hands in his pockets. "Just as well I'm not headed to the lighthouse."

"Where are you going?"

He hesitates, gaze lowered as he scuffs at the dirt. "The Four Fathoms," he says.

I frown. "Why?"

"Because"—he digs the toe of his boot deeper into the soil—"I need a drink. Not a crime, is it?"

I blink at him. "No, but you don't—" I stop, uncertainty knotting my stomach. It's as though I've lost my footing, my entire perception of Jude Osric pulled out from under me. "You don't drink, Jude."

Voice bitter, he says, "How would you know?"

Something's wrong. I can see it in his hunched shoulders, his shuttered expression. I shake my head and say, "Because I know you, Jude Osric."

"No." He steps back. "No, you truly don't."

"You're being absurd," I snap. "Why you're doing this I've no idea, but if—"

He turns away from me. I close my hands into fists as he walks off, a tall lonely figure on the path toward Dunmore. Taking a deep breath, I shut my eyes, and when I look again, I stand alone in the disquieting silence.

CHAPTER FOURTEEN

I CLENCH MY JAW until it hurts, granting myself time to fume as I walk. Jude was clearly upset, whatever he said. Upset enough to wander into Dunmore and into the smoky corners of the Four Fathoms. I hope he knows I won't be the one to fetch him once he's drunk himself under the table. Perhaps he'll see just how unpleasant it is as soon as he steps over the threshold and come running back. I pause, glancing behind me, imagining his silhouette amid the fog and shadowed trees. But the path is empty.

Ahead of me lies a stretch of grass that runs toward the inky blackness of the sea. A slice of moonlight peeks out from beneath cloud cover, bathing the landscape in silver. The lighthouse stands as the last pillar before the cliff's edge, the first warning to sailors of the rocks below. I head for home and make it halfway there before I pause. A strong wind rattles the closed window shutters of nearby houses; tree branches scrape against one another, leaves rustling in the breeze. After a moment of indecision, I turn sharply on my heel and start for Dunmore.

The Four Fathoms is one of the oldest buildings on the island. It's a black-fronted tavern with fogged glass windows and heavy oak doors, light spilling over the threshold and onto the street. In bygone days, it was a renowned hideout for criminals—cutthroats and smugglers, pirates trading in contraband—but now it fills every evening with fishermen and dock workers up from the harbor. I pull open the door, letting myself in alongside the cold.

The low-beamed ceiling and flagstone floor give the place a closed-in quality. The bar is dark, polished wood, and ship masts are built into the structure, said to be taken from the first ships that came ashore. A fire burns in the cobbled fireplace, casting the room in a warm glow.

Next to the bar, Warren Knox puts out the remains of his cigarette in an ashtray. The shadows accentuate the deep lines at the corners of his eyes; he's a few years over thirty, but he looks older. The sea and the sirens both have aged him. He glances my way and seems taken aback by the sight of me here in this place.

I can only hope my own expression doesn't show my discomfort so readily.

"Mr. Knox," I say, calm and steady. "I'm looking for our Wick."

"Ah. He's here."

Warren tips his chin to indicate somewhere farther into the pub, and I nod my thanks, eager to be away. I realize I'd expected to find Jude Osric alone at a barstool, drinking away his sorrows, only when I happen across the opposite. He sits at a crowded table, his face rosy in the firelight. Several empty glasses take up space in front of him, and he smiles in a loose, faraway manner, making it clear he's already plastered. He laughs, leaning forward, and a vicious pang of something like envy strikes me near the heart.

However reserved he is, however shy, Jude has never set himself apart. He likes belonging—and he knows how to in a way I can't seem to match. I recognize the others at the table, of course. Gabriel Flint and Peter Atherton, Killian Riley and Hamish Tully. As I get closer, it's Peter who's first to notice. He nudges Jude with an elbow, murmuring in his ear.

Jude looks around. Catching sight of me, he says, "Oh." Then he grins, hooking an arm over the back of his chair. "Hallo, Moira."

Everyone else at the table appears to find this hilarious. They snicker into the backs of their hands, into their glasses, and I deliver them all a dirty look in return.

Putting a hand on the table, I say, "Get up, Jude."

Peter gestures as if to wave my words from the air. His dark eyes are glassy from drink, but I can tell he's still sharp enough to have his wits about him. "Just leave him. He's fine."

Jude pushes up from the table. He braces himself with one hand on the chair back, looking like he might keel over without it. I glare at Peter. "Fine? Fine, is he? Tell me, how was he supposed to get home like this?"

"He told us you'd show up eventually," Flint breaks in. He tilts his glass toward me. "And here you are."

Jude lets out a giggle before biting down on his hand to stifle it. I take him by the arm, and he sweeps his cap off the table, holding it in his fist. "Gentlemen." He moves to bow, but I jerk him away, pulling him toward the door.

"Moira," he says, "I know you're cross. I *know*, all right?"

I swallow hard. We get out onto the street, and at this hour Dunmore has settled for the night. The sound from inside the pub is shut out as the door swings closed, and I'm left to study Jude under the lamplight.

He puts on his cap, glancing back at the door. He smells of whiskey and smoke. We make it a little ways down the cobbles before he says, "I'd like to sit. May we sit? I'm so dizzy." And he sits right there on the sidewalk.

"*Jude.*" I've no hope of pulling him up without his help.

He squints. "I think if I were not so drunk, I'd know what to say to make you not so cross." He pats the ground next to him, smiling like he can't help it. "Come, Moira. Come sit by me."

I rub my eyes. Taking a seat on the curb, I ask, "Why did you go off like that?"

His smile slips as a shadow passes over his face. "I couldn't stand it—being in that house." Ducking his head, he presses his forehead to his knee. "It's my fault," he whispers. "It's my fault he's dead."

"Connor?"

"I'm meant to watch the shoreline. I'm meant to—if I just . . ."

I press my fingers into the fabric of his coat. "You can't blame yourself for his death. It's the murderer's fault, no one else's."

Jude scrapes a hand over his face. "Oh, Moira." He looks up into the night, openmouthed. "I didn't mean to get like this," he says, edging into a whine. "They kept buying me drinks. It was so kind, I couldn't—"

My eyes narrow. "Who did?"

He grins, lopsided. "I like very much that you came to get me." He flattens a hand on the pavement. "I like—Moira, you know, I've missed you so much."

"I haven't gone anywhere."

"You know what I mean." He lists forward, as though we're sharing secrets. "You stopped coming to visit. You're still—you still feel far away sometimes."

My pulse goes *tap-tap-tap* like rain against a rooftop.

His mouth twists. "I oughtn't talk. I don't know—I don't know what I'm saying."

"Come on." I reach out, taking his hand. "Let's get you home."

Jude picks himself up, staggering, and grips my hand tight. I lead him from the streetlights and cobblestones to the well-trodden path over the moors. His balance is completely shot; I imagine whoever plied him with alcohol thought it amusing. Jude isn't in that pub every night like the rest of them. They probably made a game of it. Once more I ask, "Who bought you drinks?"

"Oh, they all did." He grins wide. "'Keep up, Keeper.' That's what they said to me."

I grimace. "What did you talk about?"

He rubs at his eyes. "They kept asking me things. About . . . about being in jail and Connor and . . ."

"What?" My pulse jumps. "What about Connor?"

Jude makes a face. "They wanted to know how I found him. Why the police reopened the case." Wavering on the path, he claps a hand over his eyes. He says again, "I oughtn't talk!"

Irritation touches the top of my lip as I steer him straight. "Jude Osric," I growl, "what did you say?"

I imagine Jude rambling on about our suspicions for anyone to hear, too drunk to keep his mouth shut. Losing patience, I take him by the collar. "Who was it?" I say, yanking him down. "Who asked after Connor?"

He stares back at me. "I don't—" He stops. A little crease

appears between his brows as he considers. "I mean, it was everyone but—Flint, I think. He started it."

I press my lips into a hard line. "Right."

Jude swallows. Our faces are very close now, his shirt soft beneath my fingers. I release him, step back, and reach up once more to fix his wrinkled collar.

In the stretch of grass behind him, I spot a light in the distance. Someone else crossing the moors toward us, lantern swinging in the dark. I let my hands fall from Jude's collar, eyeing the light. The slow sway of it is almost hypnotic, the glow strengthening as the person nears. Then a curious thing happens—the light goes out.

My heart stutters in my chest.

"Jude," I whisper. "Jude, we need to get off the path."

"Hmm?"

He looks over his shoulder. I seize him by the hand, pulling him after me. We stumble down the hillside, through the wet grass and heather, tripping on loose shale. Blood rushes in my ears as I tug Jude down, the two of us lying still along the dark slope. "What on earth—" he starts, but I clap a hand over his mouth.

"I think someone may be following us." I lift my head a little, trying to see over the hill. "They just put out their light."

I'm abruptly glad we haven't a lantern of our own. I wait, willing Jude to keep quiet, listening for the sound of footsteps. Above us, the stranger draws close, and I turn my face into Jude's shoulder, my hand still pressed to his mouth. The person continues on for several paces, before I hear them pause and turn back around. I dare not move until long after their footfalls have receded.

I roll away from Jude, sitting up. Thoroughly unnerved, I brush dirt from my coat with trembling hands. When I look back, Jude is still lying in the grass, watching me through half-lidded eyes.

"You know . . ." I realize I'm raising my voice and lower it. "You know, I imagine you'd be a touch more concerned right now if you weren't in such a state."

He smiles sleepily. I wonder what might have happened had I left Jude to stagger back to the lighthouse alone. It would've been quite easy to come up behind him, to draw a knife and slit his throat. Reaching over, he pats my arm in a clumsy manner and says, "It's all right, Moira."

I shake my head. There's no telling who the stranger was. It could've been no one of consequence and I've dragged Jude halfway down a hillside for nothing.

Caution over carelessness, I suppose.

"Come on, then," I say, offering my hand. "Almost there."

We start back up the hill, walking the rest of the way to the lighthouse without incident. At the door to the keeper's cottage, I turn to Jude. "Where's your key?"

There's a long pause, while Jude no doubt has to piece together the word "key" before attempting to locate one on his person. He pulls the old skeleton key from his coat pocket and passes it to me. It feels like a heavy weight in my palm. I twist the key inside the lock, but it won't catch.

"It's—you need to lean on it," Jude tells me.

"You have a shoddy door," I reply, but it works, creaking open into the entryway.

I light an oil lamp, and the sudden brightness offers me a better view of him. Burst capillaries thread the whites of his eyes, the circles beneath them dark as bruises. I pull off his cap, gently, his hair looking unkempt in the hall light.

"Oh, Jude."

He smiles, uncertain. "Yes?"

But there are no words, I think, for what I want to say. "Nothing," I murmur. "Come, let's get you to bed."

"Tired," Jude agrees with a nod.

We take the stairs up to his bedroom. I push open the door, settling him on the narrow bed against the far wall. The space is plainly furnished and has a vacant feel to it. Jude probably falls asleep in the watch room more often than here. I slip off his coat and boots and pull the blankets over him.

"Thank you," he whispers.

"You're welcome."

Just as I move away, he catches at my wrist. "Stay."

"Jude . . ."

"Please," he says, his voice heavy with sleep. "Moira, please stay." His eyes are already beginning to close.

I kneel, the hem of my dress brushing the floorboards. Jude's hold on my wrist turns slack as sleep takes him. I comb my fingers through his hair, and he sighs, pressing his face into the pillow.

"Good night, Jude."

When I leave, I close the door behind me, starting on the pathway home.

I sneak into my house as quietly as possible, but my mother waits in the drawing room. She sets her knitting down, and I come to a standstill, unable to meet her eye.

"Moira," she says. It's a great deal different from the way Jude said my name not a half hour ago.

"Mother," I say, imitating her tone.

Moonlight seeps through a slit in the curtains, and the room is made colorless, somber, and drab. I take off my coat and hang it on the rack.

My mother says, "Where have you been all day?"

"Visiting the Sheahans," I reply, thinking it's the safest answer.

She picks up her knitting again. "With Mr. Osric in tow, no doubt. I heard you were by the harbor when the alarms went off."

My hands curl into fists, but my voice comes out as nothing more than a whisper. "Russell killed two of them." I take a breath, trying not to remember the shape of his grin. "Someone gave him siren poison."

"Yes, I heard that, too."

I rest a palm against the doorway. "The police took him away."

"Well, that's something, isn't it?"

I don't have an answer for her, and the soft click of her needles fills the silence. I think back on Jude Osric, asleep in the lighthouse, how he clutched my wrist and asked me to stay.

I need my violin. I want the certainty of my grip on the bow, to play until my fingers are raw. I need the sound of the sea at night, its white-capped waves like a string of pearls in the blackness. As I head down the hall, all I can see in my mind's eye is the lantern light out on the moors. The haunting sway of it—and the moment it went dark.

CHAPTER FIFTEEN

IN THE EARLY-MORNING HOURS, Dunmore is a pocket of inertia. I walk through backstreets even more worn down than the main ones, finding comfort in the stillness. Pale sunlight shines over the terraced houses, lace curtains still drawn and shutters closed up.

Tucked away among the winding streets lies Dunmore's abandoned church. It's a small structure, lonely and forgotten, both very dark and very old.

The stone exterior has weathered over the years. I suppose it had once been beautiful, when its painted murals—now colorless and cracked—gleamed in the light, and its tower bell rung the hour. The bell tower still stands, but the bell itself was removed a long while ago, to its new home in St. Cecilia's.

This church has no name, or if it did no one can remember it.

I stare up at the tympanum above the arched doorway. Carved into the rough stone are a pair of angels, drowning in the sea, faces eroded by time. Their wings are bent in odd ways, spread wide across the arch.

I open the door.

Brendan's promise to meet me is one I clung to last night. As I enter the nave of the church, I find him there already, sitting in the front pew opposite the altar. Light spills into the building through broken windows and cracks in the stone. It makes the shadows darker somehow, and I shiver walking up the aisle.

Brendan Sheahan inclines his head in greeting as I sit down beside him. "Morning, Moira."

"Hello."

He looks at the dusty pulpit, and I follow his gaze to a large wood carving set into the wall. Two engraved sirens stare back at us. They stand on the shoreline, their eyes wide and teeth bared, as a ship sails unsuspecting in their direction. It makes me wonder just how long sirens have dwelt in Twillengyle waters and how abandoned places always seem to hold more magic than others.

Brendan says, "Bit cloak-and-dagger, meeting like this." And despite us being inside a church, he begins to smoke, striking a match and slouching back against the wooden pew. The tip of his cigarette is the brightest thing in the room.

"Thank you, though," I say. "For coming."

He breathes out a cloud of smoke into the already stale air. He wears a cable-knit sweater, like Jude's, yet instead of his cuffs being frayed, they are covered in dark stains. Oil or ash. Also like Jude, Brendan is nineteen, but I remember him from back when he played his frame drum at the summer dances, before he gave it up for fishing, smoking, and the sea.

"What do you want, Moira?" he asks.

"To talk about Connor."

"Ah." He smiles, too sharp to be taken as kind. "Of course."

"I *am* sorry. Everything you're going through . . ."

Brendan waves away my apology. "Don't be," he says. "It wasn't you that killed him."

I look down at my hands, folded together in my lap. "Please, Brendan. I just want to understand what happened."

The old pew creaks as Brendan leans forward, resting his elbows on his knees. Cigarette smoke drifts toward the crumbled altar. In a soft voice, he asks, "Did you see him? On the beach. Were you there?"

I don't have the heart to lie, not about that. He glances back at me. I nod.

"I saw him afterward. When they—in his coffin." He swallows. With the back of one hand, he scrubs at his eyes. "What did he look like on the sand?"

I press my lips together. The sea takes what it wants, and some say that those who are taken by sirens are those who are wanted by the sea. Connor was left to bleed out in the shadow of the cliff. His blood had soaked his shirt, colored the surf, stained the foam red.

It wasn't sirens who took Connor from us.

Brendan makes a small, choked sound and tosses his still-burning cigarette to the ground. He crushes it with the toe of his boot, immediately lighting another. "What do you want to know?"

I let out a shaky sigh. "Why was Connor down on the beach?"

"Haven't the faintest," he says. "Might've been heading back to the docks for some reason and got turned around in the rain."

"But you don't believe that."

Brendan exhales a breath of smoke. "No. Our Connor knew the way from the harbor like the back of his hand. He could've made it in the dark."

I nod in understanding. Islanders need compasses for our hills and paths little more than one might need a compass in one's own house.

"Do you think he could've been meeting anyone? Or that someone brought him there?"

"Careful, Moira." Brendan smirks. "You're beginning to sound like your father."

My brow furrows. I stare at the carved sirens on the church wall. Their mouths are open wide, revealing teeth of jagged wood splinters. Brendan clears his throat, and his voice is rough as he continues. "People always thought he had one foot in the sea. They'll say the same of you if you carry on like this."

I look at him: another dark shadow amid the rubble of the church. "Do not patronize me, Brendan Sheahan."

"Then don't interrogate me." His cigarette burns red in the dimness, and I watch more ash flutter to the ground. "You're looking for something that isn't there. This—*this* is sirens, through and through." A pause. Quieter, he says, "This is just the way of things."

I feel a sudden loneliness, sitting beside Brendan, in the pews of a long-forgotten church. My heart aches for things beyond my grasp, for something I could not even name. I simply *want*.

Straightening up, I smooth a hand over the front of my coat. "Thank you again," I say, though I don't know what I'm thanking him for. Talking with Brendan has made me more uncertain than assured.

He smiles. "I've nothing else to do. Haven't even been back to the docks yet."

His voice sounds strange in this place, echoing off the stone walls. The air here is thick with smoke and dust, magic and time.

I take a step toward him, hand outstretched, and hesitate. I don't know what I can say to this boy. Brendan Sheahan, who spoke as if his own words did not hurt him.

"I only want to help," I say finally. Without waiting for a reply, I start back through the shadowed nave. Just as I come to the door, I hear the strike of a match in the darkness.

There are times, brief moments, when I think of Twillengyle as a balancing scale, poised carefully between kindness and cruelty. But now—perhaps for the first time—I find myself wondering if the scales ever tipped.

And if they did, which side is tipping now.

CHAPTER SIXTEEN

I MEAN TO HEAD for the lighthouse after meeting Brendan, but somehow I end up at the old well. It's in a little courtyard by St. Cecilia's, away from the shops and stalls cluttering the main road.

No one ever comes here.

Most say it's haunted by long-dead spirits, but I know the real reason why everyone avoids the well is because of the siren story attached to it. The tale is told to children at bedtime, or whispered among a circle of friends on the verge of a dare.

It's said that decades ago an islander came to this well to fetch some water. Sometimes he is named Ian, other times it's Isaac, but by all accounts he is dirt poor and lonely, a ragged soul cast out on the fringes.

So he arrives at this well, drops down his bucket, and begins to hoist it back up. Only when he does, he hears a voice, beautiful and echoing, coming from the depths below. He thinks it's someone trapped, but it is not—everyone knows it is *not*—and the man peers over the side.

He calls back to the voice, and the voice answers in song. It's the most gorgeous sound he's ever heard; the man barely even notices when the siren rises from the darkness and drags her claws across his skin. She steals him away into the well, and neither are seen again.

So no one uses it, because after so many years there might still be a siren waiting inside.

It's not that I use it either, but I've always liked coming here. A stone bench is next to the well, sheltered under the branches of an ash tree. I brush some dried leaves from the stone and sit down.

Not too far off, I hear people, their voices and footsteps carrying with the wind. But there's no one in sight. If there were, they'd only look at me strangely, wonder what I'm doing so close to a siren-haunted well. Or perhaps not. I am my father's daughter after all.

Brendan's words echo back to me: *People always thought he had one foot in the sea. They'll say the same of you if you carry on like this.*

Gavin Alexander was often seen as odd. People didn't understand why he couldn't let things alone—not realizing that my father hoped to better the island with his research. He knew of the dangers, but he also knew sirens belonged in our waters. I can only imagine what he'd think about an islander trying to frame them for their own wrongdoing.

I watch a leaf flutter up to the side of the well, turning over the case in my mind. I always arrive at the same questions. Why would someone kill Connor? Why frame the sirens? If there was something to be gained by killing him, I couldn't begin to guess at what.

Jude finds me eventually. Just as he always does. When he reaches the bench, he removes his cap, coming to a standstill before me. He looks neat and pressed, but his eyes still have that glazed shine to them, telling of his headache. Quietly, he says, "You weren't at home."

"So you thought you'd wander Dunmore all morning?"

He winces. "Moira," he says, "I'm so—"

"You did a fool thing last night, Jude Osric." Looking away, I set my gaze on the leaves falling from the ash tree. A hard wind blows in off the sea, heavy with salt. The chill of it sneaks past my collar and into my bones.

"I came to apologize." Jude takes a step forward, casting his eyes down. "I know it was thoughtless of me. I can only hope I wasn't too much of a bother."

"You mean to tell me you don't remember?"

He rubs the back of his neck. "I remember enough." He flushes. "I wish you hadn't seen me that way."

I brush more leaves from the bench and pat the space beside me. Jude glances at the well before taking a seat. Bracing his hands on the stone, he asks plaintively, "Why do you come here?"

This isn't the first time he's found me by the well.

The graveyard is a sea of people dressed in dark suits and dresses, black gloves and netted veils. I run out the gates, wet grass slipping under my feet, and Jude runs after me. I curl up beside the stone well, my hands pressed to my eyes. "Don't say it's all right," I whisper. "Don't say it."

Jude remains silent for a moment. Then, in a voice as quiet as my own, he says, "Of course it's not." He embraces me, and he seems so much older, so much kinder, so much of everything I am not. I cry into his shoulder, and Jude doesn't say a word about it.

Now I scuff my heel against the ground and tell him, "I met up with Brendan Sheahan."

Jude lets out a sigh. "What did he have to say?"

"He doesn't know what Connor was doing down there. Or anything else really. I couldn't get many answers out of him."

I watch Jude's hand skim back and forth over the stone. His gaze fixes on the base of the well. "What of the person you saw last night? The one following us?" He looks at me, studying my face. "Or did I dream that?"

"No. That was quite real." I swallow, recalling the terror in my heart as I tugged Jude down the hillside. "Though whether they were following us—whether it was indeed Connor's murderer—I can't say."

Jude shudders. "Gosh," he says. "I was rather hoping it was a nightmare." He gets up abruptly, to begin pacing back and forth. "All the while I was no help at all. Moira, forgive me. If they were following us, it was because they heard me talking. I should have—"

"Oh, sit down. There's nothing to be done about it." I curl my fingers around the edge of the bench as Jude sits back down. He does so with care, his expression contrite. I look him in the eye. "I do forgive you, Jude. I know you were not yourself."

He takes one of my hands, holding it between us. With his eyes lowered, I see only the fringe of his lashes, dark against his cheeks. "I would've never forgiven myself," he says, "if any harm came to you."

I stare at him for a moment, wordless. His touch is warm and solid, his palms hardened by calluses. An instant later he draws away from me, returning his gaze to the well. "We ought to discuss our suspects," he says, a somewhat uneven quality to his voice. "Those who were near the harbor."

"Right." I blink. "Well, if we're to believe the killer was out on the moors last night, it can't be your uncle, can it? He's all the way over at the offshore light."

Jude hesitates, seeming to weigh his words. "You said yourself it might not have been the killer. Last summer, before he left, my uncle and I—we had a bit of a row."

"I see."

I wait, but he doesn't appear eager to expand on the answer. "This row is enough to suspect him of murder?" I ask.

Jude twists his hands together, looking toward the ash tree. He says, voice soft, "Perhaps."

More secrets. I close my eyes, trying to center myself. I don't see how much longer we can go on like this. Jude spoke of it already, last night, his words slurred but truthful. *You still feel far away sometimes.* I wonder if he realizes he distances himself as well.

I tell him, "I've got to tutor today."

He turns back. At this angle his eyes shine amber in the light. "Who?"

"Eve Maddox."

Jude rubs his mouth, contemplative. "And the investigation?"

"Well, Eve is around Connor's age. Perhaps she knows something. If Connor planned to meet someone on the beach, he might've told his friends ahead of time."

Jude heaves a sigh. "That isn't what I meant, but all right." He presses the heel of one hand to his temple. "I suppose I've work to do."

"Like what?"

"I need to polish the lens, still, and clean the chimney. I ought to start on the monthly report, too—Daugherty will have my head if I'm late with it."

Folding my hands in my lap, I imagine Jude knocking at my door earlier: his coat unbuttoned, the bags heavy under his eyes. Had he rushed out of the lighthouse? Did he think I had abandoned him after last night?

My heart feels twisted in knots.

A sudden breeze whips up the leaves near us in a flurry of red-brown-yellow. I glance toward the courtyard. "I'd best be off," I say. "Eve will be waiting."

"I'll see you at Mass tomorrow?" He phrases it like a question. We've always seen each other at church; I don't know why this Sunday would be any different.

I nod. "Of course."

My answer seems to put him at ease. I stand, cross my arms over my coat, and wander closer to the well. I place my hands on the damp stone, peering over the edge. Algae rings the inside, stone blocks circling into blackness.

"Moira," says Jude. There's the faintest trace of anxiety in his voice.

Pushing away from the well, I turn around. "You ought to have been a sailor," I tell him. "So superstitious."

"Just because you can't see something," he says darkly, "doesn't mean it isn't there."

The words put my teeth on edge. Twillengyle seems riddled with secrets and half-truths, things seen and never quite forgotten.

We head out of the courtyard together, leaving the well behind us.

• • •

Eve's grandmother is the one to answer the door when I arrive. I grip my violin case tight as she looks me over. She wears a thin shawl across her shoulders, a nettled expression on her face. "You're late, dearie," she says.

"Sorry."

"She's waiting for you in the garden."

I nod, brisk, and head around the side of the house. The gate is already unlatched, and I step through into a tiny, cluttered yard. Empty flower pots and loose bricks line the edges, gardening tools piled against a tumbledown shed. Eve Maddox sits on a wood bench, her brown hair braided in a single plait and tied with a ribbon. Her violin is laid out on her lap.

"Afternoon, Miss Alexander." She smiles.

"Afternoon." I set my violin case beside hers on the bench, and motion her up. "Sorry I'm late."

"Where were you?"

"Nowhere you need worry about," I say. Eve flips open the clasps on her case, and I watch as she rosins her bow. "Have you been practicing?"

"Yes. I did scales just yesterday."

I take her violin in my hands. Plucking at the strings, I begin tuning it for her. Eve doesn't have the natural ear for intonation that Connor did—not yet at least. I've been tutoring her for almost two months now, and while she practices, she is absentminded: daydreaming about music rather than concentrating on the composition at hand.

"Did you try the piece I gave you?"

Eve makes a face as she twists the bow back and forth. "Yes, but it's incredibly dull, miss. When can I play something faster?"

"Once you improve," I tell her.

She places the violin on her shoulder, looking for my approval as she holds the bow just above the strings.

I reach out to tug her left elbow farther from her side before saying, "Good. Now, let's go through the A major scale; then you can show me how you're playing that piece."

Unmoving, Eve says, "Did you hear about Russell Hendry?"

"I was there."

The words escape my mouth without thought. I don't want to talk about this; there's no use talking about it. Russell's in police custody, and the sirens are dead. All for Connor Sheahan, buried in the cold ground. *Dead, dead, dead.* My heart throbs with the truth of it.

"I think it's awful," says Eve, "what he did. The sirens were only doing what's natural to them—shouldn't have to be punished for that."

I study her, head tilted, puzzled at this reflection of my younger self. "They still could've hurt someone on the dock, Eve."

"Not if they had iron on them. Isn't that what all those charms and things are for? To keep the sirens away." Eve looks earnest now. Her violinist posture has come undone: bow limp at her side, her grip too tight on the neck.

With her questions ringing in my ears, I try to smile. "Yes, that's what they're for," I tell her. "And it's what Mr. Hendry should've used."

"But he didn't," Eve says quietly.

"No." I take her bowing hand in mine, rearranging it over the strings. "That is why he'll get a good long prison sentence."

She manages to play through half a scale before asking another question. "Were you with Mr. Osric earlier?"

I pause, eyes narrowed. "Why do you ask?"

She ducks her head, worrying her bottom lip. For a long moment she doesn't answer. Until, finally, she says, "No reason."

I don't know what to make of that. I give her a curious look, knowing there must be a reason and somewhat peeved she won't offer it freely.

"Finish the scale, please."

This time Eve seems chastened. She goes through the scale from the start—slow, careful, concentrated—before we move on to the piece I gave her to practice.

Connor had played the same composition just last year. I search for the memory, for the sound of his violin when he hit that first note, and my chest tightens with the realization that I *can't*. The music distorts, past and present becoming one. Eve's melody blots out the fine distinctions that made up Connor's.

She finishes the piece—slightly out of tune, sometimes shrill—and brings the violin to rest at her side. "How was that, miss?"

"It's an improvement. You still need to work on playing slower."

Eve nods, and I hope she takes the words to heart.

I sit down on the little garden bench. Eve Maddox follows my lead, moving her violin case to sit in its place. She turns to face me, expectant. "Now," I say, "since you've asked me your questions, could you answer one of mine?"

"What is it?"

"Connor Sheahan"—I watch her expression shift, become solemn—"do you know if he said anything to anyone? That day? Perhaps why he was going to the beach?"

Eve holds my gaze. Her eyes are very dark and very young. She's seen the horrors of this island only at arm's length, not yet close enough to touch. "Angus Llewellyn told me Connor said he knew something," Eve whispers. "Said it was secret."

"Connor told Angus this?"

"Yes, miss. Said he had to meet someone after helping his da at the harbor." She pauses, staring down at her violin. "Obviously the sirens got to him first."

Taking a breath, I close my eyes. I lay my hands flat on the bench to stop them trembling. "Have you told anyone else?" I say, looking back.

Eve shakes her head. "No one else has asked." A lock of her hair loosens from her braid, and she tucks it behind her ear. "But, miss, you should know . . ."

"What?"

"Wick. Mr. Osric. Connor wanted to speak with him before he"—she swallows—"I don't know if he got a chance to."

My mind races. "Did he say why?"

"No," she says softly. "Not to me anyway."

I feel my skin flush hot, then cold. What could Connor have wanted to talk to Jude for?

There's so much I don't know. Every time I feel close to lacing a single thread, the whole thing seems to unravel in my hands.

"Right," I croak out. "I'll be sure to tell him." I stand, taking hold of my violin case. "If you practice that piece a little more, I'll bring you something faster next lesson. And remember to do your scales."

"I always do," Eve says, indignant.

"As you should."

I go into the house to let her grandmother know I'm leaving, and then I'm back on the pathway home. It's a short walk, not enough time by far to get my thoughts in order. So instead I cut across another trail and head for the moors.

The lighthouse comes into view, streaks of rust running across its blue-and-white spirals. I walk to the cliff's edge, where the grass is patchy and dried out, a bit of old fencing set along the crag to mark the fall.

My fingers are numb as I undo the clasps of my tattered case.

I wonder if Jude sees me.

Music hums in my chest, my pulse alive with it as I tuck the violin under my chin. I play until I am empty, thoughtless, stark as the salt air.

Until all I can hear is the sea.

CHAPTER SEVENTEEN

IT HAS RAINED DURING THE NIGHT, so the cobbles leading to St. Cecilia's are smooth and slick underfoot. I walk with my mother through the streets as the tower bell tolls the hour. The inside of the church is warm—a respite from the morning damp—but also stuffy, close, with so many islanders already present. We've arrived just five minutes early; there's not an empty pew in sight.

A few short from the back is Jude Osric, sitting where he usually does. After some *pardons* and *excuse me*, I get to the end of the pew. Jude shifts his coat and cap, and I take a seat next to him. My mother sits on the other side of me, leaning forward to exchange quiet hellos with Jude. We kneel, and I close my eyes, my hands folded on the worn edge of the pew in front. The familiarity of it calms my nerves, an imperfect mend for all that has shaken me in the past week. When I sit back, I whisper in Jude's ear: "I spoke with Eve about Connor."

He splays a hand on his knee. "Oh?"

"She said he planned to meet someone on the beach."

Jude's eyes stray to the altar ahead of us. "I don't know if you should be discussing murder while we're in church."

I scowl at him before casting my eyes toward the other pews. I'm looking for Warren Knox, and find him on the opposite side of the aisle. He is stocky and broad-shouldered, wearing his Sunday best. It doesn't stop me imagining the worst of him. He could've given those cans to Russell, could've led Connor down the cliff and slit his throat.

Beside me Jude murmurs, "Something wrong?" His forehead is creased with worry.

I swallow, shake my head, but my conversation with Eve continues to play out in the forefront of my thoughts. Connor had words for Jude Osric—and I need to tell him so.

Jude looks prepared to say something else, but whatever it might be is cut off by the sound of the choir. Everyone rises to their feet, and Mass begins. It's grounding, the songs and motions that follow in kind. I kneel once more and think of my father. I wonder if this hole in my heart will ever fade, if I'll ever be able to bear it without feeling so wretched.

Jude's eyes are still closed when I open mine. I watch him, contemplating what it is he prays for. It's not a thought I should have—somewhere I've no business prying. He sits up, brow furrowed, and I glance away.

When the service is over, Jude and I walk behind my mother, following the flow of people out onto the street. I blink in the cloudy sunlight. Jude scuffs at a dried leaf with his boot.

Usually, after Mass, Jude heads for the churchyard to visit his family's grave. I've seen him there when I've lingered in the yard myself, seen the careful way he brushes debris from their headstone, how he'll sit for some minutes, then set his hand atop the marker in farewell.

My mother starts chatting with several women nearby, and I take the opportunity to catch hold of Jude's sleeve. "Come back with us," I tell him.

He looks down at my hand on his arm. "Why?"

"I want to go through my father's books. I think they might help with the investigation."

"I've seen your father's books, Moira. They're just full of siren tales."

And it's sirens the police seem set on condemning. Two have already suffered in the wake of Connor's death. I meet Jude's gaze and hold it. "They're worth a look."

He gives me the slightest nod in return. "Very well."

My mother turns back to us. She raises her eyebrows, and I say, "I've invited Jude over, if that's all right. We're going to have a look through Da's trunk."

For a moment she regards me, dark eyes searching my face. I can't tell what she's thinking, and the obscurity needles me to the point of frustration. But when she glances at Jude, it's with a smile. "You know you're always welcome, Mr. Osric."

Jude inclines his head, cheeks pink. In that instant he is once again the little boy who planted flowers alongside me in our garden, rolled marbles across our kitchen floor. He and my mother maintain a stream of small talk as we head for home. I let their conversation wash over me, distracted as I realize this marks Jude's first real visit since the day of my father's funeral. We pass a cluster of trees, and the shingled roof comes into view, then green shutters, spotless white siding. My mother opens the door, and we move into the entryway.

Jude hangs his wool coat and cap on one of the wall hooks. The line of fabric against our wallpaper is quite the picture, Jude's coat hanging like it belongs there.

My mother disappears into the kitchen, and I lead Jude down the hall, into the drawing room. It's crowded with furniture: a threadbare sofa and odd chairs, end tables and a dusty old piano. Paintings cover the walls, and a hooked rug obscures the hardwood floor. Jude looks about the space as though it's new to him—or like he's trying to find some difference made in the years of his absence—but it's the same as it always was.

It's peculiar to think he must have as many memories here as I do in the lighthouse.

My father's books are kept in a large trunk tucked between the wall and the writing desk. A stamped plaque bears his name: GAVIN ALEXANDER. It's held together with brass fittings, and I pry up the heavy clasp, lifting the lid back.

Large leather-bound volumes take up most of the space inside, journals and loose bits of paper crammed in the gaps. Jude settles himself on the rug as I start pulling out volumes. Taking the topmost one off the pile, he cracks it open. "Going to take a while to sort through all this," he says. "What exactly are we looking for?"

I sit back. Numerous parts of this murder don't make sense to me, but the false blame makes the least of all. The killer could've disposed of Connor's body out at sea, buried him in the remote north of the island. Instead, they orchestrated the whole thing to mirror siren kills.

"They wanted him found." I look to Jude. "Perhaps it's not important *who* was killed but that *someone* was. The killer could've framed the sirens to undermine the ban. It's likely that same person gave Russell those cans of poison. They may want the Council to crack down on the siren population again."

Jude swallows. His gaze falls back on the book in his hands. "That's awful, Moira." He says it like I didn't know it was.

"It's murder," I reply. "What did you think it would be?"

Jude doesn't meet my eye. He flips through thick, yellowing pages, but his mind seems elsewhere. "That night in the pub," he begins, "I said . . . I told them you thought Connor was murdered. Just not murdered by me."

I press my fingertips to my father's trunk. I can hear the blood rushing in my ears. "Did you, now?" I say, voice low.

He pinches the bridge of his nose. "I wasn't in my right mind."

Gabriel Flint could've followed us from the pub that night. I'd seen Warren Knox there as well. I mention this to Jude and watch his brows knit together.

"I don't know, Moira," he says finally. "Part of me doesn't even want to picture it."

"Would you rather it be someone else?"

"That's not what I meant."

Lowering my gaze, I pick at a worn thread on the rug. "Eve mentioned another thing." I look up to meet his eye. "She said Connor wished to speak with you. Did he . . . ?" I falter. "Did he come by the lighthouse?"

A long pause stretches out between us. After what seems like an age, Jude turns over my words as though he doesn't quite understand them. He says, "Speak with me?"

"Yes."

His gaze cuts away.

"She said Connor knew something. Something secret."

At that Jude blanches, but still he says nothing.

"Jude?"

Looking back he asks, "What sort of secret?"

"Eve didn't know." I tilt my head to the side. "He could've been going to tell whoever he met on the beach. Perhaps that someone didn't like him knowing what he knew."

Jude sits very still, the line of his mouth pressed thin. The ticks of the grandfather clock in the corner become the loudest thing in the room.

"He didn't," he says at last. His voice is raw and rasping. "He didn't come to the lighthouse."

It's so obvious he's withholding something, I'm inclined to push him.

Yet his expression keeps me from it.

I haven't seen Jude look like this since the day he saw the washed-up bodies of his family. He'd stood among the crowd on the beach, ashen and motionless, the same bone-deep terror in his eyes. Back then my father took him by the shoulder, turning him away.

Don't look.

The only way I can think to remedy it now is to move on entirely.

I say, "All right," and pretend not to notice the breath of relief that hisses out between his teeth.

Digging a hand into the trunk, I pull out a leather journal. It's faded, stiff when I open it, my father's handwriting familiar and comforting. An inscription marks the first page, an old island rhyme.

*A flash of silver under sea, where siren song hath
taken me. Absent of color, absent of light, absent of
all that I knew in life. Bolt the latch and watch the
waves, pray sirens do not take me tonight.*

My father and Llyr Osric would spread out large maps of
Twillengyle, jot things down in notebooks, trek across the moors
no matter the weather. I remember watching them, wondering, a
small hand pressed to the plate-glass window.

Jude must be following my train of thought. Some color has
returned to his cheeks, and he stretches out on the rug. "We're
getting like them," he says, staring up at the ceiling. "This . . .
This is something they would do." I study his expression as he
speaks, but he seems neither pleased nor disturbed by the notion.

Biting my lip, I pile more books between us. I'm ever so careful
not to touch the one Jude mustn't open, the letter between its
pages conveying what he mustn't know.

I ought to burn it really. I should have years ago, the very
moment I found it—but the idea of destroying yet another piece
of Jude's family is a task I can't easily stomach. I may be heartless
in many respects, but my blood doesn't run that cold.

Jude gets to his feet suddenly, his eyes on the doorway. I turn
to follow his gaze. My mother stands there, hand on the frame,
her apron dusted with flour. She says, "Just wondering if you're
staying for dinner, Wick."

"Oh." Jude looks down at me, wringing his hands. "I don't . . ."

"You should," I say. I'm aware of what Jude's diet must consist
of: fish and porridge and biscuits. It's probably been ages since
he's eaten a proper meal.

"All right," he says to me, and to my mother, "Thank you."

We spend the next few hours poring over the contents of the trunk. A majority of the papers are charts, records of when and where sirens took to shore. There are strange navigational symbols beside paragraphs of description. I point them out to Jude. "Do you know these?"

He squints at a pattern of triangles grouped together. "They're danger signs. That one's for riptides." He taps another near the bottom. "This one is for sunken wrecks."

"Is there any for sirens?"

Jude studies the page before tapping a symbol in the top corner. It's a dotted circle around a small *s*. "For the sirens," he says.

There are many tales of how the sirens came to be. Their origins sway from one theory to another, all of it guesswork. Some think they were once ordinary women—shipwreck survivors, or those pushed off ships to drown—whom the sea took in, fashioning them into sleek and lovely weapons. Most others believe the sirens are creatures unto themselves, like the fair folk, with music as their lure and teeth as their hooks.

Whichever is true, they are like homespun magic: an ingrained part of the island, yet elusive as smoke.

"Moira," my mother calls from the kitchen, "come set the table for our guest."

I pick myself up, glancing at Jude. The tips of his ears go pink. He opens his mouth, closes it, before dropping his gaze back to the chart he holds.

It's been far too long since I last set our table for three. My mother's friends come to call in the morning hours, usually to whisk her into town. It's dinner for two, always, at the Alexander household. Yet when Jude sits in the place I've prepared for him, I feel that shift. Something changing. Water rising toward high tide.

My mother, for her part, has cooked a considerable amount of food. It's more extravagant than what we'd normally eat on Sundays, and I know she's done it only because of Jude. I root around for something derisive to say about it but end up holding my tongue. It wouldn't be fair of me to put Jude Osric in the middle of an argument. And as dinner progresses, every inane topic under the sun is brought forward and discussed. It's one of our greatest talents as islanders—to talk about nothing for such a long while.

Jude mentions how the Council plan to have a telephone installed in the lighthouse. My mother says, "Oh, that would be novel, wouldn't it?"

He nods in agreement.

"I think it's ridiculous," I say. "What good is a telephone when no one else on the island has one? Who would you call?"

Jude pushes around the food on his plate, brow creased. "They'll be putting one in the police station, too. And town hall. It's for emergencies."

I wrinkle my nose at him. A grin cracks through his annoyance, and I think he'd laugh if my mother weren't present.

Once we're finished, my mother piles all the dishes onto the counter. Jude gets up to help, but my mother just gives him a *look*. I recognize it as the one she used when we were young and did something that displeased her. He sits back down at the table without a word, only to fidget with the edge of the tablecloth.

And it doesn't stop her from enlisting my help. As I'm drying plates, I say to Jude, "You can borrow some of those books, if you like."

He flattens his hand on the tablecloth, smoothing the creases. "All right."

Back in the drawing room, we tidy the journals and charts left scattered over the rug. Jude gathers a few books into his arms, brings them to the door, and sets them down to put on his coat and cap. My mother comes out from the kitchen, and he nods at her. "Thank you for having me, Mrs. Alexander. It was lovely."

"Anytime, dear," she says.

On the front step, he pauses. Curling my fingers around the doorknob, I ask, "Shall I come by tomorrow?"

He nods, shifting his grip on the books he carries. "Yes," he says. "That is, whenever you like."

I smile. "Night, Jude."

"Good night."

He sets off down the walkway. I close the door and turn to look at my mother.

Under the lamplight, her eyes shine to a dark polish. Bunching a tea towel in her hands, she says, "That boy is getting just like his father."

It's an unwitting echo of Jude's earlier words. *We're getting like them.* Though I feel my mother implies something else entirely.

I follow her back into the kitchen. Leaning on the table, I ask, "What do you mean by that?"

"Just an observation, Moira." She folds up the towel, places it on the counter. "I had hoped some of his sensibleness would rub off on you."

I glare, hoping she can see the daggers in my eyes. "You think I'm a poor influence?"

She stares out the window at the leaden sky. "That lighthouse was falling into neglect before Llyr Osric died," she says, voice soft. "There was even talk about removing him from the post.

Your father filled his head with fanciful notions of the sirens— made him curious, excitable. The two of them together were more concerned about the past than the present, the magic of Twillengyle over its realities."

I swallow, not knowing what to say. My mother talks as if the magic and reality of this island are somehow separate. I've only ever understood them to be the same.

She continues. "Your father was charming as siren song when it suited him. The way he spoke and smiled and laughed. He could make people forget themselves, their responsibilities." My mother looks at me then, like she means to see into my soul. "He taught you things most fathers are not wont to teach their daughters. You wanted to know it all, and he loved you for it."

"Fathers are meant to love their daughters," I say stiffly.

"He could see himself in you." She pauses. "And you're diverting another Osric from his work, just as your father did."

"You're wrong," I say. "That's not what I'm trying to do."

"Perhaps you don't mean to," she says. "But you are."

I push away from the table. I feel doubtful and precarious— standing beneath her gaze—things I never felt in Jude's company, yet they are so quick to resurface with one word from my mother.

There's a bitter feeling in the pit of my stomach.

Though the sun has not yet set, I tell her, "I'm going to bed," and escape down the hall before she can say anything further. Once I reach my bedroom, I make a nest of my blankets. I want to remember Jude's smile at dinner, but instead my mind is packed full of the sound of my mother's voice, speaking words I've no desire to hear.

I know already I'm not fit to be a friend of Jude Osric's. I've lied to him, hid things from him, isolating myself in the process.

The past haunts us still, hanging over us like a knife point strung above our heads. I've kept my father's secret, but I do know this: We are not our fathers.

We are Moira and Jude, no more and no less than that.

Whatever decisions we make, they will be ours.

CHAPTER EIGHTEEN

IN THE NIGHT, I FALL ASLEEP quickly, lulled by the quiet and the dark. When I wake, it's still dark—but not so quiet. Something knocks against my window, three short raps.

I sit up in bed. Shadows envelop the room, but I can tell by what light there is that it's close to dawn. I feel sleep-heavy and clouded; perhaps I dreamed the knocking.

Then it comes again. This time the knocks continue past three, adamant, like someone wanting to be let in.

Cautious, I creep out from under the blankets. I shiver in my nightgown as I try to peer through the lace curtains, but all I see are glimpses of my own reflection in the glass. With a sigh, cursing the night, I draw back the curtains, flip the latch, and push open the window.

Jude Osric stands outside of it.

I wonder if this is indeed a dream. Though I don't believe I'd dream Jude looking like this. He holds a lantern high, casting his face in lamplight. His curls are windblown without his cap, his eyes shadowed by the lantern's glow. In the murk, there's something wild about him—an intensity to the lines of his expression.

"I thought about waiting until morning proper," he says, "but this can't wait."

Even his voice is strange. Low and quiet, a hard undercurrent to it.

I whisper back, "What is it?"

He holds out a hand, insistent. "Please, Moira."

I straighten up from the windowsill, nerves crackling beneath my skin. I am, at once, very much awake. "All right," I say. "Just let me . . . let me get dressed."

I shut the window on him. I head to my wardrobe, tug on stockings and boots, a dress and my knit cardigan. I do up my hair and place an iron ring in my pocket. I'm about to lift the window again, when I dash back, grab a pen off my desk, and scribble out a note for my mother.

Jude offers his hand as I climb over the ledge. I don't think he knows just how many times I've done this without his help. I jump down onto the grass, dusting off my palms.

"What's this about?"

"I'll show you," he says. "Come on."

We start in the direction of the lighthouse, the sky above us a mottled blue-gray. I shiver, hunch my shoulders against the chill, and wait in vain for my pulse to settle.

It's unlike Jude to keep me in the dark this way. Whatever he wishes to reveal, it must be terrible, to have him at my window before the sunrise. As we walk, he pulls out his pocket watch, checks the time, and rubs his thumb over the face of it before tucking it away.

Reaching the keeper's cottage, Jude hands me the lantern. His fingers tremble as he unlocks the door, his face pallid as he opens it. I snuff out the lantern light, setting it down on his desk in the hall. When I look back, Jude stands motionless at the door, eyes unfocused like when the police came to arrest him. I draw my lower lip between my teeth. "Jude," I say softly. "What's wrong?"

His brow furrows. He doesn't meet my gaze, but joins me at the desk. Pulling open one of the drawers, he takes out a piece of paper. It's folded, creased, and in the manner of dreams, I know just what it is.

He offers it to me. "You ought to read this," he says.

As if I haven't read it a hundred times over.

I take hold of the paper. The letter is two-sided. It's like part of a conversation, a section cut from a longer sheet of music. The first is a message from my father, calling Llyr by the name he used to, the one that now belongs to Jude. It reads,

> Wick,
> I say if you go without iron, you'll have a better chance. Sirens will be wary of the boat otherwise. I did so only yesterday and it's quite safe, if you're thinking of taking Pearl and Emmeline along.
> —Gavin

And on the back, Llyr had written his answer:

> I'll take the boat out tomorrow if the weather's right for it. Jude knows

well eɴoᴜɢʜ to keep tʜe light foʀ a
few ʜoᴜʀs. He'll like ʜᴀᴠiɴɢ tʜe place
to ʜimself, but cʜeck oɴ ʜim if we'ʀe
late back, would you?

—L

It's their last piece of correspondence. I want desperately to
scrub the words from my mind, the knowledge that my father
sent the Osrics to their deaths that day. It was no strange mishap,
no coincidence. Llyr went without the means to protect himself
and his family, forgoing iron because my father advised him to,
because my father told him it was safe.

How did Jude find it? The letter wasn't in one of the volumes
he borrowed. I hadn't taken it from the trunk.

I lift my eyes to him. "How did you get this?"

He places one hand on the plaster wall. "It was in one of your
father's books," he says. "You . . . It was all that was left in the
trunk, so I . . ."

"So you opened it." My breath comes shallow. "You opened it
and took what you found."

He looks at me strangely. "It was my father's handwriting,
Moira. Don't tell me you wouldn't have done the same." His
hand falls from the wall, his eyes flitting over my face. "You knew
about this."

I bow my head, shoulders hunched. "Only after the funeral—
my father's funeral. I found it sorting his things."

When I venture a glance in Jude's direction, it's like someone's
struck a match to him. He doesn't look lost as he did on the
night of Connor's death, or empty as he did when I accused him
of murder. He snatches the letter back, holds it to his chest, and

the searing anger in his eyes is something out of my nightmares. "That was four years ago," he says. "All this time, you . . . You had *no right*."

I swallow. "I knew you'd be upset."

"Oughtn't I?" His face crumples. He clutches the letter hard against his shirtfront, as if hoping the ink will bleed into his heart. "This is why you never visited, isn't it? Because you were keeping this from me."

The day sirens stole away his family, Jude spent the night at our house. My father brought him into the drawing room, and though I'd been sent to bed, I crept back down the hall to spy from the doorway.

Jude sat on the sofa by the hearth. A cup of tea steamed on the table before him, but he didn't touch it. He stared into the fire burning in the grate, a wool blanket wrapped around his thin shoulders. "I want to take a boat out as soon as it's light. If I can find something . . . I'd like to have something to bury." His voice was so flat, so hollow, it scared me.

In the chair across from him, my father leaned forward. He looked bone-tired in the firelight, as though he'd aged a decade within the day. "I won't be one to keep you from the harbor, but you needn't be out there. There's plenty of other men to handle this. I'll handle this."

Jude didn't answer for a long while. When he did, he simply repeated, "I'd like to have something to bury."

"Aye," said my father. Fire crackled in the hearth, charred wood shifting. "Aye, I know."

I shivered from where I hid behind the sideboard. I knew I was intruding on private matters, matters of Jude's grief, but I couldn't find the will to move. As I watched, Jude turned to face my father. He said, "I don't want to fall asleep."

"Would you like me to stay with you?"

"Yes." Jude's voice cracked, halfway to a sob. "I don't want to be alone."

In the hall of the cottage, I curl my arms around myself. I'd kept this secret dreading Jude would fault my father, blame him, never mind the fact that this was what our fathers did. They were all fascination and no fear when it came to chasing sirens.

"I used to lie awake at night, wondering how it could've happened." Jude pales markedly. "I could never puzzle it out. It didn't occur to me, you see, that they might've gone out there without any iron."

I cast my eyes down, tears blurring my vision. "Jude . . ."

"Your father . . . He just—" The rest of his words seem to catch in his throat. He pauses, taking a breath. "You should've told me. I deserved to know."

I look up to see his gaze has returned to the letter. He clings to it as though it might vanish at any given moment, his hands red and chapped against the page.

To think just yesterday I considered burning it.

"What can I do?" I ask. "How can I . . . ? How can I put this right?"

He shakes his head. "This isn't something you can put right, Moira."

I hesitate. His words feel like a door closing, like a ship leaving port. Panic jolts my heart into beating twice as fast. "What does that mean?" When he says nothing, I hide my hands in the pockets of my cardigan, biting my lip. "Connor's murderer is still out there. We still haven't questioned—"

"All right, enough." He closes his eyes. "I need to be alone."

I try to keep my voice regular. "For how long?"

He stares, incredulous, and I wish to disappear beneath the floorboards. More than anything I want to be away from here, on the cliffs, with my violin in hand and salt air filling my lungs. I move toward the door, pull up the latch. "I'll be off, then."

Jude remains quiet, but he looks over just as I step out. For a second, for a heartbeat, our eyes meet.

I shut the door behind me.

I reach the harbor before the fishermen set out for the morning. It's still early and dark enough for lanterns, the small lights traversing the docks as men ready their boats with lobster pots and trawls. The sun has yet to appear, but the sky lightens each passing minute, the horizon streaked pale yellow.

Heading down the main pier, I look about for Gabriel Flint. He's not at the dockside; instead, I find him gathering rope in the boathouse. The building is old, made up of clapboard siding and open archways, the wood faded by the sun. The inside smells just like the outside—like kelp and fish and brine. Nets hang from the rafters, creels and lobster pots stacked against the walls.

Flint pretends not to see me until I'm too close to ignore.

"I have words for you," I say.

"Well, poor timing, Moira. I'm busy."

Patience is a virtue I've never had in abundance, and I certainly don't have room for it now. As he hoists the corded rope onto his shoulder, I snatch hold of it. "That was hateful what you did to Jude Osric. You know good and well he doesn't drink."

"I don't see him taking issue with it." Tugging the rope from my grip, he adds, "What concern is it of yours, anyway?"

"He told me what he said to you. About Connor." I cross my arms. "What concern is that of yours?"

"Just being curious." He smirks. "I suppose you think that's criminal of me."

My lip curls. He pushes his cap back, turns away, and heads for the line of boats still anchored at their moorings. He'd questioned Jude that night and gotten answers. He knows I believe Connor was murdered—though when we sailed to Lochlan, he didn't seem opposed to the idea either. At least when Jude was set to take the fall for it.

I'm out of the boathouse and on Flint's heels in an instant. "What do you think they'll do with Russell Hendry?" I ask.

He spares me a glance. "I hear they're keeping him locked up till trial."

I still can't comprehend what drove Russell to tip that poison in the sea. Did he really have so little interest in his freedom? Was he that enraged over Connor's death? He could've been coerced, perhaps, blackmailed—any number of possibilities.

But I want more than possibilities. I want facts and hard evidence, all lined up in front of me. I want *answers*.

Flint says, "And I don't know where he got those cans, before you ask."

Through gritted teeth, I ask something else entirely. "Do you know where I can find Warren Knox?"

He raises a brow, perplexed, but nods toward the boats. "He'll be setting off, same as everyone."

I start in that direction, my boots clacking against the rotting wood of the dock. Men turn to watch me, pausing in their work, the lines around their eyes crinkling. A few of them—of the elder generation—tend to keep rowan sticks in the pockets of their overalls alongside the iron nails they have for protection. They're the ones who took to blood sport in the past. I think they worry the sirens might smell that blood on their hands and desire some in return.

The last of the lobster traps are stacked on deck. Crews begin casting off their mooring lines. I spot Warren Knox on a boat with half a dozen other men and dash over, calling out to him.

"You oughtn't be down here, Miss Alexander." He says it friendly-like, but I know where I'm not wanted. Lately, it's quite a number of places. The harbor, the police station, the lighthouse. Only those at the dance hall seem in want of my presence—or rather, in want of my fingers on violin strings and my hand around a bow.

The realization leaves me cold. "I wanted to ask you about Connor," I say.

Warren's expression clouds over. He doesn't say anything at all, disregarding me as someone passes the stern line over to him.

I can do nothing but watch as they push away from the dock. Morning fog skims the water, waves ebbing into foam. Warren's boat makes its way out of the harbor, and I turn to make my way back up the cliff.

Once I reach the moors, my gaze shifts unerringly to the lighthouse. I tear my eyes away, silently berating myself. I ought to be glad for Jude Osric. Now he knows better than to treat me kindly. Now he's free of my treacherous self.

I go home only to grab my coat. I've other business to attend to, and though it feels like eons since I woke to Jude standing at my window, it's still the dawn of that day. Slipping my hands into my coat pockets, my fingers touch upon a bit of paper. I take it out, unfold it, and realize what it is.

It's the note he left me when I stayed the night in the keeper's cottage. A note I tucked away and promptly forgot about. I picture him writing it, taking it down the hall, sliding it under the guest room door.

Morning, Moira.

I crumple the paper in my fist.

CHAPTER NINETEEN

CATRIONA FINLEY APPEARS both mystified and exasperated to observe me at her desk again. "What's the nature of your visit this time, Miss Alexander?"

On the other side of the room, two gentlemen sit, quietly conversing. From the corner of my eye, I catch the pair glancing in my direction. I turn fully to stare at them until they look pointedly elsewhere.

To Catriona, I say, "I'm here to see Russell Hendry."

"He hasn't been put on remand for you to harass him."

"I'm not here to harass him." I put a bit of steel into my voice.

She returns her attention to her typewriter, typing something and pushing the carriage back. "I can give you an hour with him. *If* he agrees to see you."

My mouth quirks in a half smile. "I'd be much obliged."

An officer escorts me to the cells just as when I came to visit Jude. I walk down the now-familiar hall, unnerved by that familiarity. It's worsened when I realize Russell has been placed in the same cell. He sits on the wooden bed, leaning back against the wall. I can imagine Jude seated in the corner as before—the memory impressing upon reality until I see him there, head ducked, one knee to his chest.

That ghost of Jude Osric looks up to hold my gaze.

On the bed, Russell folds his arms. A shard of sunlight enters through the barred window, casting lines over his pale face. He leers at me in such a way that my hands curl into fists.

"What do you want, Moira?"

"To talk."

He looks away, eyes half-lidded. "That so?"

I bare my teeth as he did at the harbor. When his attention slides back to me, I level him with a glare. "Tell me where you got that siren poison."

"Told you on the dock it was none of your business."

"It wasn't your business to kill two sirens," I snap. "But you went and did it anyway."

He grips the edge of the bed. "I heard tell you paid Wick a visit in here," he says.

I swallow. For some reason the words twist my stomach, quickening my pulse. That phantom likeness of Jude is still pressed against the wall. He watches me, waiting for my answer.

"That's the truth," I reply.

"Aye." Russell rubs the stubble on his chin. "I reckon they see rightly now."

"What's that?"

"No human person killed Connor. It's our blood in the sea, but we're not the ones to spill it. Those sirens will pick us clean off this rock if we let them."

My insides roil. "We've spilled more of their blood than they have ours."

"I'm not arguing with you about this." He scoffs. "I know what you're like. What your father was like. They'll have hunting parties organized soon enough, and you better stay out of the way."

I imagine the boats going out with harpoons and poisons, returning with siren bodies piled on deck. I was so young when they were hunted; the occurrences seem closer to myth than the here and now.

Fear snares me in its claws. How could I play music on the cliffs while others sharpened their knives the very same morning? How could I sell pastries at my mother's stall as vendors hawked necklaces strung with siren teeth?

I ask Russell, "Did someone give you those cans?"

Sitting straight, he scrubs a hand through his hair. His eyes fix on the floor, his profile split between shadow and light.

Beyond the jail corridor, a door slams open like a thunderclap. The sound sets my heart pounding, and I turn my head toward it. Voices echo from the lobby, rising in volume.

I take off without another word.

When I open the door, my lips part, the sight before me prickling the hair at the back of my neck.

Jude Osric stands in the center of the room.

At first I think it's another apparition, but no—this is the real Jude, flesh and blood, breathing hard like he's run across the moors. It's plain he left the lighthouse in a hurry. He wears neither coat nor hat, his work shirt rolled to his elbows and missing a front button. A streak of ash marks the curve of his jaw.

"Moira." He takes me by the shoulders, wide-eyed. "Are you all right?"

I frown up at him. "How did you know I was here?"

He looks around, eyebrows drawn together. "I—I got a note. It said . . . you'd been arrested." His gaze returns to my face. He breathes in, exhales. "I see . . . I see now that's not the case."

"No." A sense of unease creeps over my spine. "I only came to speak with Russell."

Jude steps back, his expression now mirroring my confusion. I watch his Adam's apple shift as he swallows, and the unease I feel transmutes into something akin to dread.

Why would someone leave Jude a note like that? Deliberately false, so easy to expose, unless they knew he'd race over as a result? Unless they just wanted him gone.

Numbness seeps through my skin, through my bones, down to the very marrow.

"Jude," I say, "I think we ought to get back to the lighthouse."

We pass the walk through town and over the moors in painful silence. Recovered from his initial fright, Jude seems to recall his grievances against me. He sticks his hands in his trouser pockets, his eyes on the ground. The wind picks up, freeing strands of hair from my bun, and dense clouds gather above us, predisposed to rain.

"Weather's turning," I say.

"Yes," says Jude, without looking up.

It's my one and only attempt at small talk.

The lighthouse looms ahead, austere before the gray sky. Jude quickens his pace, then takes off, breakneck. I speed after him. He skids to a stop on the path, staring at the cottage door, and raises a hand to cover his mouth.

Deep gouges mar the wood in a crisscrossing pattern. Stepping closer, Jude presses his fingertips to them. He makes a faint, distressed sound and pulls his skeleton key from his pocket, hands trembling as he tries the lock. It clicks open, the door swinging inward. A folded bit of paper lies in the entryway, as if slipped through the mail slot. Jude picks it up, looking it over. His eyes widen. "Moira," he chokes out. "*Moira.*"

I take the paper from him. On it only two words are written.

Stop looking

Connor's killer was here, today, just moments ago. I glance around, half expecting to see them in the distance, as I saw that figure walking toward us on the moors. Instead, my gaze latches on to something else. Part of Jude's garden is just visible from here. I see green sprouting from the dark soil—alongside a grooved stick of polished wood. "What's that there?" I ask.

Jude sets his sights on where I point. His mouth turns down at the edges. We head over together, and he kneels, pulling the object free.

The blade of the knife is grimy and stained brown. It could be dirt, but the smear across the steel looks more like blood. Jude stares, frozen. It's another moment before he uncurls his fingers from the handle, the knife dropping with a *thud*.

"In my garden," he whispers.

I crouch beside him. "It's meant to scare us. That could well be animal blood."

Jude doesn't appear to hear me. He says, "They put this in my garden," and pushes his fingers into the earth, trying to tether himself. His breathing turns shallow, ragged at the edges.

Anger coils about me. Someone sent Jude off so they might damage his home, leaving a bloodied knife for him to find. The longer I dwell on it, the more furious I become.

"They're watching us," Jude gasps. "They *know* . . ."

"Breathe, Jude. Just breathe."

He does so, squeezing his eyes shut. Minutes pass, and after a while he says, "I can't have this. I need to . . . If the police ever . . ."

I pick up the knife. The handle is sun-warm in my grip, the edge of the blade still looking sharp enough to cut. Jude's eyes dart to my face. "What are you doing?"

I meet his gaze. "I'll get rid of it."

He shakes his head. "I won't ask that of you." When he holds out a hand for the knife, my fingers tighten around it.

"You needn't ask," I say quietly. "Let me do this."

Jude considers me. His expression is grave, his eyes so dark I see my own reflection in them. Finally, he nods and sets his hand back on the ground.

The knife fits neatly into my coat pocket.

Taking my leave, I look toward the beach. Swells break as they kiss the shore, the water blue-black and endless, stretching out into forever.

I do not bring the knife to the sea.

Instead, I walk over the hillside and bury it deep beneath the heather. It's slow going, as I have only my hands, but I don't begrudge the work. If it saves Jude from doing something so ghastly, I'll be glad for the dirt under my nails.

There's no sign of anyone as I dig, but I feel watched all the while. We're caught between the start and the close, racing to meet whatever lies ahead. My blood sings in my ears.

I am so, so ready.

CHAPTER TWENTY

THE DANCE HALL IN DUNMORE is a large, open space, made up of gleaming wood and lofty chandeliers. Windows line the walls, high and arched, reaching for the rafters. I make my way across the length of the room, my boot heels loud against the floorboards.

It's been two years since I was last here. Two years since I last stood on the stage, took up my violin, and played for a crowd of people. There are dips in the floor, black marks, from all the nights islanders and tourists filled the emptiness. It's an effort to push down those memories—of my father playing onstage, of Jude's hand in mine as we spun around, dancing together—but I've practice in snuffing out such ruminations.

Next to the stage is a door to the back room. It has no lock, but I tap my knuckles on the wood before letting myself in.

The inside is just as I remember: small, cramped, woefully untidy. Dust covers every surface, from the stage equipment to the piano pushed against the back corner. An oil lamp burns atop the desk. Behind it, Peter Atherton sits, looking over sheet music. When he glances up, his jaw goes slack. "Moira." He sets down his papers to place his hands flat on the desk. "Please, tell me you're back."

I put my fingertips to the desk's edge. "I don't think so."

He shifts, leaning back, now watching me with something like suspicion. At twenty, he's the oldest of us, the one trying to hold everything together in my absence.

I feel only a little sorry for him.

"Then why are you here?" he asks.

Skimming my fingers along the desk, I stare at the lines made through the dust. "I'm wondering if Flint was at rehearsal yesterday."

I'd left the harbor without seeing him set off. If he hadn't gone out, he'd have had time to leave a note at the lighthouse, and if he didn't show up for rehearsal, he could've planted that knife in Jude's garden. There had been a similarly stained knife in his boat—now I wish I'd gotten a better look at it.

"We didn't have rehearsal yesterday." Peter catches my eye. "You'd know that if you were back with us."

I grind my teeth. "Why didn't you?"

He shrugs, looking away. "Bree was feeling poorly. We've moved it to later this evening, if you'd like to attend."

Even if I wanted to, I'm not sure I know how to return. I've gotten used to playing in the wind, above the roar of the surf, without recognition or applause. But at the hall, my violin accompanied other instruments, giving layers to a song. People waited for my music, listened to it, danced to the melodies I performed.

"I know you're still cross with him," says Peter.

"And you," I bite back.

"It's been two years, Moira." He lifts a hand, palm up. "Surely your pride has recovered by now."

I press my lips thin. "Flint insulted me."

"He apologized."

"Only after I demanded it. Only after you said naught about it."

Peter rubs his forehead, eyes closing for a moment. "It was a bad night," he says.

That much is true. I remember it down to the date, as it was the day before the anniversary of my father's passing. I was ill-tempered, as such, and after dealing with a crowd of mostly tourists, everyone was a bit short with one another. Once Peter, Flint, and I were the last musicians in the back room, Flint had it out with me.

"Third figure of the set," he said. "Don't think I didn't notice when you came in late."

I huffed out a breath as I opened my case, placing my violin inside.

"And you can't start a reel like that out of the blue." He took me by the arm, my hand still gripping my bow. "Might come as a shock, but you're not the only one up there."

Peter stopped fidgeting with his chanter reed just long enough to look in our direction. He said only, "Flint."

Flint paid no mind. Seizing my bow, he held it as if to snap it in half.

I looked him dead in the eye. "Give that back."

And he did. Right after he offered up a gleeful smile and split the wood in two.

I'd walked out with no intention of playing at the hall again. Now I stand in front of Peter's desk, contemplating that very idea. If I'm to keep tabs on Gabriel Flint, this is the best way to do so.

I gaze through the open door to the stretch of floor beyond. Come this weekend, islanders will arrive as the sun goes down. The place will fill with music, the click of heels, couples whirling, laughing, kissing.

I do miss it. I really do.

Turning to Peter I ask, "What time this evening?"

When I enter the hall for the second time that day, it's with my violin case in hand. I clutch it tightly as I walk to the stage. There's Peter with his bagpipes, Flint with his flute. Bree Cairns stands with them, watching as I make my way over.

"Why have you come back?" she asks, more curious than vexed. She's a fine singer and an adept pianist. Her dark hair is done up in a chignon, her eyes shining in the evening light coming in through the windows. That light falls upon the stage, turning the wood a burnished gold.

"Because I've decided to."

The answer is a simple one—too simple for something that feels momentous—but Bree takes it at face value. She looks to Peter, as I do, and his eyes meet mine.

"Leave your case in the back room," he tells me.

Just that. It's like the three of them were waiting for me all along, knowing I'd return, and now that I have it's business as usual. I slide my gaze to Flint, and he grins back, devilish. I grip my violin case that much tighter.

In the back room, I find someone else waiting for me. He steps away from the desk when I come in, holding his cap at his side.

I stop in my tracks. Then I hurriedly close the door behind me. Through it, I hear Peter laugh, but it's muffled by the rush of blood in my ears. "What are you doing here?" I ask.

Jude presses his knuckles to his mouth. I don't think he's ever stood in this room, but he doesn't look wholly out of place. The shadows give weight to his solemn expression; he's little more than a silhouette in the dim. My heart hammers as I wait for him to speak. He says, "Peter told me you'll be playing at the dance this weekend."

"That's right."

"I didn't believe it. It's all anyone's talking about at the docks."

I shift my violin case from one hand to the other. "Jude," I say.

He seems to grasp the uncertainty in my tone. "I think"—he pauses, biting his lip—"I think we ought to talk."

"Don't worry. You made yourself quite clear." Unexpectedly, my voice breaks, and I clamp my mouth shut.

Jude looks down, kneading his cap. I don't know what he wants from me, but having him here, so close, tugs at my heartstrings. "Moira," he starts, only to pause again, searching for words. He flicks his gaze back up, eyes dark. "You are—you have always been—my closest friend. I don't wish to spend another few years apart because of this. It's hypocritical of me to be upset with you for keeping secrets, when I've done the very same."

I'm not sure what he means, but now seems a poor time to inquire. I lay my violin case on the desk, pressing my fingers to the clasps.

"I can't fault you for your father's actions," he says. "Nor can I fault you for shielding such actions from me. I know you were only trying to protect his good character." In the dimness, I see his grip tighten on his cap. "He didn't force my family out there iron-less. My father made that choice."

I swallow. "I am sorry, Jude." I look up at him, at his dark eyes, the set line of his mouth. "I should not have kept it from you—certainly not for so many years."

He offers me a small smile. "Well," he says, "I understand why you did it. Now, I'm sure I've taken up quite enough of your time. I oughtn't intrude upon your practice any longer." He moves for the door, but I catch hold of his sleeve.

"You can stay, if you like."

His lips part. As I watch, a blush rises in his cheeks. "Yes," he says. "Yes, I would like that very much."

Warmth kindles to life in my chest. I can't help but grin as I unfasten the clasps on my case and rosin my bow. Jude opens the door once I've finished preparing, and the others eye us without comment. Onstage, I take up my violin. Jude sits with his feet dangling over the edge, the pink across his cheeks not yet faded.

We manage to play through our entire set. In perfect moments, everyone is wonderfully in tune, the song permeating the hollows of my heart, humming through violin strings. Realizing I've closed my eyes, I open them, and find Jude watching me.

His expression is soft, his own eyes far away. I imagine him at the dance, the sound of his laugh entwined with the music, the brightness of the hall spilling out into the night. Bree begins to sing "Over the Moor," and Jude smiles at me as though we're sharing a secret. I want to memorize that smile—to preserve its image and place it beside all the compositions in my mind—but the song ends all too quickly, and Jude's gaze breaks away.

When Peter calls an end to rehearsal, Jude gets to his feet. He waits on the dance floor as I head into the back room. On my way out, I catch him looking up into the rafters as if studying the woodwork.

"How was I?" I ask.

He tucks his hands into his pockets. "You know I always love your music, Moira."

I grin back. "I do hope that means you're coming to the dance."

"Wouldn't miss it."

We step out of the hall together. The sun has dipped below the nearby shops, casting shadows, the smell of burning leaves sharp in the air. I swing my violin case back and forth, content with a job well done. That feeling soon dulls when I remember why I was there in the first place.

"We need to keep an eye on Gabriel Flint," I say.

Jude turns on his heel, walking backward to hold my gaze. "I reckon most of our suspects will be in attendance at the hall," he says, "once people find out you're playing."

I kick a stray leaf down the sidewalk. "Mr. Sheahan said he saw the Brackens walking home that day. We've yet to question them."

The sisters are also Jude's closest neighbors. It'd be easy for them to put a knife in his garden and take off back home before anyone noticed. Whoever might be at fault for Connor's fate, we'll have to build a case against them. Someone we could place at the crime scene around the time of Connor's death, at the harbor before Russell tipped that poison in the sea.

We reach the edge of town—cobbled streets disappearing into heather and moss and sprawls of shingled houses—and I pause as the path diverges.

Jude says, "I can meet you tomorrow, if you want to visit them."

I stare out at the wide sweep of grass tinted red by autumn.

After today I ought to feel gladness, some sense of satisfaction. Jude is once more at my side, once more willing to help me investigate. My hands are still warm with the memory of my violin, my fingers still pleasantly sore after playing for such a stretch.

Yet dread continues to gnaw at my insides. It seeps through my rib cage, winding tight around my heart. I think of the scratches marking Jude's door, the knife in his garden. The police have made no other arrests as far as I'm aware. It doesn't sit right with me, and the longer this goes on, the longer the killer is out there, watching us, aware of our investigation.

"We'll go in the morning," I tell Jude.

We part ways, and I look back, regarding him until he's but a figure in the distance, cast in relief by the setting sun. Gripping my violin case, I start for home.

CHAPTER TWENTY-ONE

JUDE APPEARS ON MY DOORSTEP just after breakfast. When I lead him into the kitchen, my mother looks him over, lips pursed. "Finished all your morning duties?" she asks.

"Yes, ma'am." He smooths a hand down the front of his wool sweater, nervous, as if we're at town hall and my mother is Mr. Daugherty.

Our table is still cluttered with odd plates and silverware, the butter dish flanked by my teacup and a tiny basket of bread rolls. Jude sits down opposite me, and I push the basket toward him. "Have you eaten breakfast?"

He shakes his head, but he doesn't take a bread roll, either. He twists the loose threads at his cuff, pulling at the ones that have come undone. His expression is drawn, and he looks so tired; I fear he's passed another night without sleep.

My mother pushes a cup of tea into his hands. "Eat, Wick," she says. "I won't have you wasting away in my kitchen."

Jude nods meekly, setting the teacup on the table beside him. He looks to me and says, "I repainted the door." His voice is quiet, but it wavers nonetheless. "It was in need of a new coat anyway."

I want to say something like *you shouldn't make excuses*, because it's foul, intolerable, for Jude's home to be treated in such a poor fashion. But another part of me understands his desire to bury this, to render the event mundane. This is Jude's way of coping.

At the counter, my mother picks up a basket of pastries. She says, "I may not be back until late, Moira." She nods at Jude. "Take care, Wick."

When she's gone, Jude heaves a sigh and starts diligently buttering one of the bread rolls. Confirming my suspicions, he mumbles, "I didn't get much sleep last night."

I tap my fingers against the table. "Well, you're not sleeping now. We've got to go question the Brackens." Though even as I say it, my heart aches in sympathy. It's easy to see why Jude might have trouble sleeping. He lives alone, at the island's edge, and his nearest neighbors may be the persons responsible for Connor's death.

Imogen and Nell Bracken reside in a small cottage by the cliffs. It's a quarter of a mile away from the lighthouse, close to the crime scene, close enough to observe Jude's comings and goings if they wished to leave him a message.

They are among the few people Mr. Sheahan mentioned seeing around the harbor, aside from Jude's uncle.

I want it to be them. I don't want it to be them.

I rack my brain for recollections of their family history. It's rare for families on this island to go completely untouched by siren song. Somewhere down the line, there's the great-grandmother who survived an attack, the happily married fisherman lost to sirens at sea. My father's father had been lured in by their song, stolen away when Da was just a child himself.

To have killed Connor, Imogen and Nell need a motive.

Jude rubs his eyes. "Nell was our schoolteacher," he says, as if this excludes her from any wrongdoing.

"Their cottage is near the crime scene," I reply. "They could've met Connor on the beach and made it home before the storm got bad."

It makes me feel a little sick, envisioning how the murder could've been planned, and Jude's expression reflects my thoughts. "I still don't think it's them," he says, but doubt lingers behind his eyes. I just can't tell whether it's doubt over the Bracken sisters, or simply everyone on the island.

We leave the house and make our way over the hillsides, toward the cliff's edge. As we approach, I hear the rush of waves against the rocks, salt air ruffling the heather.

The sisters' cottage is a timeworn accompaniment to the windswept moors. It's made up of old stone and weathered wood, with a garden of roses, foxgloves, daisies. Jude removes his cap and knocks on their door. Through the wood, there's nothing but silence, and I hope the sisters haven't already left. Imogen works as a secretary at town hall, but surely she hasn't already set off. School doesn't start for another couple of hours, so Nell should be in.

"Perhaps they're not home?" says Jude.

Then the door opens.

Detective Thackery stands on the other side of the threshold.

Next to me, Jude freezes up. His breath comes quick, and I feel my pulse thrum in response. I can only imagine what ideas must be racing through his head. The last time I talked to Thackery, Jude was behind bars for someone else's crime.

Thackery smiles as though he's been anticipating our arrival. "Ah, Miss Alexander, Mr. Osric," he says. "A good morning to you both."

I try to see past him into the cottage.

Voice hoarse, Jude says, "Good morning, sir."

What's he doing here?

"I was just asking after you, Wick. You're a hard man to track down."

"Am I?" Jude holds his cap in front of him, white-knuckled. "Did you . . . ? Did you try wiring me? I check for messages every morning. I didn't see . . ."

Thackery waves him silent. At the end of the entrance hall, Nell Bracken emerges from another room. She pauses, hands clasped, watching us with a curious expression. I meet her eye.

"I caught word your lighthouse suffered some damage," says Thackery.

"Oh." A number of emotions play across Jude's face. Relief and embarrassment war with each other. "Oh, gosh, that. I've already sorted it, sir. The door, that is. Some resin, some paint—good as new."

I make sure to study Nell as he speaks. She blinks back at me, brow furrowed.

Thackery narrows his eyes. "This is a serious matter, Mr. Osric. If you wish, I could have some officers investigate the incident further."

"No." Jude shakes his head. "Thank you for your concern, sir, but that won't be necessary. I'd rather put the whole thing behind me, to be honest."

"That's one way of dealing, I suppose." Thackery straightens his coat before glancing back at Nell. "Thank you for your hospitality, Miss Bracken."

From the front step, I see the soft line of her smile. "It was no trouble, Detective."

Thackery takes his leave, and Nell comes forward to usher us into the house, talking all the while. "What's that about your lighthouse, Wick? You haven't been getting into trouble, have you? Goodness, you haven't visited us in such a long while. Would you like a cup of tea? Imogen! Put the kettle on!"

Nell walks us through the hall into the drawing room. I remember times when Jude and I had visited and been afraid of knocking something over. There are cabinets full of books and crockery, tables laden with knickknacks. I skirt around the maze of it to sit on the sofa near the bay windows, looking out at the open fields behind the house. Jude sits beside me, eyes searching the room. He puts his hands between his knees as if to keep from disturbing the surroundings.

When Nell joins us, it's with a tea set and Imogen Bracken in tow. They take seats on the opposite sofa, and Nell spends a few moments fussing over tea. She seems pleased at the very sight of us, while Imogen looks sullen—like we are a bother to her, arriving unannounced. She is the elder sister, I know. The both of them are in their forties, and they're graceful and tall, fair-skinned and dark-haired.

"Is there a reason for this visit?" Imogen asks.

Jude looks to me. Clutching my teacup, I say, "Jude's front door was marred the other day. We were wondering if either of you saw anything."

Nell tsks. "When was this? We were at work for most of the day."

"Detective Thackery mentioned something of that nature," says Imogen, nodding. "Probably just some little urchins having a go at you, Wick. I'd pay no mind to it."

Jude nods. He stares down into his tea, expression pensive.

I drag my attention back to the sisters. I can't tell whether or not they're lying.

"We were both elsewhere at the time," I say, careful with my words. "I thought it would be charitable to visit Russell Hendry. It's a wonder, isn't it, how he got ahold of that poison?"

"Hendry?" Imogen snorts. "What a disaster. Thinks himself a saint, I bet. He'll change his tune once the trial's over."

"Unpleasant business," Nell adds. Her fingers skim the edge of her teacup. With a shake of her head, she shifts topic. "Have you seen the garden? The lilies are still doing well."

"Yes," I say. "Lovely. Now, are you quite—"

"Already feels like October," she continues. "End of the harvest. Will you be playing at the festival, Moira dear?"

Jude says, "She'll be playing this weekend," and it's the first time I've seen him smile all morning.

Even Imogen's interest seems piqued by this. Nell grins, delighted. "Oh, that's wonderful," she says. "We'll most definitely be there for that."

Jude wasn't wrong when he said people would come just to hear me play.

"Right," says Imogen, setting down her teacup, "this has all been very nice, but my sister and I have to be getting to work."

I clench my teeth. Not yet, *not yet*. We still have no answers, nothing to indicate the Brackens' innocence or guilt. It could be them. It could be them . . .

Whereas Nell ushered us in, Imogen is the one to see us out.

I'm rattled by the speed of it. We snatch our coats, then find ourselves back on the cottage's front step.

Jude eyes the closed door. He says, "That didn't go at all well."

I grab him by the sleeve, pulling him away.

"It's fine," I say. "You can question them at the dance."

He looks out across the hillsides to his lighthouse. A breeze cuts past us, sweeping over the moors. "Why has it got to be me?" he asks.

"You don't expect me to interrogate people and play violin at the same time, do you?"

"I suppose not."

We reach the keeper's cottage, and the door is freshly painted, bright blue and marvelous. A smile pulls at the corner of my mouth. "You'll be all right," I say. "You're Dunmore's keeper. People trust you."

Jude looks fairly amused by this assertion.

I think of him sitting down at my kitchen table, graciously exhausted.

The investigation is wearing on him, just as I feel the grit of it behind my eyes. It's a wheel, circling us, never quite near enough to grasp. I'm left hoping, wondering, reaching for answers. I'll pry open every secret on the island, if it comes to that.

CHAPTER TWENTY-TWO

THE NIGHT OF THE DANCE, I journey along the path to the lighthouse. The fading light streaks pink and gold across the sky, clouds thinning out above the horizon.

My dark hair is pinned neatly and curled owing to the rags I wore earlier to shape the strands. As I walk, the cool salt wind seems set on undermining my efforts, twisting my hair into a tangle. I swing my violin case from one hand to the other, taking pleasure in how the wind sweeps my long coat back, fluttering at the ends of my dress.

Tonight the island is singing.

I near the cliffs and the sea plays its own tune: the soft *shhh* of waves, water crashing over jagged rocks. Heather bows to the breeze, and it's all I can do not to unfasten my violin case and start playing where I stand.

Approaching the keeper's cottage, I admire once more the marks of Jude's productivity. New brass hinges shine against the door's blue paint; the front steps are swept clear of debris. I knock against the wood, stepping back to wait.

Jude answers the door still dressed in his work shirt and worn trousers. His eyes widen a fraction, a blush staining his cheeks.

I grin. "Evening, Mr. Osric."

He swallows hard. "Evening." He moves back to let me in. After bolting the latch, he turns to face me. "You look beautiful, Moira."

I take my dress in hand, swishing the fabric back and forth. "I do hope so. This is my best dress." It's long and the dark blue color contrasts with my pale skin. The sleeves are short, trimmed with white lace. I've sewn beads onto the bodice and the glass sparkles in the low light.

Jude says, "It's lovely, certainly," before looking elsewhere. He leads me into the kitchen, where an ironing board occupies the floor space between table and counter. He holds up the stiff white shirt laid across it, running his fingers over the sleeves, checking for wrinkles. His touch is careful, as though he handles something finer than cotton.

I set my violin case on the table. My father's books are stacked there in a pile. Volumes I don't recognize are scattered over the counter, and I guess Jude has brought out Llyr Osric's records too.

In the past dance nights were a great, joyful, chaotic affair between our two families. No matter if the Osrics came to our house, or we Alexanders found ourselves walking over to the keeper's cottage, my father would take up his fiddle and start playing in the kitchen. Emmeline would tug Jude into a dance. He'd catch hold of my hand, so it was the three of us all together.

The memories are easy to sink into, mesmerizing as siren song.

Jude continues ironing his shirt, his face pink from the heat. I tell him, "Just put it on already. We haven't got all night."

He nods dutifully and heads upstairs. I open one of the books nearest me, flipping through the pages. Inside, there's a copy of an old petition, listing names of those against the hunting ban. A door opens and closes above, and I look in the direction of the hall as Jude's footsteps sound on the stairs.

He appears in the doorway dressed in his dark suit and trousers. He fidgets with his cuff links, and I clear my throat to get his attention.

"Have you seen this?" I ask, pointing to the petition. "If someone's looking to dismantle the ban, they might be on this list."

Jude frowns down at the page. "There's more than a hundred names here, Moira."

"We'll have to go through it later."

He smooths a hand over his lapel, his gaze shifting to meet mine. That night, walking back from the pub, we'd stood just this close. I remember reaching up to fix his collar, and I itch to trace the line of it now.

"You look very handsome in that suit," I say.

Jude turns red-faced and flustered at the compliment. He opens his mouth, but before he can speak, I step away. "We better hurry," I tell him. "We're going to be late."

Out on the moors, I look toward the cliff's edge. The sun has set, bands of burning red accentuating the western skyline. I breathe in the salt air, the smell of earth and dried leaves. I feel Jude's presence beside me, the leather of my violin case warming my palm. The evening quiet surrounds us. There's anticipation in it, an expectant energy that twists with the wind, over the hillsides. Tonight I'll set the hall in motion as I haven't done in years. I'll give the island my music—and it will sing.

From a block away I hear the sound of people gathered outside the dance hall. Once we turn the corner, light and color spill out from the doorway and onto the street. Someone calls my name, but I can't tell who. I spot councilors, namely Thomas Earl and Calum Bryce, mingling with the crowd.

Warren Knox is among them, his back to me. He turns as though sensing my gaze, and I stare back, jaw clenched. He ducks his head, disappearing into the hall.

I look to Jude. "I'll see you in the break, all right?"

He nods, distracted. His eyes survey the street before looking my way. "Good luck tonight, Moira."

The words amuse me. "You need it more than I do."

"Suppose so." His smile is winsome in the lamplight. "Associating with murder suspects."

"Warren Knox is here. Keep an eye out for the Brackens."

"Will do."

I squeeze his arm, reassuring, then head around the side of the building. As I enter the back room, heat rushes over me, prickling my skin. Peter and Bree stand near the desk, murmuring to each other. Flint sits on the piano bench, piecing his flute together.

"We thought you weren't going to turn up," he says.

"Well, I'm here now." I set my violin case on a chair. "I'd be perfectly on time if I weren't waiting for Jude-takes-all-the-time-in-the-world-Osric."

Straightening up, Flint looks me in the eye. "Osric? You came here with Wick?"

Before I can snap back at him, Peter points at Flint from across the room. "Don't start anything," he says in warning.

"Aye, aye," Flint mutters. He cuts his gaze back down, seemingly chastened.

I take out my bow to rosin it, rubbing the block over the hair from end to end. I take out my violin, tuning it with care.

To make my first violin, my father brought me into the forest to collect the necessary wood. Late-afternoon sunlight winked through the leaves above us, and my heart thrilled when he led me off the beaten path. We hiked through underbrush, deeper and deeper, to where the trees grew thick and close as old neighbors.

"For the neck and back," he said, "we'll use maple."

Chopping spruce for the front, he cured and cut it to size. I watched him work with a knife to carve out a neck and scroll from the maple; I brought my fingers to the instrument in wonder.

"Look now, Moira, and remember," he told me. "You'll be crafting the next one."

After that, he said he'd build me a ship. "But not out of maple and spruce," he added. "I'll fashion you a ship from oak and cedar. Wood that can hold off the sea."

On our next visit to the lighthouse, I showed Jude my fine new violin. I told him I'd take it aboard my future ship of oak and cedar, and his eyebrows pinched together.

"Where will you go?" he asked.

We sat facing each other on the floor of the watch room, and

I shifted my gaze to the map of our island on the wall. "I don't know," I said truthfully. "Lots of places."

"You'll come back, though, won't you?"

I put my fingertips to the violin's strings. They trembled beneath my touch, waiting for the glide of a bow across them. "Yes," I said in answer. "I'll always come back."

He released a breath. "Oh, good." Then he leaned back on his hands, grinning at me. "I shall keep the light burning to guide you home."

Now, years later, I've neither a ship nor a violin constructed by my father's hands. The violin I hold is a result of my own labor, my own craft. I knew it when it was only strips of wood, when it still smelled of fresh air and evergreen.

To Peter I say, "Let me play the first few figures."

He nods, gesturing for me to go on. I carry my violin by the neck, my bow in my other hand. They are extensions of me, light and familiar in my grip. I walk up the steps to stand at center stage, and Bree follows, taking a seat at the piano.

A hush falls over the hall.

The dance floor is packed with islanders, and I look for Jude among them. He stands near the window; when our eyes meet, he tips his chin up, grinning. My pulse soars as I bring the violin to rest on my shoulder. Bree gives me my cue, and I touch bow to strings, sending the first note into the air. It glides out, sharp and true, and I set into something lively, so I might do away with the starch in Jude's cuffs.

The music lifts to the rafters, clearing the dust from my memories. I stand where my father once played, where I once played, and it's like rejoining a piece after trailing a full bar behind. Only at a distance do I feel the slow ache of my muscles. I am alive, centered, focused on the notes. Heels click against the floorboards, keeping time.

And surely, surely, *surely* siren song is something like this. Music that makes my heart sing and call out for something ancient and forever, for the secrets in the deep, in the fog over the moors.

I close my eyes, head tilted to my shoulder. In the dark, I listen to my heartbeat, to the song I weave—for a few precious minutes, nothing exists but that.

I play the last note, and the applause crashes over me.

Opening my eyes, I smile at the crowd, holding my bow out to the side as I dip into a curtsy. I head for the stage steps, cheeks warm. People part in my wake, and I'm quick to place my violin in the back room. After doing so, I move through the sea of islanders, hoping to spot Jude Osric.

Someone taps my shoulder, and I spin to find him standing there. I note his flushed face, his bright eyes, his missing suit jacket—just before he embraces me. I link my arms around him in return, leaning against him, feeling the quick tempo of his heart.

"You were incredible, Moira." His whisper is a warm breath at my ear. "If I weren't dancing, I wouldn't have taken my eyes off you."

I pull back to look at him proper. He grins, luminous, and I say, "Tell me you haven't been drinking."

He bursts out laughing. I revel in the sound—so guileless, so *happy*. I can't even recall when last I heard him laugh. "I'm just pleased for you," he says. "Can't I be pleased?"

"It isn't like you've never heard me play."

He drags a hand through his hair. "Not like tonight." He swallows, looking down at me. His dark eyes gleam in the light. "Tonight's special, Moira."

Onstage, others take my place. There are Lochlan fiddlers who've come to play, a frame drum player from up north. Peter calls to me, questioning, but I wave him off.

Right now I want to dance.

Jude rolls up his sleeves, catching my eye. When he holds out a hand, I grin, clasping it tight. The fiddlers fire straight into a reel; we whirl onto the dance floor, laughing, our fingers intertwined, Jude's hand on my waist.

My heart plays its own wild tune. My curls unravel. My feet remember every step. I press close to Jude, gazing up at his face. He smiles back, bright and daring, the way he did when we spun in circles, clutching on to each other, faster and faster until we tumbled into the grass.

He tells me, "I spoke with Imogen Bracken," and I blink, realizing I've forgotten all about our suspects.

"What did she have to say?"

"I asked if she was hoping the ban would be lifted." He pauses for a moment's consideration. The music swells, and the shoes of other dancers clatter in rhythm. "She seemed pretty indifferent either way. She didn't take part in the initial opposition."

"And Nell? I thought she'd be here. Did Imogen tell you where she was?"

"Waiting for a *suitor* apparently." Jude wiggles his eyebrows. He lifts our joined hands, twirling me.

Once we've resumed, I ask, "What about Warren?"

"I talked to him, yes. He's all for keeping the ban in place."

"He could be lying."

I look around and everything comes to me in flashes. The flutter of a dress. Hands tangled together. A smile in a man's sea-wrinkled face.

Jude says, "We can check the petition to see if he's on it."

At those words I wish we were already back at the lighthouse. We could be assessing suspects, cross-referencing them with that list of names.

Though Gabriel Flint isn't old enough to be on a petition made ten years back.

From the stage, the fiddlers' reel bleeds out to become a waltz. Our steps slow.

"I didn't get a chance to speak with Flint," I say.

Jude bows his head. "We have the rest of the night."

When the musicians break, Peter Atherton heads through the crowd in our direction. I'm ready to take up my violin again, but he sets his sights on Jude instead. His expression is pensive, worry knotted into his brow.

"Wick," he says, "someone ought to tell you . . . You ought to know . . ."

Standing this close to him, I feel Jude tense. "What is it?"

Peter rests a hand on his shoulder. "There's been another siren attack," he murmurs. "I hear the body's still on the beach."

"Who?" asks Jude.

"Not sure. Police are down there now, I think. A couple more officers just left."

I squeeze Jude's fingers. He looks over, wide-eyed, the laughter dashed from his face. Setting his jaw, he turns to Peter. "I'll see what's going on."

"Right." Lifting his hand from Jude's shoulder, Peter rubs the back of his neck. "I thought you may need to write it in some report."

I watch him edge his way back toward the stage. Jude's hand tightens on my waist. "Moira," he says.

I hiss out a breath. "I know."

Another murder.

Without pause, without letting go of each other, we leave the light of the hall behind us, taking off into the night.

CHAPTER TWENTY-THREE

DUNMORE'S SHADOWS PLAY tricks with my eyes. Every alley seems a gaping hole, every reflection off a shop window like the flash of a knife. A gust of wind sends leaves skittering across the cobbles, making Jude start horribly, and the adrenaline in my veins surges in response.

I feel *watched*.

"Moira," says Jude. "God, Moira, it's just . . . It's just like . . ."

"I know."

"I'm going to be sick."

"You are not." I tug on his shirtsleeve. "We can still catch the police if you hurry up."

Yet once we reach the pathway to the moors, brambles and low-hanging branches slow our progress even further. Jude says, "That's two people now. *Two.* I mean—" He stumbles in the dark. As I throw out a hand to steady him, realization hits me.

"The killer wasn't anyone at the dance."

"That rules out Warren and Imogen." Jude ticks them off on his fingers, then hesitates. "Flint?"

"I didn't see him." I bite my bottom lip, trying to think. "He was in the back room when I came in, but after . . . I thought he'd be onstage after me."

Jude runs a hand over his mouth. We continue walking in silence, the unknown spooling out ahead of us. Clouds shift across the night sky, the moon shining through, casting its pale light onto the long grass and heather.

Softly, Jude asks, "Do you think it's another child?"

I remember Connor—his body left in the wet sand, his throat stained red—and a shudder travels up my spine. The thought of finding something similar tonight pinches my stomach. "We oughtn't assume anything," I say.

Jude swallows. I hear the click in his throat.

We pass up and over hillsides until we reach the flat stretch leading to the cliffs. Picking up my dress, I dash forward, and Jude runs after. We both skid to a stop near the rocky edge.

The police are still there, all right. Five of them—two with lanterns in hand—stand over the crumpled body. They remind me of spirits, ghosts circling the dead, until one of the men lifts his lantern, shedding light onto the lines of his face.

Inspector Dale.

"Aye," he calls. "Who's there?"

I start down the wayward path, slow and careful. Jude answers before I can.

"Jude Osric," he says, "and Miss Alexander. I heard there was an accident on the beach. Came as quick as I could."

Another of the men, Detective Thackery, turns as we get to the shoreline. His white teeth flash in the darkness. "We'll have the relevant information wired through to you, Mr. Osric." He looks at the both of us, and his eyes linger over me, no doubt questioning my presence. "We're waiting for the coroner. Nothing more to be done, I'm afraid."

"Who is it?" I ask. From this angle, I can see only a tangle of long brown hair, the twisted fringe of her dress. Lantern light glints off the blood pooled around her body, shades of black and crimson.

An officer, fair-haired and young, replies, "Miss Nell Bracken."

Beside me, Jude makes a soft *oh* sound. I set my gaze on Inspector Dale. "And you've already determined it was sirens? Were there witnesses?"

I see him look quite pointedly from me, to Jude, and back again. No doubt he's expecting Jude to do something about me; when Jude remains both silent and unmoving, Dale heaves a sigh. "An anonymous message arrived at the station," he says, "but that's hardly any business of yours."

I fist my hands at my sides. "I believe it's every islander's business, indeed, if—" A hand comes to rest on my arm, and I pause, glancing at Jude. He shakes his head slightly.

Inspector Dale clears his throat. "I'll have to ask you to leave the area, Miss Alexander, Mr. Osric. The situation is in police hands, I assure you." He touches the brim of his hat, his gaze steely as he regards us.

I spin on my heel, making my way back up the path even as Jude murmurs in reply. A moment later he follows after me. On the moors, a cool breeze tugs at my hair, brushes over my bare arms, and I hardly feel the chill. If I unclench my fists, they'll start shaking; if I speak, my words will hitch. So I don't do either.

"She's dead," Jude whispers finally. "Nell's dead. I thought—" He stops, takes a breath. There's a quiver in his voice when he asks, "What are we going to do?"

Something inside me breaks then, like a branch snapped underfoot. I stare down at my boots, dark and scuffed in the moonlight. "I can't stand it, Jude."

He says nothing, for which I am grateful. Wonderful, quiet Jude Osric, always the listener. The night is still, and I want to sink down beneath the soil, to sleep for a decade.

Jude's hand reaches across the space between us, as if to take hold of mine, but he falters at the last moment, stuffing it into his trouser pocket.

"We should've kept an eye on her," I say. "I should've known when she didn't show up at the dance that something was wrong."

"We'll solve it," he says.

"Will we?"

Suddenly I'm not so sure. The threads I've spent days lacing together unravel in my mind; loose connections held in fragile balance begin to slip.

Jude stops walking, and I look back around. His face is shadowed, his expression unreadable. "Don't," he says, and it's a voice I've never heard him use before. "Don't start doubting now, Moira. Not when . . ." He hesitates, only to ask, "Can I trust you?"

I nod, not entirely understanding his train of thought. "Of course."

Jude nods too, as though steeling himself. His eyes look black in the darkness. "There's something I need to show you," he says. "Something secret."

I pause, thinking of the cracks in the lighthouse walls, running through white plaster, each said to hold a secret. I think of Jude standing on the cliff's edge, watching as he threw a slip of paper into the sea. I think of Connor knowing something he shouldn't and someone taking a knife to his throat.

"All right."

And we continue on, walking toward the glow of the lighthouse beacon.

It doesn't occur to me what secret Jude could be referring to until he leads me through the cottage, to the door at the end of the hall. It's the space below the guest room, one that echoed with thumps and voices in the night. I turn to Jude. His hand trembles where it rests on the knob.

"I heard you that night," I tell him. "You said you weren't talking to anyone. That I was dreaming."

Fear darkens his eyes. "I must confess I lied." Then he asks his previous question, but in reverse. "Do you trust me?"

"With my life."

The words surprise me. *With my life.* It's true, yet I wonder just how long it's been that way.

Jude's gaze falls from mine as he knocks twice, softly, against the wood. He reaches into his pocket, pulling out a key. It looks smaller, older, than the one used for the front door. He turns it in the lock. I hear the faint *click* as it catches. Glancing back at me, he says, "I'm sorry, Moira." He swallows and lets the door swing open.

I stare into the room.

It is cold inside, and dark, the one and only window shuttered up. Moonlight sneaks through the gaps, sliding across the floorboards in silver lines. Dust hangs in the air, and it's as if the chamber has been forgotten: an unused space that has fallen through the cracks. The space, however, is not empty.

I stare into the room for a long, long time.

When I look back at Jude, he hangs his head, though I cannot say whether it's in shame. He seems to be waiting—for me to shout at him, or hit him, or run down the hall and out of the cottage entirely. Instead, I am frozen. Slowly, unwillingly, my gaze returns to the darkness of the room, to the figure cast in pale light by the moon.

Jude Osric has a siren locked away in his lighthouse.

CHAPTER TWENTY-FOUR

SHE IS THIN, her skin ghost white, long black hair matted with knots. It is not these features, common enough among sirens, that are unusual about her appearance. It's the look in her eyes, hollowed and empty—lost in a way I've never seen a siren to be. She sits against the wall, atop several quilts laid out on the floor. In the corner, there is a length of rope, the glint of a chain. They must've once been used to manacle her. Pale scars mark her face and arms, the long, straight edges of a blade. I turn away.

"Please tell me . . . you did not do this."

"My uncle," says Jude. His voice sounds unsteady. "I didn't know anything, Moira. I tried to . . ."

I take a step into the room. The siren watches me with dulled interest, tilting her head to one side.

"How long?" I ask.

"Just . . . just over a year."

Another step, and the siren pulls back her lips in a quiet hiss, revealing thin and pointed teeth. I'm afraid to ask why she does not sing, why the shuttered window is not cracked through from the sound of her voice. But I say it anyway. "Why hasn't she begun to sing?"

Jude is very still behind me. If I didn't know better, I would think he wasn't there at all.

"Her tongue was cut out."

Yes. Yes, that would do it.

I walk out of the room, pausing in the arch of the door. I look at Jude, but he doesn't meet my eye.

"And you did nothing?"

He looks up at that, indignation sparking in his gaze. "I *tried*, Moira." His fingers knot around his shirt cuff, his breath shuddering out of him. "I was sent over to the offshore light for a few months after Mr. Irving took ill. When I came back, my uncle—he showed me what he'd done." Jude stares past me to the open doorway. "He said he did it to avenge Da, like . . . like an eye for an eye, but this is the last thing Da would've wanted. I know that."

I swallow hard. "Your uncle is gone, Jude. Why is she still here?"

"That's what our argument was about. Before he left, I told him we should let her go, give her back to the sea." He shakes his head. "He laughed, said it wouldn't matter even if we did; she wouldn't survive a day. What with . . ." Jude gestures with one hand, as if trying to convey the damage inflicted upon the siren, everything she has endured. It's a rather poor attempt.

"When I saw those dead sirens on the dock, it just reminded me of her being trapped in here." His mouth twists. He scrubs hastily at his eyes. "I bring her raw meat from the butcher's. I try to . . . I try to give her a bit of peace."

I grit my teeth. "She is suffering."

Jude looks at me with a lost expression. His shoulders sag, as though the heaviness of his burdens is the weight of an anchor, pulling him down into the cold blackness of the sea. "What else am I supposed to do?"

My heart thuds inside my chest, the steady rhythm at odds with the rest of me. I place a hand on his arm. "We'll return her to the sea," I say.

"She'll die out there. We can't—"

"Sirens are not solitary creatures, Jude. They'll care for her. I'm sure of it."

He closes the door, shutting the siren away. His hands are still trembling, but his expression is no longer so bleak. His eyes shine bright and feverish. "And if we're caught? What then? We'd have to carry her all the way down to the harbor. The police might still be on the beach."

I tip my chin up. "We shan't get caught."

Jude laughs, a single, broken exhale.

I forge on. "We'll have few better chances than tonight. Most are still at the dance; the harbor will be empty. We'll go without a light and take your rowboat out."

Closing his eyes, he links his hands around the back of his neck. I watch him in silence, the downward tilt of his head, the tense line of his shoulders. He swallows and says, "Very well," before reaching under his shirt collar, drawing out the plain iron ring he wears on a length of cord.

I narrow my eyes. "What are you doing?"

"I'll not touch her wearing iron," he says, looking over. "Do you have any on you?"

After a pause, I shake my head, realizing I'd left what iron I had in my coat at the hall. Jude passes me the corded rope. "Take this, then. It'll have to be enough for both of us."

I bite my lip, uncertain, even as I slip it on. "Jude, you can't get into a boat without iron. The sirens—"

"I know," he says softly, "but I won't—I won't hurt her."

I curl my fingers around the ring. Never would I imagine that Jude might head out onto the water iron-less, as his family did all those years ago. Never would I imagine that I might let him.

My gaze returns to the closed door. The wood looks black as oil, there's so little light in the hall. I take a slow, even breath.

"We'd best get going," I say. "We have until dawn."

Before we set off, Jude tends to the light. He disappears into the tower to check over fuel, trim the wicks, wind the clockwork. While he does, I collect a thick wool blanket from the drawing room, then wait for him in the kitchen. I stare out at the darkness beyond the window glass, his iron ring like a weight around my neck.

Jude enters the kitchen wearing his wool sweater over his dress shirt. He has his oilskin jacket with him and offers it to me. I have to roll back the cuffs a couple times to free my hands. Together, we walk through the cottage and stand before the door at the hall's end.

I pass Jude the blanket. Taking it, he opens the door, stepping into the room. I watch from the doorway—as the siren tips her colorless face up to his, as Jude kneels in front of her.

"Hallo," he says gently. "It's me; it's only me."

He wraps her in the blanket, taking her into his arms.

"Are you all right with her?" I ask.

"Yes." Jude's voice is hollow as he turns to me. "She's very light."

The siren's eyes are wide-open and dark in her pinched face, but she remains quite still in Jude's arms. I look away, heart hammering, and make a start down the hall. Jude follows after, and we step out into the damp night air.

This past evening, I'd left the lighthouse with my violin in hand, Jude Osric at my side, the sunset warm and lovely along the horizon. Now I'm here as mist carpets the moors, bundled up in Jude's jacket, while he stands holding a scarred siren to his chest.

Fear splinters my bones. We head for the stone walls that mark the way to the harbor, and I imagine the police coming upon us, someone waiting on the docks. Reaching the cliff's edge, I survey the beach, but I see no lanterns in the darkness. I hear only the rush of the surf, the breaking of waves against the rocks.

I say, "They've gone," yet I whisper as though we're not alone. I glance back at Jude, and he looks as pale as the siren, his eyes just as wide.

We take care on the wooden steps down to the docks. Jude's boat is tied neatly to a cleat; I fetch the oars from inside the boathouse. Jude gazes out at the stretch of blue-black sea, his breaths quick and uneven in the quiet. I can see the beat of his pulse at his throat.

His grip tightens around the siren. "Moira, if you would . . ."

I nod. "I'll row us out."

Settling into the boat, I untie the rope from the cleat and lock the oars into place. Jude sits facing me, and I've some childish, desperate urge to grab him by the sleeve, as if my hold could protect him as well as iron, as if I could keep him in the boat once a siren sang to him. The siren in his arms shifts, her attention fixed on the water. What a strange thing it is, seeing her so close. Her clawed hands curl around the edges of the blanket, her lips parted to show her needle-like teeth. She could scratch Jude's eyes out from where she sits, but perhaps she isn't strong enough for that. I imagine she's been kept on land longer than any other living siren.

We push away from the dock, and I row out into the bay. The oars scrape my hands, but I concentrate on keeping them balanced, the heavy thwack as they hit the water in time with each other. My arms soon tire, sooner than they would had I not spent so much of the evening playing violin. In front of me, Jude has his head down, whispering to himself or to the siren; I can't hear him over the wash of the breakers. I pull the oars from the water, resting them against the gunwales.

"Quickly," I say. "Release her here."

Panic crawls up my throat, lacing into my words. Our boat in the otherwise empty bay surely hasn't gone unnoticed by sirens. Now that I've stopped rowing, I'm all too aware of the night, of the dark depths below us. I wonder if they already realize Jude is iron-less, if they're watching him . . .

He lowers the siren over the side of the boat. She pulls free of the blanket, flitting into the deep, swift and silvery as a fish. It happens so fast, both of us are left staring down after her, motionless even as the boat begins to drift.

Jude moves first. He gathers up the blanket, the wool now soaked through and dripping. Looking to me, he says only, "I'll row back."

I pass him the oars. He steers us back toward the island,

toward the beam of his lighthouse on the cliffs. I put my arms about myself, pressing my fingers into the cotton of his jacket. We dock at the harbor, and Jude helps me out of the boat before securing it to the cleat. His expression is unnervingly blank, but his silence is what truly worries me.

As we reach the steps, he slumps to his knees, head bowed as he clutches the blanket to his chest. "A year," he whispers. "More than a year, and I . . ." He squeezes his eyes shut, tears slipping down his cheeks. "God forgive me, I did not know what to do."

I crouch beside him. "Jude . . ."

"I tried to be kind to her. I tried to keep her alive."

"And you did." I place a careful hand on his shoulder. "She's safe now. She's free."

This does not soothe him as I hoped it might. He presses his forehead to the dock, taking great, heaving gasps like he can't find air to breathe. "I didn't . . . I didn't dare tell anyone," he says. "I thought they would kill her. Oh God, I couldn't . . ."

My throat tightens. Tears flash down my cheeks before I can push them back. "Jude," I say softly. "Jude, you're not the one at fault here. You didn't put her in that room. You didn't bring the knife to her skin."

He chokes on a sob, covering his eyes with one hand. I want badly to take him from the harbor; he is still without iron, still too close to the ever-present dangers of the sea. Instead, I wrap my arms around him, pulling him into an embrace. I let him cry into my shoulder as he let me the day of my father's funeral.

Drawing away, he wipes his face with the sleeve of his sweater. "I apologize for not telling you sooner. You. . . You always know just what to do." His red-rimmed eyes look out to sea. "I hope she's all right."

I bring a hand to his cheek, turning him back toward me. He swallows.

"She's home," I say. "Now we ought to return to ours."

He nods. "Yes." He breathes in deep, steadying himself. "Moira—thank you."

His voice cracks like glass. I move my hand to grip the front of his sweater. "I'll stay with you tonight, shall I?" I look over his face, the tracks of his tears plain even in the dark. "I don't want you to be alone."

Jude nods again. The wind ruffles his hair, the boats around us creaking. Just behind him, something winks above the sheer wall of the cliff. For an instant I think it's the shine of the lighthouse beacon, but this light is too dim for that, too low to the ground.

It's like someone's lantern—like someone is there at the cliff's edge, looking down upon the harbor.

My expression must shift in some way, because Jude chances a look around. The light is already gone, but the memory of it ghosts eerily across my vision.

"Moira?" Jude says. "What is it?"

I shake my head even as dread creeps over my spine. "Nothing," I murmur. Releasing his sweater, I try my best to smile. "Just my eyes playing tricks on me."

CHAPTER TWENTY-FIVE

AFTERWARD, SLEEP DOES NOT COME for either of us. I hang Jude's oilskin jacket on its peg in the entryway, climb the stairs, and settle into bed in the guest room. His iron ring presses against my skin. I draw it off, leaving it beside the oil lamp on the nightstand. The hours pass erratic and fitful, all twisted sheets and half-remembered dreams. Throwing back the blankets, I step out into the hall. It's there, against the heavy morning silence, that I hear muffled bars of music playing. I follow the tune over to Jude's bedroom.

It takes only a moment for me to place it. I recognize this music: slow and mechanical, off-key and dolorous. It's the tune of Emmeline's old music box. My heart feels weighed down by the knowing, and even as I close my eyes to listen, I try not to picture

Jude on the other side of the door, holding the tiny box that once belonged to his sister.

As he winds it a third time, I turn away. This, I won't intrude upon. After the murk and melancholy of last night, Jude deserves a moment to himself. I head to the kitchen and make us both a cup of tea.

Jude shuffles down the stairs soon after. He appears in the doorway, rubbing his eyes. When he catches sight of me, his mouth curves in a small smile.

"Oh." He takes the tea I offer with careful fingers. "Thank you."

"What's the time?" I ask.

"Just past nine. I've observations to do on deck, if you want to join me."

We start up the lighthouse and step out onto the narrow gallery deck. A breeze tugs at the hem of my dress. It's a clear day, clouds streaked thin across the sky, sunlight dazzling the sea.

It's been mere hours since we released a siren to those waters. During the night, the two of us had knelt together in the empty harbor, Jude's sorrow piercing my heart as he cried into my shoulder. Now it's morning and the past is just a memory. Connor Sheahan and Nell Bracken will be added to this year's record of siren deaths, their names pressed into the pages of a book and forgotten. I grip my teacup, its heat warming my palms. Far below, white-capped waves break over rocks near the shore. Jude sits with notebook and pencil, but his page remains blank. I think perhaps he has trouble observing the weather when he's busy observing me.

I turn and give him the first real look since last night. His dark eyes are still shadowed, auburn hair still tangled. Still Jude Osric.

Just something about the way he carries himself has changed. He's grown up from the soft-cheeked boy he once was. And I realize, too, I am no longer that little girl who came visiting alongside her father.

The past has altered us into something altogether new.

He blushes under my gaze, tearing his own eyes away. He begins writing things in shorthand: visibility and wind direction and tide conditions. It's a routine worn into him, passed down to him, from father to son. The lighthouse is as much a part of him as the moors and cliffs are part of me. Despite the dangers of this island, the horrors of it, there are few who know how to leave. I imagine those who manage it spend the rest of their lives trying to knock Twillengyle soil out from the soles of their boots.

Twin flashes of silver catch my eye. I look over the gallery railing, but there's nothing to see. Perhaps a glimpse of sirens as they slipped between the waves. To the west, a group of them bask in the shallows. I can't tell how many from this distance, but there's a peace to them, a stillness, the cool composure of hunters at ease.

"Jude." I turn my gaze on him, his notebook propped on one bent knee. "How did your uncle capture that siren?"

His pencil comes to a stop. After a pause he says, "With a net and iron, I imagine."

"He didn't tell you?"

"We didn't discuss the particulars, no."

I lace my fingers over the rim of my teacup. "I'm only wondering," I start, "if perhaps he had help. It would've been difficult to accomplish on his own, don't you think? Even more so to keep her hidden away."

Jude looks stricken. He sets his pencil down, staring at the open page of his notebook. "That's certainly a possibility." He splays a hand over the words he's written, his voice dipping into a whisper as he says, "You don't suppose it's connected, do you? To Connor's murder? To Nell's?"

I recall the shadowy figure who followed us from the pub, the light I saw from the harbor. That person couldn't be Dylan Osric simply because Dylan Osric wasn't in Dunmore at the time. It wasn't his handwriting on the note left in Jude's entryway.

Stop looking.

I bite my lip. "We ought to visit Imogen," I reply. "If Nell was waiting for a suitor, it could've been the killer. Imogen likely knows the person."

Jude lifts his head, looking out toward the cliff's edge. "My uncle has wanted the ban dismantled since the day my family passed," he murmurs. "But you must know I've never . . . I've never blamed them, Moira. The sirens. I never wished to hunt them, to hurt them as he did."

"I know." My fingers loosen around my teacup. "I know."

Jude closes his notebook and stands, tucking the pencil behind his ear. He still gazes at the sea, at the sirens by the shore. I press my palm against the railing.

"I need to fetch my violin," I tell him. "I left it at the hall."

He looks over. His face is awash in sunlight, his cable-knit sweater snug across his shoulders. If it weren't for his bloodshot eyes, I might be inclined to believe last night was nothing but a nightmare. "What of our investigation?"

Stepping toward the gallery door, I say, "I'll come straight back from Dunmore."

Jude smiles. He tips his head down, the gesture shy, and

fidgets with the pencil behind his ear. "All right, then," he says.

I hurry down the stairwell to the cottage. In another few hours we might have our answers.

Halfway across the moors I realize I'm still wearing my evening dress from last night and decide to stop at my house in order to change. I would've preferred to avoid my mother in the interim, but I find her doing laundry by the side of the house.

She stands next to the wooden tub, her hands wet and soapy, as she rubs a sheet against the metal ridges of her washboard. Several tin baths are scattered on the ground nearby, filled with water and rinsed clothes. She pauses in her work as she catches sight of me.

"Come here, Moira."

A vitriolic edge accompanies my name when she says it.

This is precisely what I don't need right now.

I walk toward her, keeping my eyes on the tin baths, the sides of the tub. I can feel my mother's gaze on me like the prick of a hundred needles. "Yes, Mother?"

I chance a look at her face. She glares, anger emanating like the heat off our stove. I duck my head, penitent, in the hopes of deterring the worst of it.

"You don't seem to realize," she starts, "how many eyes this island has."

I wince. "I can—"

"No." With the hand not gripping the washboard, my mother gestures sharply. "I've no desire to hear excuses. You think you can leave the dance with Mr. Osric and no one notices? I assume you spent the night at the lighthouse?"

"Yes, but—"

"I try to give you space, Moira. Really I do. Ever since your father . . ." She takes a breath. "And I know Mr. Osric has always been a good friend to you, but you're not children now. Either of you. I would expect—"

My own temper sparks in response. "My comings and goings are my business," I tell her. "There's no need for you to worry over me."

She sighs, rubbing chapped fingertips against her temple. It irks me how concerned she seems about islanders gossiping. Rumors unfurl from a glance, a whisper. They mean very little altogether; they simply give people something to talk about.

"Moira," she says, and the vitriol in her tone has disappeared, replaced by fatigue. "I just want—"

I take a step back. "Please," I say. "Please—just let me alone."

I turn away, run into the house, and slam the door shut. My heart pounds against my rib cage. I'm shaking with the knowledge I hold, the secrets I've kept from my mother. *Two people were murdered, and Jude and I are trying to catch the killer; Dylan Osric tortured a chained-up siren, and we released her out in the bay.*

So many secrets.

In my bedroom I slip on simpler clothes: a long-sleeved dress of pale-blue cotton. I walk over to the kitchen and steal a seedcake from the batch on the counter. Heading back out, I edge around the opposite side of the house to evade my mother.

Sparrows flutter from branch to branch as I start on the path to Dunmore. I break off pieces of cake for them, and their whistles follow me until I reach the brick buildings and narrow cobbled streets.

The market is slow today, as it often is the morning after a dance. Young women in neat shirtwaists and skirts stroll arm in arm, heads bent in private conversation. Mothers pull their sleepy-eyed children from shop to shop. Men go about with their caps tugged low, hands in pockets.

Brendan Sheahan stands just outside the bakery, smoking. Even from across the street I see his red-rimmed eyes, his face white as paper. I swallow, avert my gaze, and continue on to the hall. I pull the door open and silence envelops me.

Without music, without people to fill it, the place feels ghostly. Dust motes drift in the light shining through the tall windows. As a child I believed the golden specks to be faerie dust, something able to grant wishes if only I could catch them. I step out from the shadowed entryway, stretch a hand toward the rectangle of light, but the particles slip away, too intangible to grasp.

Someone coughs. I look up, suddenly self-conscious, and find Peter Atherton leaning against the doorway to the back room. Sunlight threads into his dark hair, lighting the angles of his face. It warms his eyes to amber just as it does Jude's.

"Morning, Moira."

I head over to him. "I'm here for my violin," I say. "I left it behind last night."

"I noticed. Your coat, too." He lets me pass into the small room. "You and Wick cleared out quick as anything. He didn't bring you down to the beach, did he?"

"And what if he did?"

"Dear God, Moira, you're not the police."

"Nor is Jude Osric, last I recall." My coat and violin case are set on a chair next to the piano. I open the case, taking stock of my instrument.

"No, but he is keeper. I wouldn't have troubled him if she wasn't at the shore."

I run my fingers along the neck of my violin, down to the

bridge, the graceful spruce front. I think back on Jude winding up his sister's music box, the melancholy tune of it. I close the case and snatch up my coat.

"Moira, listen," says Peter, "the Council's not best pleased. Apparently there's been discussion over the hunting ban, whether they should be looking at the restrictions."

I predicted as much, suspected it at least, but hearing him voice the situation puts a hard lump in my throat. "Why?" I ask. I don't know what else to say.

The look he gives me is a sympathetic one—the kind given when there's nothing left to be done. It's the look I received from nurses when they told me my father was dying. "You know why," he replies. "Two islanders are dead and the month isn't even out. They can't ignore that."

Curious, I hold his gaze. "Don't you think their deaths odd, Peter?"

"You're still going around imagining it's murder? I'd let that idea sink."

I tighten my grip on my violin case. "I'll do what I like."

He rests a hand on the doorknob, releasing a sigh. "There's going to be a meeting about it—they're holding it here, a few days from now—if you want to attend."

I nod and walk back out onto the sunlit dance floor. I feel Peter's eyes on me as I leave. Specks of dust still hang suspended in the air, and I want to trap them all in the palm of my hand. But I need more than just fanciful wishes now—I need a miracle.

A hard wind gusts over the moors as I make my way across it. I tuck my chin against my coat collar, the hem of my dress flicking back and forth. My eyes set upon the blue-and-white tower of the lighthouse. Heading up the path, I try the doorknob, on the off chance Jude has left it unlocked.

Of course he hasn't.

I knock my knuckles against the wood. I wonder if he's still up on the gallery deck, if he's within the glass walls of the lantern room. Minutes pass. I knock again, my fist hammering the door of the cottage. I look around to the empty garden, the hillsides beyond it. A dark melody whispers at my pulse, quickening my heartbeat.

Jude knew I was coming back. I'd told him so, hadn't I?

The wind changes direction. It pulls strands of hair from my chignon, stings my eyes, and I put my violin case down, turning from the door.

Against the sun's glare, I track someone coming up from the harbor. My breath rushes out of me, relief sinking in. Jude must've been needed at the docks.

I step forward and raise a hand to shade my eyes. As the person nears, however, I realize it's not Jude at all. A smaller boy runs through the heather in my direction—Terry Young, red-faced and wide-eyed. He almost crashes into me.

"Miss Alexander." He stares as though seeing something terrible in my place. "Oh God, they told me to find you."

Fear pricks my heart. Jude still hasn't answered the door—and I don't think he's inside to answer.

"What's the matter?"

Terry leans over, hands on knees, panting. "Wick," he says. "Jude Osric." He glances up. The terror in his eyes is black and hard as stone. "He's been attacked."

And the alarm bells sound, high and clear, from the harbor. *Sirens.*

CHAPTER TWENTY-SIX

WHEN WE WERE YOUNG—I was perhaps nine, Jude eleven—our fathers set us to the task of fixing broken lobster pots. We sat together on the floor of the boathouse, and I threaded twine with a needle, while Jude took up hammer and nails to set the frame to rights. I didn't see it happen, but I heard it when he slipped, slamming the hammer against his thumb rather than the nailhead. He inhaled, sharp, shocked, right before his mouth opened in a silent scream.

That's the moment I seem caught in now. A place somewhere between the shock and the scream. My ears ring as the alarm bells echo, too loud for thought. Cold floods my veins. It feels as though I'm trapped beneath an ice sheet, everything slowing to a halt as the chill steals through me. I run until the harbor comes into view and the ice in my blood turns to fire.

Men dash from pier to pier, shouting orders over the alarm. I look around, panicked, and my throat closes when I see a group holding Jude down on the dock.

He's alive.

Then I realize why the alarm hasn't been silenced. Two sirens remain at the pier's edge, keeping to the water. Their indigo eyes glitter as they watch, and they smile, close-lipped, as though hoping to draw me forward.

I take careful, silent steps, the surrounding chaos receding like the tide. Slipping a hand into my pocket, my fingers brush metal—my small iron ring. I toss it up and into the sea. It hits the water with a splash, and the sirens disappear, twin flashes of long hair and pale skin diving beneath the waves.

At once the sounds of the harbor come blaring back. I don't let my eyes stray to Jude just yet, but I lend my voice to the commotion. "Why do you still have him by the water?" The men look to me, and I lift my chin a little higher. "Get him to the lighthouse. There should be a key in his pockets."

One of the fishermen, Emyr Llewellyn, says, "He's bleeding, miss." He tilts his head toward Jude's left arm, where three long gashes stretch from shoulder to elbow. Blood seeps through the fabric of his oilskin jacket, staining the dock red.

I swallow and crouch down to study Jude's face. His eyes are shut tight, jaw clenched, his breaths coming fast and shallow. Blood runs from his nose, smeared across one cheek. I touch his shoulder. "Jude," I say softly. "Jude, it's Moira. Can you open your eyes for me? Can you do that?"

He must hear, because he does as I ask. His gaze flits over my face, the whites of his eyes threaded with burst capillaries. The size of his pupils, huge and dark, turns the stare into something unnatural. He opens his mouth, but no words come out.

Taking my hand away, I dig in my coat pocket for a handkerchief, tying a rough tourniquet at his elbow. His eyes shut once more, as if to avoid the sunlight, and he keens, a high, pained whining in the back of his throat.

I look up. "We need to move him."

Next to Llewellyn, Gabriel Flint sets his hands on Jude. Hands that might've sent Connor and Nell to their deaths. Rage seethes inside me, coating my throat. "Don't you touch him," I snarl.

If anything, his hold tightens. "I'm trying to help."

Another of the men, Benjamin Carrick, says, "Can someone turn off that alarm?"

In the quiet that follows, they pull Jude up. His eyes snap open. His breaths catch in his chest. When he speaks, his voice is strange and reedy. "Get off," he says. "Get off, get off, get off of me!" He pulls against them, struggling, twisting under their grip.

I seize his hand. "Jude, it's all right. We're bringing you to the lighthouse."

He stares, eyes feverish. "Moira?"

"Yes. Yes, it's me."

He tugs on my hand. "Please, Moira, tell them—tell them to let me go." Blood drips from his nose, running down his chin. He doesn't even seem to notice.

"I can't give you to the sirens, Jude. They'll kill you."

"*No*. No, no, no. You . . . you don't know that." He shudders, teeth gritted, the blood on his face only emphasizing how pale he looks. "You don't understand."

I brush the sweat-damp hair from his forehead, feel the burning heat of his skin. "I do understand," I whisper back. "How much you must want to go to them. How you would dash off the pier if we let you. You've got the song's magic running through you. We can't let you go until it's run its course."

His next breath hitches on a sob. He thrashes against the hands restraining him, but the men hold fast. "Please," he says, voice choked. "Please, I'll do anything. Just let me go. Let me go!"

He is so unlike himself in that moment, it hurts.

I draw my hand away, his blood dotting the sleeve of my coat.

There have always been survivors. As long as sirens have hunted on the shores of Twillengyle, there were survivors. Islanders and tourists, few and far between, escaping the siren's song. Some who survive and get better, recovering until the attack is nothing more than a faded scar on their past. And some who descend into madness, who waste away slowly, never truly here nor there, never truly *living*.

My heart smashes against my rib cage, a terrible fog filling my mind, because in one of these fates lies the future of Jude Osric— and I do not know which one.

Exhausted by his efforts, he slumps back. His face is grayish white and his eyes roll up in their sockets, unfocused. "They sing to me still," he murmurs. "I can hear them."

It's the last thing he says before he falls unconscious.

Benjamin Carrick picks him up as easily as if Jude were a child. "Lead on, Miss Alexander," he says. "I've got him."

Flint and Llewellyn follow along as we journey over the moors to the lighthouse. The midday sun hides beneath a patch of clouds, shadowing the way.

I ask, "What happened?"

"Carrick saw him by the shore," says Llewellyn.

I look to the man carrying Jude Osric in his arms. He's in his early thirties, dark-haired and broad-shouldered, his skin light brown. His expression is tense with worry, and his hands tighten protectively around Jude. "He wasn't paying attention," he says.

"Do you know what he was doing down there?"

"You'll have to ask him, miss. He'll be back to his senses in due time, I'm sure." He shifts Jude's weight, glancing at the tourniquet around his arm. "It'll be a nasty scar, that will. She caught him by the shoulder before I could pull him away."

I bite my bottom lip. "I don't know many others who would risk going so near the sirens to save another."

"It was Jude Osric," says Carrick, as though this explains everything.

And I nod, because I understand. Jude's kindness has never been for my eyes only. "Thank you," I say, words unable to convey just how thankful I am.

The lighthouse looms ahead of us, and I search through Jude's torn and bloodied jacket until my fingers close around a large skeleton key.

The cottage door swings open on its new hinges. I tuck the key into my pocket and take up my violin case I'd left on the step. "He keeps a first aid kit in the kitchen. I'll get that. His bedroom is just up the stairs, second door on the right."

I make my way into the kitchen. I've seen the first aid kit brought out many times during my visits. It's a plain metal box tucked into a cupboard; I flip the clasps and find it well stocked with bandages, salves, a needle and thread. I grip the handle, white-knuckled, and head up to Jude's bedroom.

I pause outside his door, just for an instant. Placing my hand flat on the wood, I close my eyes, breathing in. Then I walk into the room.

Jude is laid out on the narrow bed. Someone had the sense

to remove his boots, but he's still wearing his tattered jacket, his blood already staining the sheets. *Oh God*, I think. *That will vex him terribly*, and for a moment panic threatens to overwhelm me.

Carrick, Flint, and Llewellyn all stand in the middle of the small room. Flint catches my eye as I enter, but he says nothing. I sit at the edge of Jude's bed, removing the tourniquet from his arm. There's no saving the jacket, nor the sweater he wears beneath it. Both are wet with blood, the sleeves shredded. I take a pair of scissors from the first aid kit and begin cutting through the cloth. Silence cloaks the room as I work. There's only the blood rushing in my ears, the quiet whisper of Jude's breathing. I don't look at his face, how pale he is, the dark hollows under his eyes.

"Moira," Flint says finally. "Do you not think it best we bring him to the hospital?"

"No." I shake my head. "I can care for him better here."

A pause. "No one's saying *you* have to care for him." His tone is all hard edges.

I finish cutting away Jude's clothes, leaving him in his thin undershirt. I turn to face Flint and say, "Why not? Do you think me incapable?"

"No—"

"Well, then." I swallow hard. "I'll keep watch on him until he's recovered. I've seen my father nurse other survivors. Nothing I haven't done before."

"And if he doesn't recover?"

Benjamin Carrick glances sharply to him, but I've already stepped forward. I tip my face up, meeting Flint's pale gaze. "You will not condemn Jude Osric under his own roof," I tell him. "I will not allow it."

A muscle in his jaw twitches. He could very well be the killer we're after, perhaps even the reason why Jude was on the beach. The possibility puts my nerves on edge.

"Get out," I say.

He does so without another word, his footsteps heavy on the stairs.

Carrick and Llewellyn linger in the room, their eyes fixed on Jude. I clasp my hands tight to stop them shaking. "Thank you both," I say, "for bringing him here."

Carrick nods. "No trouble, miss." His gaze falls back on Jude's sleeping form. "The island would be all the poorer without him."

The men take their leave, closing the door softly in their wake. I am alone, and the reality before me settles cold and terrible in my chest.

No—not alone. I'm with Jude Osric.

Although I've never felt so distanced from him.

I sit back down on the edge of his bed. I clean his wounds and prepare new bandages. My hands tremble only a little as I stitch the gashes closed. "Mr. Carrick was right in saying these will scar," I tell him, knotting the thread. "But not to worry. I suspect they'll look quite dashing." A tinge of pink flags his cheekbones, the fringe of his hair damp with sweat. I take a cloth and clean the blood from his face, watching his eyes flit beneath closed lids. I hope it's not nightmares that plague him now. Siren song has a way of addling the mind, racking the body with fever, chills, hallucinations.

No iron ring hangs about his neck. I'd left it, unthinking, on the bedside table in the guest room. If only I'd handed it to him— if I'd simply tucked it into his jacket . . .

Had there been a moment when he realized he wasn't wearing it? Had he tried to turn back before the sirens happened upon him?

A crease appears between his brows as he dreams. I bandage his arm and smooth his hair back. "I know I've asked much of you," I whisper. "More than you've ever asked of me. But if I may ask one other thing, I ask that you survive this." The words scrape my throat. I rest my head on his uninjured shoulder, my eyes burning hot with tears. "Please, Jude. Please don't leave me."

Only last night, he'd returned a siren to the sea. Now they wish to steal him away into the darkness, to fill his lungs with salt water and sink their teeth into his skin. The sea takes what it wants, and perhaps the sea has wanted Jude since the time he'd fallen out of my father's rowboat. Yet the siren we saw that day had not taken him.

His quiet voice echoes inside my head. *I've never blamed them, Moira. The sirens.*

I feel as though something inside me is splintering. I love the sirens as I love the island. They are a link to my father, my childhood, an integral part of myself. They are a double-edged sword, and I admire them for it.

Sirens are not the ones I have given my heart to.

When I look at Jude Osric, I can still see the young boy who showed me the lighthouse, pointing out and explaining everything in sight. I see the wild expanse of the moors and two children, running and stumbling after each other while their fathers were away. I remember Jude, twelve years old, bowing his head during his family's funeral, when he wanted no one to see him cry. And just a few years later, when he stood among the gathering at my father's grave.

Then I cut him from my life, heedless of the consequences, fixating on music and siren watching so that I might fill the loss. Now, I realize, Connor Sheahan's death came as things often did in Twillengyle—as a blessing and a curse. For it brought me back to Jude Osric before I even knew how much I needed him.

Sitting up, I wipe the tears from my cheeks. I go down to the drawing room, open the linen chest, and find a quilt I haven't seen in years, stitched by Jude's mother. The needlework is beautiful, precise, the patchwork blue and white like the lighthouse. I shake the dust from it.

When I take it up to Jude's room, placing it over him, he makes a small noise, a soft sigh in his fitful sleep. I press my fingers to my mouth, but he looks no closer to waking.

In the kitchen, I light an oil lamp as twilight falls. Wind howls its way across the moors. Before I know it I'm fetching a lantern from the desk and unbolting the door.

I shiver as a breeze catches at my open coat. Clenching the lantern, I tug my collar up. The evening air carries all the scents of autumn: burning leaves and dried grass, the sharp smell of salt and brine. I head for the path down to the beach, my boot heels sinking into mud and peat.

On the shoreline I take in the height of the dark cliff wall before surveying the length of the beach. My eyes alight on the nearest crevice, a narrow fracture in the rock. I duck into it, press back against the hard, damp surface, and snuff out the lantern's dim light.

If Jude were here, he'd tell me I was mad to be doing this. Except he's half the reason I'm here to begin with—and I've always been a little bit mad anyway.

So I wait, the last shreds of sunlight disappearing into the sea. I'm reminded of Jude's hand in mine as we danced, of his warm, dark eyes, and the look he gave me, like I was the most remarkable thing in the world.

Leaning forward, I peer out at the beach, and there they are.

Two of them step from the shallows onto the wet sand. Their heels kick up foam, but on the beach they are soundless, pale nymphs slick with salt water. Adrenaline sharpens my eyesight, and I press back into the crevice when their gaze slides to the cliff. My heart races as indigo eyes flick to where I stand, their enlarged pupils dark as midnight. The sirens move on, and I swallow, wondering if it's the same pair who lured Jude earlier.

The thought makes me reckless, pulls me out of hiding. It's then I remember I threw my iron charm into the sea. The sirens have only to turn around to notice me.

They need only sing a single note.

It would be a quick death. Once they got hold of me, I'd be dragged down into the depths. Dizziness from blood loss would make drowning almost pleasant. I wouldn't struggle—not with their song pressed against my eardrums.

And there is a part of me that wishes to hear it, to feel it in my heart and in my veins, a cacophony of salt water and blood.

But I think back on Jude Osric.

Jude, who is a steady hand in the dark, a compass, surefire and true. He has stood by me, lent patience when I had none. I cannot, will not, abandon him now.

I take a step out of the crevice, just as one of the sirens turns.

And everything in me freezes.

We stare at each other, unblinking, both uncertain of the other. Behind her the second siren carries on down the beach. I hardly dare breathe as my thoughts become a whirlwind. I try to remember how fast sirens are—fast, but slower on land, surely? Can I make a dash for the path before she starts to sing? Unlikely. It's several feet away. I'll be caught between the cliff wall and open sand.

If she takes a moment to call for the other siren, I might have a chance. A slim chance. Will they follow me up the cliff path? How far inland will a siren follow her prey?

But I pause, hesitant, when I notice the siren hasn't even opened her mouth. I take another, careful step out from the narrow crevice. The siren tips her head to one side, watching me, her eyes wide-open and dark.

But she does not sing.

My hands ball into fists. "Go on," I whisper, knowing her sharp ears will hear perfectly. "What are you waiting for?"

She takes a step toward me, and my breath quickens. It's as if I'm enchanted already; I can't move. *Caught in siren eyes*, they say, like a rabbit frozen in the arc of a lantern's light.

A breeze off the sea sweeps back her dark tangle of hair. Her face is pale and colorless, except for the red flush across her cheekbones and at her lips. She's beautiful like only a siren is, beautiful like dangerous things so often are.

And she just looks at me.

"Why did you sing to him?" I ask. At a whisper my voice still cracks. "You spare me and not him? He's *dying*—" I swallow against the lump in my throat, tears pricking my eyes. "You took his entire family and he never raised a hand to you."

The siren tilts her head once more, her eyes flitting over my face. Then her gaze drops. She turns away, and her bare feet scarcely leave a print on the shifting sand.

I let out a shaky sigh. It takes a minute before my fists slacken, before I let my eyes look from the beach to the cliff path. With numb and unsteady footsteps, I make my way back up to the moors.

• • •

They say the sea can grant wishes. For the price of a secret.

I stand on the cliff's edge, under the night sky, and glance in the direction of the lighthouse. The beacon light is still burning. It turns in a slow circle over the hillsides, out to the black horizon, the darkness of the deep.

They say the sea can grant wishes, and I'm in desperate need of one.

My fingers hold tight to the piece of paper folded in my hand. Closing my eyes, I whisper, "May Jude get well," and let the paper flutter from my grasp. I watch as it drifts downward—until it's a speck that vanishes against the white-capped waves. In tidy cursive letters, I've printed out the secret of my heart. A secret I now murmur, quiet and breathless, to the clouded moonlight and distant stars.

Because I love him.

CHAPTER TWENTY-SEVEN

I WAKE, HEART POUNDING, to a knocking at the door. Pale morning light marks the floorboards, and I realize I've fallen asleep on a chair at Jude's bedside.

I stretch, stiff neck cursing me. Last night's dream returns in jerky flashes: thunder and lightning over a dark sea, Jude holding fast to my hand before the waves tear us apart, watching him drown . . .

I look over to where he lies in bed. His face is shiny with sweat, his chest rising and falling beneath the quilt.

During the night, he cried out in his sleep, restless and feverish. He said my name, an anxious edge to his voice, as if he were looking for me. Yet when I placed my hand over his, when I told him, *I'm here, Jude, I'm here*—he only pulled away, turning his head against the pillow.

It was worse when he called out for the dead. He shouted for his sister, and I can't remember a time he's said her name since the funeral. I set a damp cloth across his forehead, hoping to bring his temperature down, but it did nothing to ease his flushed cheeks. His body burned with the song's magic; I'd kept watch in fear he'd leave this life before the sun rose.

The knocking starts up again. I hesitate, eyes on Jude, before getting up and hurrying downstairs. Unlatching the door, I step back.

"Mother?"

Her dark eyes meet mine. "Mr. Flint let me know you were staying here." She adjusts the basket she carries in one hand. "He told me what happened—to Jude."

The way she says his first name, like he's a child again, twists my insides. I think of how many people will know what transpired at the harbor yesterday, how swiftly words travel on Twillengyle. My jaw tightens. "I'm looking after him."

"How is he?"

I pause, considering. "I—I don't quite know," I say honestly. "He's asleep."

Something like pity crosses my mother's face. I thought, at first, she'd come here to lecture me again, but I see now that's not the case. I open the door wider, and she steps over the threshold. She sets down her basket, hanging her coat in the entryway. We head up to Jude's room, and I watch her take a seat at the edge of his bed, put a hand against his forehead. His restlessness from last night has drained away; now he lies unmoving, his breathing slow and too quiet in the surrounding silence.

I swallow hard, clasping my hands together.

When my father nursed survivors, he made them drink tonics,

encircled their wrists with charms, pressed bars of iron against their skin. It worked; it always worked. Yet here I am—tossing fool wishes into the sea instead.

My mother says, "I'm going to fetch Dr. Grant," in a way that leaves no room for argument. She stands, turning to me. "Moira—"

"He'll be all right."

I mean to say more, but my throat closes, cutting off the rest of my words.

I'm scared he won't wake up.

I'm scared of what will happen when he does.

Touching my shoulder, she says, "I suppose I can't convince you to come home?"

I shake my head. "I want to stay here until he's better."

And it isn't like Jude has anyone else to care for him. He hates his uncle, wouldn't feel comfortable stuck in the hospital. Most of his life has been a lesson in self-sufficiency.

My mother nods, conceding. I walk with her back down to the entrance. Donning her coat once more, she says, "If you're staying, expect Mr. Irving's arrival later. He'll be keeping the light in the meanwhile."

"Mr. Irving?" I pause. "Not Mr. Osric?"

"That's what I heard."

I gather her basket, hand it to her, and unlatch the front door. "Will you be returning with Dr. Grant?"

She smiles back at me. "Of course."

A pang of guilt pulls at my heartstrings. I remember running out on her, telling her to *let me alone, please.* Now she's allowing me to care for Jude, island gossip notwithstanding. Standing on the doorstep, she places a hand on my arm. "You do well by your father, Moira."

I don't know what to say to that, so I just smile, wondering if I really have. Not yet, I think. The Council is planning to undo the hunting ban—something my father worked so hard to establish— and I can't allow his efforts to amount to nothing.

Perhaps once I solve this murder, and convince the Council, and heal Jude Osric. Perhaps, then, this hollowness in my heart will ease.

After my mother sets off, I go into the kitchen. Sunlight shines through the lace-curtained window, making the cottage seem an equable space. Not at all like its keeper is dying in one of the upstairs bedrooms. I bite my bottom lip, cutting that thought off quick.

Without knowing what else to do, I make a cup of tea.

Steam rises toward the ceiling, disappearing in the light. My father's books are still piled on the table, one of them still open to the petition. I trace over the faded print. I haven't had a chance to study the names, but Jude might have done so. He must've had a reason to head down to the beach.

I drag my fingers through my hair before wrapping them around my teacup. I start up the stairs to check back on him. Walking into the room, I'm met with the unexpected.

Jude Osric is awake.

He's sitting up in bed, leaning against the wall, his temple pressed to the cracked plaster. He doesn't look at me as I enter; aside from the steady rise and fall of his chest, he's completely still. Instead, he gazes out the window, his hand on the glass.

My father used to say that siren victims are predictable in one way: Once taken from the shore, they will do anything to get back to the sea.

I set my teacup on Jude's nightstand.

This feels like precarious ground.

Softly, I say, "You're awake."

At the sound of my voice, his eyes slide toward me. They look bleary in the morning light, not quite focused. "Moira?"

"Yes." I sit on the bed in the hopes of drawing his attention away from the window.

"How long have I been asleep?"

I smooth a hand over the blue-and-white quilt. "Since yesterday afternoon." Recalling the struggle of keeping him from the siren's grasp, I worry how I'll manage on my own. "How are you feeling?"

He smiles, his eyes at half-mast. "You've been staying here," he says.

"I wanted to make sure you were all right."

"So kind." He takes his hand off the window to cup my cheek. His skin feels damp from condensation, hot from fever. "I'm quite all right."

"You don't look it, Jude."

His smile widens. I put my hand over his, bringing it to rest on the quilt instead. Our fingers lace together. Jude closes his eyes, leaning his head against the wall. "I shall miss you," he says, "when I go."

My heart lurches. "You're not going anywhere."

He raises his free hand, tapping his temple, wincing as he pulls at his stitches. "I can still hear them, you know. Singing. They want me back—I need to go back."

"If you do," I say, "the sirens will kill you. Is that what you want?" It's foolish, really, to think I can reason with him. Their enchantment is coursing through his veins, and he's the same as any other siren victim. A familiar boy made unfamiliar by siren song.

When he doesn't reply, I think he may have fallen back asleep. I shake him a little. "Jude—Jude, what were you doing on the beach?"

He opens one eye. "That's where Nell died."

"Yes—but what were you doing there?"

He blinks at me, sluggish. "I wanted . . . I just wanted to see . . ." He pauses, scratching his head. "I was looking for evidence."

"Evidence? Of what?"

His eyes slip shut again. "I need to go," he says quietly. "They're waiting for me."

With gentle hands, I urge him back under the quilt. It's no good questioning him like this. I shouldn't be questioning him at all, the state he's in. I run my fingers through his curls and tell him, "Just try to sleep for now." I wait until his breathing slows, then take up the teacup on his nightstand. I have to grip it tight to keep my hands from trembling.

Outside, clouds gather on the horizon, and I wonder if it will rain. I suppose it'd be pleasing for the weather to suit my mood. Not much else I can be pleased about—what with Jude being delirious, the forthcoming Council meeting, our investigation left on the fringes.

Most of Dunmore has probably heard of Jude's condition by now, if not all of Twillengyle. I sense their eyes like a presence I can't shake off.

It means the murderer will know also.

"What are we going to do?" I mutter, looking back at Jude. He sleeps soundlessly, nothing to indicate whether or not he'll sink into nightmares. I exhale slowly, trying to calm my nerves. "When did you become rash and I cautious?" My voice wavers, chaotic and uneven. "Why didn't you wait for me?"

That's the question I really want answered.

He must've known how dangerous it was, and he wouldn't do something so impulsive without cause. But if he went off in search of evidence . . .

A knock at the door announces my mother's return with the doctor. Grant looks decidedly grim, his face weathered like the crag. He doffs his hat, but he doesn't bother to remove his coat before we start upstairs. He holds a black leather bag in one knobby hand, setting it down on Jude's bed as he leans over to examine him.

"He was awake and talking not a half hour ago," I say, glancing in my mother's direction. "After you left, Mother."

Grant raises an eyebrow as though he's not sure whether to believe me. He unwraps the bandages from Jude's arm, checking over my stitch work.

"His wounds don't appear infected," he says gruffly.

I sit on the chair at the bedside. "He was quite feverish in the night."

"Hmm." Grant lifts one of Jude's eyelids, frowning. "I'd be surprised if he wasn't, Miss Alexander. Siren song is quite like an infection itself. Fever will set in with the delirium—his body is trying to burn the magic out." He covers Jude's stitches with a salve from his medical bag, wrapping them in fresh bandages. "It will take time."

"He'll get better, then?" I ask before I can stop myself. Leaning forward, I shift my gaze from Jude to Grant. "That is, he'll recover?"

Grant straightens up. "That depends entirely on him, Miss Alexander. Recovering from a siren's enchantment is no small feat, but neither is it impossible."

I nod, mouth tight, and look back at Jude. The color is still high in his cheeks, his fingers curling against the blankets.

I see Grant and my mother out and trail my hand along the cracked and peeling plaster in the hallway. Each crack said to hold a secret.

In my mind's eye I watch my slip of paper flutter into the sea. And with all my heart, I want Jude to be well.

CHAPTER TWENTY-EIGHT

It's late in the afternoon when Malcolm Irving reaches the lighthouse. I open the door to find him standing on the front step, hatless, his black hair tousled from the ferry crossing. He wears overalls beneath his threadbare wool coat, and though he's not yet thirty, deep creases mark the skin around his eyes when he smiles.

"Hallo, Miss Alexander," he says cheerfully. A wicker creel is slung over his shoulder. Opening the flap, he shows me the herrings inside. "Got these for tea."

"Thank you." I take it from him as he steps into the hall. "I'll put them in the pan."

"Aye." He shucks off his coat. Hanging it up, he swallows, his expression turned grave. "How is he? Our Jude?"

I clutch the strap of the creel. "Sleeping the day away," I say, trying for lightness. "You can go up and see him, if you like. Dr. Grant checked in on him earlier."

"Oh, good." Irving runs the back of his hand across his forehead before tugging at his hair. He looks down the hall to the staircase, to the door leading into the tower. "Though I reckon he'd be wanting me to see to the light first. I'll head up to the lantern room for but a moment, if you'll excuse me."

While Irving tends to the light, I bring his creel of fish into the kitchen. Unbuttoning my cuffs, I push up the sleeves of my dress, setting out a pan and fillet knife. My eyes drift to the books on the table.

Gabriel Flint is too young to be on the petition. Russell Hendry is locked in a jail cell. Nell Bracken's death provides an alibi for those at the dance. She was waiting for a suitor only to end up in a pool of her own blood—and the police thought it sirens without any witnesses. But why kill her after Connor? What secret had Connor discovered that was worth slitting his throat?

A door opens down the hall. Irving enters the kitchen, cleaning his hands with a handkerchief. He looks at me and says, rather hesitantly, "Might I see him now?"

We go upstairs, and I show him into Jude's room. He kneels at his bedside, taking one of Jude's hands in his. Jude mutters something unintelligible, and Irving turns his hand palm up, the blue veins standing out along the inside of his wrist.

"Has he been . . . ? Has he not woken?"

"This morning he did. Not for long."

The shadows lengthen across the room. Irving places Jude's hand back on the quilt. Sitting against the wall, he looks over at him. "My great-grandfather," he says, "God rest his soul, was in a similar state before he passed. I wasn't even a thought in my mother's mind at the time, but I was told he would take neither food nor water. He wanted only to go back to the sirens." He drags his eyes away from Jude to meet my gaze. "We ought to wake him—make sure he eats something."

I lower myself onto the edge of Jude's bed. "Mr. Irving, if I might ask, why are you here rather than Mr. Osric?"

"He's at the offshore light with Mr. Drummond. The tender won't be able to reach them for another day or two—there's a storm out that way." He rakes a hand through his hair and glances out the window. "I reckon it'll set upon us in the night. I only just managed to catch the last ferry from Lochlan." When he looks to me, his dark eyes are somber. "There's also the matter of my owing him this. Jude. He came to relieve me at that light when he was not yet keeper here. I couldn't get back on the tender—I was too ill—so it was Jude and Drummond taking care of me as well as the light." He smiles a little, rueful. "Drummond's about as comforting as a wet sock, but Jude . . . ah, well, you know how he is." He sets a hand across his heart, fingers spread. His hands are much like Jude's: red knuckles, dry, cracked skin. "He watched over me as if I were his own blood."

I cast my eyes down, staring at a warp in the dark floorboards. Now that Irving has mentioned it, I can almost feel the oncoming storm in the air. I take a glimpse out the window, and the clouds hang low, a uniform gray over the choppy sea. Jude sleeps on, and I stand up from the bed. "I'll get dinner ready," I say, "if you'd like to sit with him until then."

Irving nods. "Thank you kindly, Miss Alexander. I'll do just that."

Downstairs, I clear my father's books from the kitchen table, light the stove, and set about filleting the herrings, coating them in butter, salt, oats, frying them in the pan with another lump of butter. It makes the kitchen smell like wood smoke, like fried fish, so the air is no longer so stale and cold. Before I can call for Irving, I hear his tread on the stairs, alongside another—one I know as well as my own.

Irving comes into the kitchen with his hand around Jude's uninjured arm. Jude is pale-faced, swaying slightly on his feet. Blood trails from his nose, and he wipes at it with the back of one hand, considering the blood across his knuckles with glassy eyes.

He doesn't look at me.

Irving directs him to the water closet to wash up. Once Jude closes the door, I turn to Irving. "I'm not sure he ought to be up and about," I say. "I could've brought him something."

"It might do him good," says Irving. "He seemed agreeable enough."

Indeed, when we sit down to eat, Jude does so without protest. He holds his fork in his right hand, his left arm—stitched and bandaged—cradled against his stomach. He doesn't speak a word, and Irving and I take his cue, so it's a quiet affair altogether. After we finish, Irving asks him, "Would you like anything else, Jude? Cup of tea?"

Jude stares down at his plate. He shakes his head minutely.

"Then let's get you up to bed," says Irving, taking him by the arm.

I rise from my chair as well and follow them into the hall. At the foot of the stairs, Jude pauses, reaching out to touch the wall. He says, voice rasping, "I would like to go to the shore."

"No, Jude." Irving's grip on his arm tightens almost imperceptibly. "Storm's coming. We'll stay here tonight."

Jude looks over his shoulder, finding my gaze and holding it. "Moira . . ."

"Mr. Irving is right," I say. "You're not well, Jude. You need to go back to bed, get some rest."

He shudders, hand pressed flat against the wall. His nose starts bleeding again, but this time he makes no move to wipe the blood from his face. It drips onto his shirtfront as he ducks his head, breathing ragged.

"Easy, now," says Irving. He gives a tug on Jude's arm, pulling him up onto the first step. "Come, you must be tired."

He manages to get Jude upstairs. I wait, and listen, my hand curled around the banister. I hear Irving say something, low enough to be inaudible, and Jude mumble in answer. They walk into his room, the wood creaking beneath their feet.

When Irving comes back down, he smiles at me reassuringly. "He's asleep," he says. "I'll just head up to the light—wind the clockwork."

The rain starts not long after, sudden and pouring down in sheets. Irving lights a lamp and builds a fire in the drawing room. I sit on the rug before it, like I did as a child. We drink black tea and eat bread with butter, watching the logs shift in the grate, the wind outside rattling the windows in their frames.

"Good God," Irving says, "I'll be hammering shingles back onto the roof come morning." He sits in an armchair, gazing up at the ceiling. In the corner of my eye, I see him look my way. "Your violin is here, I noticed. Over in the kitchen."

I nod. Irving takes up the knitting he brought along—a half-finished sock—and I set down my teacup, staring into the fire. After a few minutes, he clears his throat and says, "You know, I don't mind if you play a tune or two."

I lift my own eyes to the ceiling. "I don't wish to wake him."

"You'll settle him, Miss Alexander. I'm sure he'll prefer it over this gale."

His words make me smile. I pick myself up and head into the kitchen. Placing my violin case on the table, I flip the clasps, opening it. Yet it's not only my violin, bow, and rosin I find inside. A slip of paper, crumpled and a little ripped, lies atop the cloth covering my violin. I take it in hand, frowning.

It's the flyer I'd pinned in the schoolhouse, an advertisement of my tutoring. Near the bottom of the page, however, are words I hadn't written. A shiver runs over me as I read them.

There are worse things I can do

I pull the cloth from my violin and realize all four strings have been cut. I put a hand on the table to steady myself, rage coiling at the back of my throat. The last time I'd left my violin unattended was when Jude was attacked, when I'd left it behind at the lighthouse as alarm bells rang from the harbor.

I know the killer is watching us. My jaw tightens as I imagine them opening my case, bringing a knife to my violin strings. I keep additional strings alongside my rosin should any break; I take my time about replacing the ruined ones, intent on the familiar task, rather than the memories unfolding in my mind's eye. I thread a string through the peg hole, trying to escape the thought of Nell lying dead on the beach. Winding the string onto the peg, I do my best not to dwell on how her blood glinted in the lantern light.

I leave the flyer and carry my violin and bow back into the drawing room. I sit on the sofa, and my mind is eased somewhat as I begin to tune up. Irving continues knitting, unaware, and asks, "What are you going to play, then?"

"What would you like?"

"Oh." He looks up. The firelight shadows his face, darkening his eyes. His needles, for a moment, lie still in his lap. "I think something slow, Miss Alexander. Something with a bit of sorrow, if you would."

"Yes." I raise my violin, angle my bow over the strings. "I was thinking just the same."

CHAPTER TWENTY-NINE

THE NEXT DAY DAWNS gray and chilly, a swathe of mist carpeting the moors. I'm awoken by the sound of Irving on the cottage roof, hammering shingles back into place. I walk down the hall to check on Jude, but he sleeps through the noise, curled up under the quilt.

Downstairs, I wash up and pull my hair into a bun. I open the kitchen window, hearing voices outside. Irving is talking to someone. I tug on my coat and make my way around the side of the cottage.

Benjamin Carrick is there, in his oilskin and cap. He stands next to the ladder leaning up against the siding, his eyes on the roof.

"Good morning," I say.

He looks around. "Morning, Miss Alexander." He doffs his cap. "I was just asking after our Wick."

"He's faring well enough." This is said by Malcolm Irving. Both Carrick and I glance up as he appears at the edge of the roof. He starts down the ladder and adds, "He has a stubborn way about him—he'll pull through." Reaching the ground, he regards me. "Are you off home now, Miss Alexander?"

"No. I'll be back. I'd like to visit Miss Bracken, is all."

Our one remaining lead. I dare to hope, though I realize I shouldn't. I try to cast the feeling aside, but it clings to me like water. Imogen has the information we need. She must know who was courting Nell, who had offered to take her to the dance.

Apprehension curls in my veins, sickly and ominous.

"That would be kind of you." Irving wipes his face with his handkerchief. He turns his gaze on the stone cottage over the moors, and I see his mouth thin. "You know, if we count our Jude, that's three islanders attacked within the year, within the *month*. I haven't seen the likes of that since . . . well, since the Osrics, I suppose, God be good to them."

I swallow. "Jude wasn't wearing iron, Mr. Irving."

He grimaces. "More's the pity." Stowing his handkerchief in the pocket of his overalls, he scrubs a hand through his hair. "You go on, then, Miss Alexander. Carrick, you coming in for tea?"

I set off a little ways and turn back to watch the two men disappear inside the keeper's cottage. Taking a breath, I pull myself together. I leave the lighthouse behind, carrying all my worries with me.

The Brackens' garden is littered with dying petals, dried and browning at the edges. I walk over to where Imogen is crouched among them, aiming a pair of shears at the surrounding rosebushes. She hasn't done up her hair; it tumbles past her shoulders in thick black waves. Her gloveless hands are marked with thin scratches from the thorns, her cheeks pink from sun and exhaustion.

"Miss Alexander," she says in greeting. The unspoken message is immediately apparent: I am not wanted in her garden.

"Morning, Miss Bracken. I hope you're well." I clasp my hands in front of me. "I was . . . I was very sorry to hear of Nell's passing." Though even as I say the words, they feel worthless, the heart of them worn down by repetition.

"I'm still making funeral arrangements, if that's what you're wondering."

"No. No, it's not that. I just have some questions."

Imogen pauses in her work to point the shears in my direction. "What questions?"

Staring at the fallen roses around us, I blurt out, "Why cut down your roses?"

"Wouldn't think you came to ask about my gardening."

"No, miss, I—"

"They were Nell's roses," Imogen says abruptly, "and now that she's no longer—" She stops, shaking her head. "Never mind me. What is it you want to know?"

I hesitate. Without Jude by my side, uncertainty threatens to swallow me whole.

"Last weekend's dance," I start, "Jude mentioned Nell was planning to come with a suitor."

"Yes," says Imogen, digging her long shears into the thicket. "She told me to go on ahead without her. He was to meet her here, but she must've wandered off to the beach. I don't understand why . . . There was no reason for her to be down there."

My pulse flutters with adrenaline. "Who was the gentleman? Do you know him?"

Her eyes meet mine. She says, "Detective Thackery," and numbness creeps over my skin. "He came by the same morning you did, remember?"

I think of Nell's smile as she bade goodbye to Thackery, of how calmly he'd spoken on the beach, standing over her body.

"Yes," I say quietly. "I remember."

Eve Maddox's voice circles back to me, soft as a whisper. *Connor said he knew something. Said he had to meet someone after helping his da at the harbor.*

Said it was secret.

Did Connor plan to meet up with the detective?

Someone had taken my flyer from the schoolhouse, likely the same person who put that note in Jude's mail slot, the knife in his garden. Had Thackery followed us from the pub? Had he doubled back the night of Nell's death to observe us at the harbor?

Imogen heaves a sigh. Looking me over, she says, "Why are you asking about this, Miss Alexander? What are you getting out of it?"

I bite my lip. "Nothing, miss. I—I'm only trying to understand what happened."

"Think it might be better if you minded your own."

A flush rises in my cheeks. She doesn't give me a chance to reply, as she continues. "Hear you've been caring for Wick."

"That's right."

"How is he?"

I feel a flicker of irritation at her question—at the irony of Imogen telling me to mind my business only to prod her nose into mine. Then I realize it's Jude she's asking after, and his business is his own. The realization is an uncomfortable one, and my voice comes out stiff as I say, "He's been resting."

"Best get back to him, shouldn't you?"

"Yes." I nod. "Sorry to have kept you."

Her expression softens. "Take care, Miss Alexander."

I smile in return—the best I can under the circumstances—before starting back toward the lighthouse. I concentrate on the whistling of the wind, the rush of waves below the crag. Distantly, I feel the press of the investigation, the urge to visit the police station, as if I'll see Thackery's guilt writ upon his face.

To do that, though, I need Jude Osric.

With Jude bedridden, I am split in two, wedged between looking after him and protecting the sirens, worrying over his health and trying to find a killer.

In the evening, I travel up to his bedroom. The floor creaks beneath me, and Jude mumbles in his sleep. I pull the quilt up where it's slipped from his shoulders. Bringing the back of my hand to his forehead, I find his temperature much improved. I sit in the chair by his bedside and tell him about my morning with Imogen, about Thackery being Nell's suitor.

His hand rests on the pillow. I take it in mine, allowing myself this. I look at his closed eyes and imagine them blinking open.

But he sleeps, and then I do too, falling into dreams alongside him.

CHAPTER THIRTY

WHEN I SIT DOWN to breakfast the next day, Irving puts aside the morning paper, leveling his gaze on me. "Did you know," he says, "that Jude has a telephone?"

I reach for a bread roll. "Oh, he made me well aware of it."

The telephone—installed just last week—sits next to his telegraph machine in the watch room. Jude had spent a good hour admiring the device when it first arrived.

"Well, his uncle rang," says Irving. "Told me he'll be here by evening."

I pause, butter knife in hand. "Jude will not be pleased about that," I say flatly.

"That's true enough." Irving lifts the teapot, pouring tea into my waiting cup. "I don't know the ins and outs of it, but I reckon Dylan must've done something awful for our Jude to turn away from him."

My stomach churns as I wrap my hands around my teacup. Dylan Osric tortured a siren in Jude's absence, leaving Jude to try to care for her. I'm not sure what he'll do when he realizes we've returned her to the sea.

I glance toward the hall. "I ought to check on him."

Quite unexpectedly, Irving tells me, "He's awake." When I snap my attention to him, he amends, "Or rather, he was. He found me in the watch room earlier. I sent him straight back to bed, though. He oughtn't be climbing all those stairs."

"How was he? That is, was he . . . ?"

"He's doing better, I'd say."

I push away from the table, smooth a hand over my dress. "I'll go up and see him."

"Here, wait"—Irving pours out another cup of tea, adding milk and sugar to it—"take this up to him, eh?"

I carry the tea upstairs. In the hall, I hear nothing but silence from Jude's bedroom. I ease open the door, and for a moment I see him as he was before I walked in. Sitting up in bed, he holds an old keeper's manual, his head bent over it, one hand pressed flat against the page as he reads. His hair is damp and curling from the ewer, and he wears a wool dressing gown, hiding his bandages from view.

When he looks over, his eyes light up. It's not the hectic burn of fever, but a glow that's dark and warm and steady. He smiles just as bright. "Good morning, Moira."

Stepping into the room, I close the door behind me. He sounds incredibly normal, worlds apart from the last few days. I bite the inside of my cheek, trying to keep my grin in check. "How are you feeling?"

"Like a wrung-out cloth," he replies, sheepish. "But other than that . . ."

"It takes time. The song had you rattled for quite a while." I put the tea on his nightstand, sitting down on the edge of his bed.

Jude turns away to set his manual beside the teacup. His left arm remains stiff at his side. I remember the slash marks as they looked at the harbor, deep and red. It must be agonizing.

He says, "It's what I deserve, isn't it? I kept that siren from the sea. She was suffering, and I didn't . . . I could've . . ." His fingers work restlessly at the cuff of his dressing gown. I cover them with one hand, bringing the motion to a stop.

"This was an accident, a fluke. You've done nothing to warrant it."

Untangling his hand from mine, he presses his thumb between my eyebrows, smoothing the crease I know is there. "I don't mean to worry you, Moira."

"And yet you do such a fine job of it."

His mouth quirks.

"Mr. Irving made you tea," I tell him. "You ought to drink it."

He picks it up off the nightstand. His hand trembles a little as he does, and I study the shadows beneath his eyes, the slight flush across his cheeks.

"What was it like?" I say, the words taking shape in my mouth. "The song?"

Jude looks down into his teacup. "It was as if the world were slipping under me."

"You were charmed?"

"I guess so." His voice is quiet, strained, but he continues. "Nothing seemed to matter except getting back to them. It was like I wasn't myself anymore. Like I didn't know who I was."

An uncomfortable heat burns in my chest. I don't know what to say to Jude—I'm not even sure his response was the one I wanted—but his words hollow out a place deep inside me, and I know I need to answer.

"Of everyone on this island," I say, "you deserved that least of all."

"I don't think I'd wish it on anyone, Moira."

I can think of a few I'd wish it on. Dylan Osric, for one. Whoever helped him catch that siren. Whoever killed Connor and Nell in cold blood. I wish the sirens would steal them all into the cold blackness beneath the waves.

Casting my eyes to the floor, I ask, "What were you hoping to find on the beach?"

Jude leans back against the headboard. "I thought it strange how the police never made any arrests apart from me," he says. "I—I thought . . . perhaps if I checked around where Nell died, I might find something."

"I questioned Imogen—Detective Thackery was Nell's suitor."

Jude's eyebrows go up. "Thackery?"

I swallow. "We need to find out what Connor knew. It could be evidence."

"When you told me"—Jude hesitates, squeezing his eyes shut—"when you said Connor knew something, I thought of the siren my uncle caught. I thought he found out somehow, and that's why he wanted to talk with me. Perhaps he wanted to report it."

I frown at the unlikeliness of this. "Jude, how could he? You told me he hadn't been to the lighthouse, right?"

"Not *recently*." He sets his teacup down and scrapes a hand over his face. "Last month Mr. Sheahan brought him up after he got a fishhook stuck in his thumb. I treated it. He might've heard something or . . . I don't know. I'm certain that door was locked."

If Connor truly knew of the siren, I find it hard to reconcile the fact that he hadn't confided in me before going to the police. I was his tutor. He never made mention of any such thing during our lessons.

Jude looks out the window with a sigh. His profile is sunlit and familiar, and every time I consider how I almost lost him my heart breaks anew. He mumbles, "I shouldn't have gone to the beach without you."

A lump rises in my throat. "No," I say thickly. "You shouldn't have."

He glances back at me, and I put my arms around him, drawing him close. I rest my cheek against his uninjured shoulder, fingers curling into the fabric of his dressing gown. "I was so afraid," I whisper, "when Terry told me. I saw you there on the dock and I was terrified, Jude." My voice catches, but still the words tumble out. "Because if you . . . If they had taken you, Jude Osric—" I can't finish the sentence. My throat feels pinhole thin, and I concentrate instead on the sound of his quiet breaths, each one promising that he is alive and safe and *here*.

Softly, he asks, "Did you manage to retrieve your violin?"

"Yes." A smile tugs at the edge of my mouth. "I have it here."

"In my dreams I heard you playing. I knew it was you even without seeing you. It was your music that led me out of the dark."

I pull back so I can see his expression. He raises a tentative hand to the side of my neck, to the small bruise left by my violin. Meeting my gaze, he bites his lip. "Moira," he says, "I've been wondering . . . That is, I've been meaning to ask . . ."

I bring my hand to his cheek. He leans in to the touch, closing his eyes.

And I kiss him.

I feel Jude go still, but then he presses close, his hand moving to circle the back of my neck. It isn't how I ever imagined we might kiss: Jude's blood staining the sheets, his arm lacerated by a siren's claws. He tastes like tea and sugar. He smells like the lighthouse and the sea. He says my name again, whispers it, and slides his hand into my hair. I draw away, looking at him. His cheeks are pink, his brown eyes warm as honey.

He smiles. "I've wanted to kiss you for quite some time, Moira Alexander."

I laugh, a little breathless. I should've kissed him ages ago.

And I want to fold this moment up for safekeeping. A single point when Jude is happy, when the sirens are protected, when an unknowing islander is not left to bleed out on the sands below.

I place a hand on his chest, just over his heart. I lean in to kiss him again.

CHAPTER THIRTY-ONE

We share a few more kisses before making our way downstairs. Irving is still in the kitchen, tidying up, but upon hearing our footsteps, he turns to study Jude.

"On the mend, are you?" He puts the tea towel he holds on the counter, motioning Jude forward. "Let me have a look at you."

I slip past to stand at the kitchen table as Irving sets his hands on Jude's shoulders. Jude is an inch or so taller; Irving peers up into his face, eyes narrowed. Then, taking Jude by the collar, he shakes him none too gently. "Being out there without iron. What were you thinking? You had me scared half to death—and worrying Miss Alexander, too."

Jude ducks his head. "I did not think." He looks over at me. "I'm sorry."

When Irving speaks again, his voice comes out raw and uneven sounding. "Dear God," he says, and pulls Jude to him, embracing him tightly. "You must grow up to be an old man, Jude Osric. Promise me."

At this Jude glances my way over Irving's shoulder. His expression is amused. "I'll do my best," he replies.

Irving claps him on the shoulder before stepping back. "Well, I ought to head off. Your uncle is coming by later, and Drummond will be needing me at the offshore light."

Like a slate wiped clean, Jude's countenance goes blank. "Dylan is coming here?"

"He is," says Irving, not without sympathy. "I reckon others will too, once I tell folk at the harbor how you're doing." He shifts his gaze to me. "Miss Alexander, you've been fine company these past few days. Thank you."

As it turns out, a great deal of people end up visiting. All through the rest of the morning and afternoon, fishermen and dockers come knocking at the door. Jude answers it each time, smiling, reassuring them of his well-being, but as the day wears on, I can tell it tires him. He is not yet fully recovered. He presses a hand to the wall, as if needing the support, and his face pales, his mouth tightening when he thinks no one is looking.

The last pair of visitors take their leave, and Jude sits down, gazing bleary-eyed at the creels of fish and tins of biscuits left on the kitchen table. His dressing gown hangs off the shoulder of his injured arm, the bandages crisp and white alongside the green wool. He folds his right arm on the table and rests his head against it.

"Perhaps you should go upstairs," I say. I open one of the

creels, inspecting the herrings inside. "I can wake you when your uncle arrives."

"I'm fine," says Jude, looking up. "Shall I start dinner?"

"I'll make it."

I bring the creel over to the counter before Jude can get up. He leans back in his chair, passing a hand over his eyes. "What am I going to say to him, Moira?"

I curl my fingers around the counter's edge. Any answer I might give seems to lodge in my throat. I look to the window, to the stretch of moors beyond the glass.

Jude continues. "What if he did catch that siren with somebody else? He's going to . . . He's going to notice she's gone."

"There's a meeting tomorrow," I say quietly. "Your uncle likely wants to be here for it. The Council is thinking about changing the restrictions of the hunting ban."

"And they're holding it in Dunmore? I would think Lochlan . . ."

I turn back to him. "Perhaps the police want to have their say."

He places his hands flat on the table. "I'm coming."

"Jude, you're not well enough."

He meets my gaze, jaw set. "Do you imagine I'll go dashing off to the sirens as soon as you open the door?"

"I'm more concerned you'll collapse after taking a step out of it."

He swallows, looking elsewhere. "Very well, then," he says after a pause. "I'll stay."

Before I can reply, there's a knock on the door. The two of us stare at each other, unmoving.

I clear my throat. "Should I . . . ?"

"No." Jude stands up, one hand gripping the chair back. "He'll be expecting me to answer."

We walk to the entryway together. Jude straightens, almost imperceptibly. He unbolts the latch and opens the door wide.

Dylan Osric waits on the front step, in his wool coat and cloth cap, looking much the same as when I last saw him. There's more gray streaking his brown curls, but he's still wiry, like Jude, and haggard in a way Jude is not.

"Hello, Uncle."

Dylan takes off his cap. "Jude," he says. Then he regards me. "Evening, Miss Alexander. Mr. Irving didn't mention you were here."

I fix my gaze on him, offering up a thin smile. "Good evening, Mr. Osric."

"She wanted to make sure I was all right," says Jude.

"Hmm." Dylan turns his attention back to him. "You going to let me in?"

Jude steps aside. In the entryway, Dylan hangs his coat and cap on an empty peg. He turns his head slightly, glancing down the hall.

Jude says, "I can build up a fire in the drawing room. If you'd like—"

"Have there been many people here, then?" Dylan interrupts. His eyes are hard, calculating; I can tell he's weighing his words, mindful of my presence.

Jude leans back against the wall. He looks ashen and vulnerable in his loose-fitting dressing gown, his exhaustion evident in his posture. I want to reach out for him, to press my hand to his, but I hold myself still. He tells Dylan, "A fair few."

"Hmm," Dylan says again. "And what were you doing by the shore? Did that day seem a fine one to be drowned?"

"I was just . . ."

"Being foolish, that's what. This is just the way your father was, you know, before he died."

Jude says nothing. Dylan sets off down the hall, past the staircase, to the storeroom he kept the siren in. He pauses near the door. "Miss Alexander," he says abruptly, "oughtn't you be heading home?"

"Moira is welcome to stay as long as she likes," Jude says. He looks over at me briefly before returning his gaze to his uncle. "Dylan, I—"

Dylan silences him with a raised hand. As he walks back toward us, his eyes do not stray from mine. "Did you send my nephew down there, Miss Alexander? Would he have been on the beach if it weren't for you?"

And my breath catches with the honesty of it, a chill settling deep in my chest, because Jude *wouldn't* have been on the beach if it weren't for me. Of course he wouldn't. I'm the one who suggested an investigation in the first place, dragging him alongside me into all of Twillengyle's dangers and magic.

"All right, that's quite enough." This is Jude, his eyes shining bright and fierce. He pulls himself from the wall, leaving my side to catch Dylan by the arm. "I need to speak with you alone."

Dylan glares back at him. "Very well." He tugs out of Jude's grip, turning toward the oak door—heading, presumably, for the watch room.

After he disappears into the tower, Jude comes to place his hands on my shoulders. He gazes down at me and says, voice low, "I'll deal with him, Moira." His face is anxious and tired, lovely and sad. "He shouldn't have spoken to you in that manner."

I touch his cheek. "Be careful."

He goes up after Dylan, the door falling shut behind him. I wait a long minute and follow in his footsteps. On the watch room landing, I stop, hearing Dylan and Jude on the other side of the door. I rest a hand against the cool plaster of the tower wall, listening hard.

"Where is she?" says Dylan, so loud and sudden that I start. "I know well enough she's not in that room. You've done something with her."

Jude mumbles something. A sharp *thump* resonates from inside the room, and I grit my teeth, digging my nails into my palms.

Then Dylan's voice, snarling, "You've no idea—"

"I do, actually," Jude cuts in. "I know you only did it for yourself. Were you even thinking of Da when you chained her up? Did you even—"

"You had no business throwing her back. Not now. Not after what I've done."

For the first time in recent memory, I hear ice crystallize in Jude's voice. "What would you have me do?" he asks. "You *tortured* her, Dylan, and I've spent the past year worried sick over her. If someone found out—"

"*Someone did find out*," Dylan growls.

I hear movement, the creak of floorboards. And very softly Jude says, "What?"

"Little wonder how they did. I had dockers asking me why you were stowing supplies out in the shed rather than the storeroom. Hughes thought you were hosting dinner parties with the cuts of meat you kept buying."

"I didn't think—"

"Now you have Gavin's daughter downstairs. Good God, Jude, you've got the song in your ears with her, never mind sirens."

"Dylan," Jude says, and he's so quiet I strain to hear him. "Who found out?"

There is a long, long silence. I feel my heartbeat, slow and dreadful, as I wait for something to happen.

"Just—tell me it wasn't Connor Sheahan. Tell me you didn't . . ."

"Now, that was a tragic mishap."

"Dylan."

"I wasn't the one to wield the knife, if that's what you're asking."

Inside the watch room, Jude curses once, and then again. He sounds wrecked, and I'm both thankful and torn I can't see his expression.

"When I was here a while back, he started asking all sorts of questions," says Dylan. "Met me on the dock soon as I was off the boat. Said he'd been meaning to talk to you." He pauses, but Jude remains silent, and he continues. "You're lucky he came to me instead. That boy was putting two and two together, nosy as anything. He thought there was something going on up at the light, and I asked him—asked him what made him think so. He went off talking about how you were never much at the harbor these days, wondering why you had that one shuttered window, why you were paying out for so much goddamn meat.

"He said he thought he heard something while he was here in the summer. A strange thing—seeing as he knew you lived alone."

Through the wall I hear Jude make a sound low in his throat, like Dylan's words have choked him. I bow my head, close my eyes, and try to breathe through the ache in my chest.

"So I dealt with it." Dylan's tone is matter-of-fact. "I reckoned he'd go to the police in time. Wasn't hard to head him off and find someone who agreed with my line of thinking. Llyr was a stone's throw away from losing this post before he died—I wasn't going to let that happen to you."

My lip curls in a sneer. It's Dylan alone who's at fault. He put Jude between the hammer and the anvil—there's no reason why Jude should be taken to task for it.

Jude says, "He was a child," and his voice is on the verge of cracking in two.

Dylan doesn't answer immediately. When he does he says only, "Worse things have come to pass on this island."

"Get out," Jude snaps back at him. "Get out. *Get out of here.*"

I step away from the door. The kitchen is too far below, so I dash upstairs, to the highest door of the lighthouse. I walk out onto the narrow deck set above the gallery. Its railing is rusted, but I curl my hands around it nonetheless; my one barrier from the cliffs beneath, from a long drop into the sea.

Below, the front door of the cottage opens, and I see Dylan Osric strike out toward Dunmore. He's a figure of sharp edges and shadow against the red evening sky. It takes a few minutes for Jude to join me. He stands beside me, hands resting on the railing. I look up at him. He stares out at the waves rather than his uncle's retreating figure.

"I heard what Dylan said to you," I whisper.

Jude swallows hard. With the back of one hand, he wipes his

eyes in a perfunctory way, like he means to catch the tears before they fall.

"He'll be spending the night at Alder's Inn." His voice comes out rough as gravel. "He wants to be here for the meeting."

I place my hand over his. "I'm sorry, Jude."

Ducking his head, he turns his face away. A pair of gulls swoop above us as he takes several deep breaths. Eventually he says, "Not surprising, is it?"

And it's true Jude suspected his uncle from the outset. I expect it's different though, to have that suspicion proven so.

I fix my eyes on the bleeding horizon, on the sea black as spilled ink. A matching darkness coalesces in the chambers of my heart. Anger is a hot hand against my breastbone, and I wonder, just for a moment, what would happen if I set it loose.

Jude, as always, is the one to pull me from the shadows. He taps once against the iron rail. "Do you know why this is called a widow's walk?"

I do know. Jude had told me years ago. Or my father had. Old island stories all blurring together in my head. But I say nothing.

"The wives of sailors came up here, in times gone past, to watch for their husband's ships on the horizon. Waiting for someone who would never come back to them."

His words send an involuntary shiver down my spine. I imagine pretty women wearing white dresses and sad expressions where Jude Osric and I now stand. His voice sounds empty, undone somehow, like he has taken the story and swallowed the heart of it.

"You should rest," I tell him.

He looks at me. Red traces the whites of his eyes. "Tomorrow," he says, "at the meeting . . . you think the killer will be there?"

"Most likely."

"Be careful, please, Moira."

I squeeze his fingers, the both of us gazing at the horizon line. We stand there, waiting, until the sun dips into the ocean and disappears.

CHAPTER THIRTY-TWO

A CROWD HAS ALREADY GATHERED in the dance hall by the time my mother and I arrive. Someone has placed a lectern on the edge of the stage and chairs where each of the four Council members sit.

With so many people milling about, my memories of the place feel distant, drowned out by the whispers of those present. In an hour or so the Council may well make a decision regarding the ban. A decision that might not be a favorable one.

I remember little of the hunts, but what I do remember is sitting in the drawing room of my house with Emmeline and Jude, our mothers making cakes in the kitchen. Emmeline was only a child herself then, and she sat with Jude and me by the fire, telling us stories. They were old folktales that changed with each telling, but the heart of them remained the same. I remember how red her hair looked in the firelight, her lovely, musical voice lulling as waves upon the shore.

And the townsfolk drove the woman off the cliff, for she had provoked their ire. She fell into the depths below, where the sea took pity, gifting her sharp teeth and a beguiling song, so that she might exact her revenge . . .

I survey the islanders around me. Dylan Osric appears out of the crowd, walking over to stand next to my mother. He inclines his head. "Good morning, Lenore. Moira." His smile is thin as a razor's edge.

My mother nods back at him. "Morning, Dylan."

Inside the pocket of my coat, my hand closes in a fist. Placing my other hand on my mother's arm, I tell her, "I'm going to find a place by the stage."

I set off through the crowd. I've nothing to say to Dylan Osric, nothing that could be said in polite company. The blackhearted part of myself, the part that yearns for siren song, wants to see him locked in his own chains—to see his expression when a knife is pressed against his skin. I feel adrift without Jude by my side.

Brendan Sheahan stands near the stage. He has a cigarette balanced in the crook of his ear and another between his fingers, but neither is lit. I don't see the rest of his family anywhere.

He glances at me. "Hello, Moira."

"You're here alone?" I wonder why he has come at all.

"They didn't want the attention. So I've come to see what happens." He smiles, close-lipped. "I'm just the messenger."

I look up toward the stage. Two councilors, Thomas Earl and Calum Bryce, mutter to each other, casting doubtful eyes over the crowd of islanders.

Perhaps I'm projecting my own hopes onto their features.

I say, "What do you think will happen?"

"They'll drop the ban," says Brendan, and perhaps he's projecting his hopes as well. Catching sight of my expression, he adds, "Why do you care for them so much?"

"They have a right to be here. They are part of Twillengyle just as we are."

"Doesn't make them good."

"They do not kill us for sport. Men can go out to sea with harpoons and call it vengeance, but that will hold up only for a time. We needn't hunt them to protect ourselves—we have iron for that."

I am like a child in love with something dangerous and desperate for others to love it too. But to sever myself from the sirens would be to sever myself from my past, from my father. I can't do it—I've never wanted to.

Finally I say, "This isn't the way. I know you might think so, but it isn't."

Brendan raises his eyebrows, only half interested in my words. Men from Dunmore's police department come to stand across the platform from us. I watch Detective Thackery pull Thomas Earl aside, head bent as he speaks, making sharp gestures with one hand.

Anger consumes me.

He put Jude behind bars without a scrap of proof. He was to accompany Nell to the dance the same night she ended up dead.

He could've helped Dylan Osric catch that siren.

It could be him. It could be him.

"How's Wick doing?"

The question catches me off guard. I look back at Brendan.

"Better," I say. "A few more days and he'll be quite well, I imagine."

Brendan turns his cigarette over between his fingers. "I'm glad to hear it. He has a good heart, our Wick. What was he doing down there?"

I'm interrupted from answering as Earl steps up to the lectern. Everyone is silent.

Thomas Earl, Dunmore's councilor, commands silence easily. Well into his sixties, he has perfect posture and a heavy brow. He says, "Good morning, everyone," and his voice is a low grind, rusty. "I assume you're all aware why this meeting was called, so I'll get straight to it. There has been a steep rise in siren attacks this past month, more locals taken this year compared to the one previous." Earl leans forward over the wooden lectern. "I realize this is cause for concern. The recent memories of Connor Sheahan and Nell Bracken are still fresh in our minds, and I speak on behalf of the Council when I say that I do not wish for one more islander to be seized from us by a siren's enchantment."

The word "death" has not been used yet—for which I am thankful. It helps make the speech formless, insubstantial words that only hint at the true gravity of the situation.

"A number of people, including members of Dunmore Police, have suggested we take another look at the hunting ban that currently protects the siren population."

The silence of the dance hall dissolves into whispers. I do not dare breathe—every part of me tuned for Earl's next words.

"How much of the population will be culled?" asks someone from the back, breaking my concentration.

I want to scream at whoever it is. *Nothing has been decided yet!*

"Well, there are multiple factors to consider," Earl replies. He folds his hands on the top of the lectern, like a grand delegate. "This ban has been in place for the past ten years. It's not something to be regarded lightly."

"They attacked our Wick."

I don't know who says the words, but the response they receive is instantaneous. The noise in the hall swells, an oncoming wave. I shut my eyes. It doesn't block out the sound of Jude's name on everyone's lips.

Our Wick.

As keeper, Jude Osric is the one meant to protect us from the sea. His encounter with the sirens—more than anything— demonstrates just how susceptible to their song we are.

"The nature of the sirens is a delicate matter," says Earl. "Heavy losses to their number could result in a decline in tourism . . ."

From nearby someone says, "So you're saying we should keep them on just so a few tourists can ogle and likely get killed doing it? Have you been addled by siren song yourself, sir?"

Others near me look decidedly torn, whispering among themselves. I hear my father's name, and hope creeps into my heart. The hunting ban hadn't come about without support— it hadn't lasted all these years without people standing by it, upholding it.

Calum Bryce rises from his chair and walks to the edge of the stage. He murmurs something in Earl's ear before taking his place at the lectern. "Mr. Earl raises valid points," he says to the crowd. "Like it or not, our island relies on sirens to survive.

"With that said, precautions must be put in place. The sirens, now more than ever, exemplify the dangers we face at sea and along our shores. It's a blessing, indeed, not to have experienced the consequences of their song within your own circle of loved ones."

Where Thomas Earl was rusty, Calum Bryce is refined. He is Lochlan's councilor and looks sharp in his dark suit and tie, polished as a new penny. He glances back to Earl, who gives a single, tired nod in return. I fear I've missed some secret conversation between the two of them.

His eyes on the crowd, Bryce persists. "The deaths of Connor and Nell should not slip by without note, as we have allowed so many others to do in the past. With this in mind, the Council aims to discontinue the ban on siren hunting, effective immediately."

No, I think, except I must say it, as Brendan turns to give me a look.

"Those in favor?"

A chorus of *aye*s echoes through the dance hall. Dozens of them, contrasting with my own silence. Brendan, also, to my surprise, does not lend his voice to the vote. Instead, he mutters, "Oughtn't we wait for Wick?"

Hearing this, some of the fishermen glance uneasily at one another. Doubt seeps into their voices—*we ought to; he is keeper*—and the words carry, pass around, until they reach Dylan Osric.

He says loudly, "I think I can speak for my nephew."

Brendan looks around to eye him through the crowd. "I think not, Mr. Osric. He is, after all, no longer your ward. I reckon he can speak for himself."

"And what do you imagine he'll say?" someone asks. "He was just attacked—sirens stole away his family!"

"Then he'll vote to dismantle the ban," says Brendan. "Either way, he has a stake in this. Miss Alexander here tells me he's on the mend."

Something flares up inside me. I shift my attention to the stage, locking eyes with Calum Bryce. "Yes," I announce. "He is quite recovered. As Dunmore's keeper, he ought to have a say. Another day or two . . ."

Bryce rubs a hand across his forehead. He looks to the other councilors.

I am so, so still.

"Tomorrow, then," he says. "We shall reconvene here. You would do well to inform Mr. Osric, Miss Alexander."

As people start filing out toward the street, I catch Dylan Osric exchanging words with Detective Thackery. They head for the back room by the stage, and without thinking twice about it, I follow after them. I duck into the unlit space just in time to see Thackery disappear through the side door, the one leading out into the alley.

He closes the door behind him. Pressing back against the wall, I set my hand on the knob, pulse heaving as I ever so slowly crack it open. Though I can't see them, they must be just a little ways from the door. The sound of their conversation drifts over to me.

"—of *course* he let her go," Thackery is saying. "Do you even know the boy at all? Your own nephew?"

"It's not him," Dylan replies gruffly. "It's that Moira Alexander."

"You shouldn't have left him with the siren."

Low and unyielding, Dylan retorts, "You shouldn't have killed Nell Bracken. Connor, aye, he needed to go, but—"

"She heard him talking in class. Did you know that? She

knew there was something going on up at the light. She told me as much."

I stare at the dusty piano. I feel fixed in place, panic seizing my muscles, my heart crashing in my chest.

Out in the alley, a boot heel scrapes against the cobbles. Dylan says, "This is getting out of hand. It has *gotten* out of hand."

"Tomorrow—if the ban—"

"Jude won't vote in favor of the hunts. You think I don't know him? He won't do it."

Thackery is silent.

And just as silently I push the door closed. I've guessed this. I've waited for this. But that doesn't stop a chill from running up my spine. There's no victory in the knowing.

The truth aches like an open wound.

I spend that night at the lighthouse. After dinner, after telling Jude all that I'd heard at the dance hall, we end up crawling into our beds exhausted just as the weather takes a turn for the worse. Heavy rain lashes against the window of the guest room. I stare up at the ceiling, contemplating my failures of the past few days. Each forms a thread like the cuffs of Jude's frayed sweaters. A thread for Connor, his blood washed away in the storm, for Nell, who found herself caught up in the same secret, a thread for Thackery, who tied the two together. A thread for the sirens and the hunting parties soon to come, a thread for Jude Osric, because I have dragged him into all of this.

I must drift off then, as I'm startled awake by a flash of blue-white lightning. Seconds later a low boom of thunder follows it. I turn over in bed. The night feels like a solid weight on my chest, pressing in from every side.

Between one strike of lightning and the next, there's a soft knock at the door. The knob turns, and I see Jude standing, glassy-eyed and pale, on the threshold.

I sit up against the headboard, wondering if this is a dream. "What's wrong? Has something happened?"

"Can't sleep," he says, in a tone that sounds heavy with sleep nonetheless. His voice is thick because of it—drawn-out, rounded vowels, like the wind caught in the long grass of the moors. And it isn't that Jude can't sleep; he just doesn't want to.

Almost a year after his family died, Jude told me a little of his nightmares. How sometimes he'll find himself on the cliff's edge, watching again as their boat is torn apart; or he's lost at sea, tossed back and forth by the waves, the sky pitch-black above him. On those nights, the sirens take him—tearing at his skin until he screams himself awake.

I pat the sheets beside me. "Come here."

Jude pads across the room, his bare feet soundless on the wood. I tuck my feet up, and he sits down on the bed, tipping his head back against the wall.

"Thank you," he murmurs.

"How are you feeling?"

Lifting a hand, he tips it side to side. "Fine for now. How about you?"

"Fine for now."

He turns his head to look at me. Lightning flashes across his face. "We can fix this," he whispers. "I promise you. We still have time."

"And if we can't? What then?"

So much effort has been put into demonizing the sirens—years spent turning them into something nightmarish—that some have forgotten not all monsters are found beneath the waves.

Islanders can be monsters too.

Jude swallows. "I'm sorry, Moira."

It's a very clear echo of my words to him yesterday evening, and that fact alone squeezes the air from my lungs. I press my hand against the mattress, fingers digging into cotton. In that same echo I say, "Not surprising, is it?"

Jude makes a soft sound in the back of his throat. "Perhaps I can convince them," he says. "If I tell them—if I speak to Mr. Earl . . ."

I let out a sigh. "You're just one person, Jude."

He cups my cheek, brushing his thumb over my cheekbone. "That doesn't mean it's not worth trying."

Pushing back the blankets, I shift until I'm sitting beside him. I draw him down, and he rests his head in my lap. Carefully, I run my fingers through his curls. His hair is not soft, but stiff from salt air, which pleases me. It marks his place here, his work, as well as his calloused hands.

"Do you know the story," I begin, "of the couple who lived in a lighthouse upon the cliff's edge?"

"My lighthouse?" he asks.

"No. This one was much older. A lighthouse on an island that did not yet have a name."

Lightning illuminates the room. There's a crack on the opposite wall I've not noticed before.

"The husband was its keeper, but his wife was the one who cherished it," I tell him. "Except the lighthouse was not built well, and there came a day when the wife leaned too far across the gallery railing only to have it snap beneath her. She fell to her death, leaving her husband to grieve—all alone in his lighthouse by the sea.

"He worked hard every day afterward, rebuilding the tower so there was not one crack left behind. It's said his wife haunted him until he died, and continues to wander the cliff side even now—singing laments to the sea that took her."

"Not a very happy tale," Jude comments, sitting up.

"Nor is this a very happy island."

His hand finds mine in the darkness. "Sometimes," he says, sounding quiet and shy. "Sometimes it is."

I smile. "Once there was a boy who loved the lighthouse that he cared for. And then a delightful violinist girl came along, and the two fancied themselves detectives."

"Much better," he says. I can hear the answering grin in his voice.

"But that story doesn't have an ending."

Jude sighs, very softly. He says, "Not yet," and I hope he'll finally allow himself to sleep.

I'm still awake when his breathing evens out, his head lolling to one side. I study his face in the dim light. I've never really noticed how fine-boned he is, or how his ears stick out a bit. I put a hand on his shoulder.

"Jude," I say, "you oughtn't sleep like that."

He drags his eyes open. "Hmm? Oh. Sorry. I'll just . . ." He shuffles off the bed. I watch him go, some part of me still wound tight with worry. How will we ever prove the crimes of Thackery and Dylan? How will we do it before sirens pay the cost?

At the door, Jude pauses. Rain pounds steadily outside, wind gusting hard against the windowpane. He says, "We'll figure something out," as though I've spoken my thoughts aloud.

I set my jaw. The hours and days we've spent investigating stretch out in front of me, worn thin, almost to the point of breaking.

"Good night, Jude."

"Good night."

He heads back down the hall, and I lie in bed, left to fight whatever nightmares await in the dark.

CHAPTER THIRTY-THREE

TWILLENGYLE IN THE MORNING is made of mist and rain. Dark greens and browns paint the moors, rocky hillsides pitted with shadows. My violin rests snug against my shoulder as I slide the bow across its strings. It's a slow song, haunted, singing of melancholy and grief. I've been playing for the good part of an hour, pouring out all the music welled up inside me.

At the sound of approaching footsteps, I set the violin down and begin to pack up.

"Have you even had breakfast?" asks Jude.

I've been on the cliff since sunrise. I watched the tide come in, clouds gather on the horizon, four sirens bask in the shallows before diving into deeper water.

Yes, I wanted to call to them. *Swim far away, so deep they cannot find you.*

This island is no longer a safe place for your kind.

Behind me Jude says, "I can make tea, if you like."

I glance around to where he stands, arms folded across his wool sweater, before looking back at the beach. I dig my teeth into my lower lip. Violin case in hand, I stand up, and Jude walks over to take my free hand in his. His cheeks are a little pink from cold, his eyes dark as autumn.

"I think," he says, "I know a way to expose Thackery."

A gust of wind off the sea tangles his hair, just as it tugs at my dress. My mind whirls back to Connor and Nell—always, *always* Connor and Nell—and I can't stand the possibility of their deaths going unanswered for.

I couldn't let the sirens be held accountable for that particular cruelty.

I squeeze Jude's fingers and say, "I'm listening."

In the kitchen we sit down across from each other. Jude taps two fingers on the table, and I look at him, expectant. He says, "We'll catch him in the act."

He gives me a moment to mull over the words.

When I have, I frown. "How do you mean?"

"I can send him a message to meet me on the beach. I'll tell him I've proof of the murders." Jude skims his fingers across the tabletop. "He's bound to want to get rid of me after that."

Leaning forward, he continues. "Then we notify the rest of the police department, tell them to head down to the beach as well. If I can stall Thackery long enough, they'll see what's going on, and"—he presses his hands together, opening them like a book, palms up—"we have him."

I raise a brow. "That," I say, "is a terrible idea."

Jude looks crestfallen. "And what's wrong with it?"

"You're not baiting Thackery with your own life. If anyone's going to be the lure, it ought to be me."

"No." He shakes his head, eyes wide. "No, it oughtn't."

"Oh, I see. It's all right for you to do it, but not the other way around?"

He drops his gaze. I push up from the table, grateful when my hands don't shake as I smooth over the front of my dress. With his eyes still lowered, Jude says softly, "You understand, don't you? Why I don't want you to?"

He looks up at me, and I tell him, "We'll think of something else."

My violin case rests on the table. Jude glances to it as he pulls at the loose threads along the cuff of his sweater. He says only, "I need to tend to the light before we leave."

When he heads into the tower, I flip the clasps on my case. My flyer from the schoolhouse is still folded up inside. I take it out, my eyes fixing upon the slight tear at the top of the page.

And I wonder if Nell suffered when she died.

And I wonder if Connor had been afraid.

The Council meeting looms over my thoughts. I'm sure Jude will be able to convince some of the fisherfolk to side with the hunting ban because they trust him—because they love him. I can't predict the rest. Thackery will be there and likely so will Dylan. I don't know what they'll do if the ban remains intact. My stomach twists as I consider the possibility of finding another islander bleeding to death on the beach when Jude and I could've done something to stop it.

We need to uncover their crimes—and quickly.

Closing my case, I wait for Jude in the hall. He comes back into the cottage, silent as he helps me into my coat, expression unreadable as he tugs on his boots. He reaches for his coat, and I grab hold of his hand. He smiles then, small but reassuring. Curling his fingers around mine, he presses a kiss to my knuckles.

"It'll be all right, Moira."

I pull him to me, kissing him on the mouth. He brings his other hand to the small of my back, holding me close. He's warm against me, and I wrap one hand around the back of his neck, my fingers brushing the rough wool of his collar.

"Moira," he says, "I need to thank you."

"For what?"

"Staying here." This time, when he smiles, it creases the corners of his eyes. My blood sings with the knowledge that I put it there. "I know I wasn't the world's easiest patient."

"Siren victims usually aren't."

He raises a hand to cup my cheek. I know what he might say—that the meeting will go well, that the sirens will be safe—but I've a splinter of fear in my heart, one I've felt since waking this morning, and I turn away before he can offer empty promises.

"Let's go," I say.

Jude puts on his coat and cap. Giving me one last look, he unlatches the front door.

I walk out into the sunless morning. However much I hope for the best, I find myself preparing, inescapably, for the worst.

This meeting is not like the last.

For starters, there are far more people. I recognize faces from Lochlan, solitary folk from the remote stone houses at the northern edges of the island.

It's all of us, together. Some are still sleepy-eyed, blankets wrapped around their shoulders, and those who look disheveled from the early ferry crossing. Children stand around barefoot outside the hall, holding cups of tea, pieces of burnt toast from breakfast.

The second thing I notice is how many eyes light up upon seeing Jude Osric.

He gets clapped on the shoulder, shaken, pulled into tight embraces—until he's as unkempt as the ones who have just come off the ferry. He looks well pleased by the attention, albeit a little dazed. Some fishermen take my hands in theirs, leaning close, telling me, *You did well, looking after him. I'll be saying a prayer of thanks for you tonight.*

My heart swells, but then we manage to get inside the dance hall, and I see the arguments have already started up. There are men who think it's a wicked act to kill a siren, while others think it can bring storms, bad luck, all manner of ills.

I touch the iron charm in my pocket, looking to Jude. His coat sleeve hides his bandages, the stitches along his arm, but that doesn't change the fact that his survival came with scars. He meets my gaze, nods, and heads off into the crowd.

On our way across the moors, I thought it'd be wise for Jude to make the rounds as soon as we arrived, to talk to as many folks as possible before the Council held its vote. He's the keeper of the light, recently recovered from siren song. Those from Dunmore will heed his words.

I start in the direction of the stage. Detective Thackery stands near it with the rest of the police department, and an uncomfortable queasiness curls my insides. The floor feels abruptly uneven beneath my feet; I concentrate on breathing past the dread blooming up through my ribs.

When Thomas Earl steps up to the lectern, Jude finds me again. There's hope in his dark eyes, in the curve of his mouth. I clasp his hand and hold tight.

Earl's gaze rests on Jude. He says, "Good of you to join us, Mr. Osric."

"I'm glad to be here, sir," says Jude, grinning back. "My father played a part in establishing the hunting ban—I feel it's only right that I do my best to uphold it."

There's some murmuring at this, whispers passed from person to person. From what I can catch, it isn't altogether disapproving.

Earl raises his eyebrows, but before he can answer, Thackery decides to speak.

He says, "A pity that Wick still sounds unwell."

My free hand curls into a fist.

Jude's smile falters. "Excuse me?"

Detective Thackery looks not to us, but to the Council. "It's quite clear, I think, that Mr. Osric is still fascinated by sirens. If he were of sounder mind, he'd surely want the hunts reinstated."

Jude pales. He says, "That's not true," but it comes out so quiet no one seems to hear him but me. Clearing his throat, he says again, "That's not true, Detective."

"And you're to be the judge of that, are you?"

I tip my chin up. In a cutting voice, I say, "If Jude Osric were still under the siren's sway, he'd be making for the sea, not standing here before you all."

Yet I see the effect of Thackery's words, the seeds of doubt they sow. I can imagine the thoughts winding through the crowd. *Poor Wick. He doesn't know what he's saying. Sirens took away his family.*

With a heavy sigh Thomas Earl says, "Those in favor of reinstating the hunts?"

The *aye*s that follow are numerous. I stand there, holding Jude's hand, and listen as my father's work unravels before me, ignored, forgotten.

"And those opposed?"

Our voices are a bleak contrast to those that came before. They echo in the crowded hall, the *nay*s too few to change the outcome.

"Very well," Earl says, sounding like a man defeated. "The ban shall be lifted as of tomorrow."

I stare up at him. I feel as though I've been dragged down into deep water—how I suppose it must feel—everything cold and endless, distorted and strange. The shadows of the hall seem to bend, twisting out of shape.

I stumble back, pulling Jude alongside. My ears ring as I push my way through the crowd, the dread I'd felt between my ribs sinking into my stomach. We reach the doors, and I yank my hand from Jude's. I stalk away from the hall, from the people on the street.

Head down, Jude follows me in silence. I can't look at him; I can barely breathe through the pain in my chest. Part of me didn't believe it would happen—even now I can't fathom that men will be hunting sirens as soon as tomorrow.

I reach the gates of St. Cecilia's. Morning fog lingers over the yard, creeping across the grass and slanted headstones.

Without looking at Jude I say, "I can get myself home from here."

He doesn't move. "Are you sure you don't want—"

I turn toward him. He takes off his cap, holding it in both hands. I can see his eyes, how soft and sad they are. "Moira," he says, "I want to help you." His voice wavers, and he swallows hard. "Why won't you let me help?"

I look back at the churchyard. The wind nips at my fingers, and I feel that numbness extend to my heart.

"I'd like to be alone."

"Moira, please . . ."

Turning on him, I hiss, "What did I say?" My hands are fists at my sides, and the darkness inside me surges, set on doing damage. "Just leave me alone, Jude Osric."

He takes a single step back. With the look on his face, it's as if I've slapped him. Guilt rushes in like a tidal wave, crushing me beneath its weight.

His eyes flit away from mine. In a small voice he says, "Right, then," and his mouth twists, as though he's trying to conceal his sorrow, to stow it away inside himself.

He brushes past me to continue down the street. I half want to call him back, but my pride is too great to allow it. Instead, I watch him go, watch as he ducks his head and buries his hands in his pockets.

He doesn't look back.

I push open the gate to the churchyard. It's quiet here, and cold, the smell of wet earth and stone so strong I taste them on my tongue. The stones are dark and discolored, the salt air eating at their edges. I wander through the rows until I come to the foot of my father's grave.

> *In Memory of*
> *GAVIN ALEXANDER*
> *Loving Husband and Father*

I sink to my knees, heedless of the damp. I trace over the letters carved deep into the stone and close my eyes, wondering if he sees me from where he is.

"I'm sorry, Da," I whisper. "I'm sorry I can't . . ."

A lump rises in the back of my throat.

"They'll be going out tomorrow to hunt the sirens. I tried to stop it. I tried to keep them safe. Now everything is falling apart, and I don't . . . I don't know how to put it right." I curl up, digging my fingers into the wet grass. "If you were here, you could fix this. I know you could." I grit my teeth as the tears I've kept in check well up and spill onto my cheeks. "I need you here, Da."

In the silence of the graveyard, I tip my forehead to the earth. "I wish you could come back. I wish the Osrics would come back. I miss you all so much. Every night I wonder if it'll hurt less in the morning, and it never does."

Then I start to cry. And once I start, once I let it out, I can't seem to stow it back away inside me. I think I won't be able to stop.

"*Da*," I choke out, "*what am I supposed to do?*"

A long while later, when I'm worn through and shivering in my coat, I catch the sound of footsteps. I scrub my face with my sleeve and look at who's come to collect me. She stands with her hands clasped, melancholic. Her eyes regard the headstone before settling on me.

"Moira," says my mother, "let's go home."

CHAPTER THIRTY-FOUR

AFTER WE GET IN, I wash up, slip on a clean dress, and look myself over in the mirror. I'm still red-eyed and wan, but neither is a lasting mark. If I'm to save the sirens, it won't be done crying over my father's grave. I also doubt it's something he'd like seeing.

In the kitchen, my mother has prepared tea, and I take my seat at the table. As I do, my thoughts turn to Jude Osric. I fidget with the butter dish, biting my lip. I'll have to go apologize to him.

My mother sits down across from me. I ask her, "How did you know where to find me?"

"Mr. Osric came by the house," she tells me. "Said I should check on you." She holds my gaze over her teacup, and her expression softens. "He seemed quite concerned."

"I kissed him the other day."

I keep my voice casual, glancing away from her as I set my teacup in its saucer. The words are meant to be an olive branch between us—a secret I'm prepared to share. And I prefer to tell her of my relationship with Jude myself, rather than have her hear it secondhand from someone else.

She stills, but the pause lasts only for a moment.

"Do you love him?"

I look up, startled. It's not what I expected her to say. Judgment, I anticipated. A lecture on impulsiveness, perhaps, a word of caution. Not questions of the heart.

My cheeks warm as I stare at the plates cluttering the table. "I think I've loved him for a long while."

My mother nods like I've told her something indisputable. "He seemed in much better health at the meeting. How's he getting on?"

"He's quite well, I believe."

Or he was before I snapped at him. I think back on his face when I told him to leave, the hurt in his eyes before he walked away.

My heart aches as I remember I left my violin on Jude's kitchen table.

"Tomorrow," my mother starts, "I don't want you going near the harbor. You'll come into town with me."

Imagined possibilities flare to life in my mind's eye: the hunting boats casting off with the tide, cans of poison piled in the boathouse, siren blood staining the pier as their bodies are carried ashore.

I swallow.

It isn't going to happen. I won't *let* it happen. Jude and I will catch Thackery, and this whole business will be put to rest.

I wish I'd not missed Mass on Sunday. A few prayers seem more than in order.

Quietly I say, "You can't keep me from the harbor forever."

My mother purses her lips, but she doesn't push the issue. Silence falls between us, but it feels tainted, burdened, weighed by the unknown.

After our tea I head out, making my way toward the lighthouse.

The sky is dove-gray and the first drops of rain land in my hair, but I tuck my chin into my coat collar, continuing along the path. The blue-and-white tower stands stark against the gloom, its light arcing out to sea. I set my sights on it as I cross the moors.

When I'm close, an inexplicable shiver runs over my spine. Something feels . . . off. I hesitate, studying the space in front of me, until I realize—the front door is ajar.

Not all the way open, just a thin gap where it hasn't been set on the latch. Except Jude never leaves the door unlatched. Not that I can remember.

I suddenly feel very, very cold.

I'm left at a standstill when I reach the threshold, staring at the bright blue door. I imagine Detective Thackery coming to call while I was busy sobbing over what was already lost. I imagine Jude dying, Jude dead, his blood darkening the floorboards.

Between one second and the next, I push open the door.

The hall is empty.

An almost palpable relief rushes over me at the sight. Adrenaline courses hot through my veins. "Jude?" I call.

In my mind I hear a voice like my father's: *Just because he's not here doesn't mean he isn't dead somewhere else. Check the rooms.*

There's a revolver tucked away in the large oak desk. I know this because Llyr Osric showed it to Jude and me one day and taught us where the safety catch was. Then he put the gun in a drawer and said, *You will never touch that.*

Sliding open the third drawer down, I find it there, looking much the same as it did years ago. It seems Jude has also taken to listening to his dead father's advice.

I lift it out, careful, feeling the weight of metal in my hand. It feels like death, heavy and cold.

With shaking fingers, I load a few of the chambers and make certain the safety is on. Holding it unnerves me; I slip the gun into my coat pocket.

"Jude," I say again, voice echoing in the quiet. "Jude, are you here?"

Thackery might be here, I realize. Yet with the revolver in my pocket, I feel invincible. It also makes me reckless, and I run up to the second floor of the cottage, checking each bedroom, before returning downstairs.

When I head into the tower, the iron stairwell echoes my footsteps. I get to the watch room and slip inside. Perhaps Jude went back to Dunmore to talk to Mr. Earl. There are any number of reasons why he isn't here now, but none to explain why his door is unlatched.

I examine the papers and navigational charts left scattered on his desk. My mouth quirks as I think of Jude bent over in his chair, reading manuals, scribbling in his logbook.

I see a single note in particular, written in Jude's hand. There's only one word—inked letters scrawled hastily—but it's enough to make the breath catch in my throat.

Beach.

I peer out at the shoreline, searching, while my brain spins out the same thought. *He didn't. He didn't . . . How could he . . . ?*

Two dark figures stand between the cliff and the sea. I make out Jude's auburn hair, Thackery's lean frame. Light glints across the object in his hand.

Then I am running, tearing down the stairwell, because Jude is on the beach—and Thackery holds a knife.

I know how to get down to the beach unseen. Years of watching sirens taught me how to walk in the shadow of crevices, place each footfall on shifting sand without sound. My heart is a trapped bird, fluttering wildly in my chest, but I do not let adrenaline betray me.

I am a ghost in the presence of a killer.

Their voices ring clear as I edge closer. Jude says, "My uncle told me what you did—how you killed Connor for him. I thought it was time we talked."

I gaze out from the rocky crevice. There's a knife in Jude's hand also, but he keeps it limp at his side.

Thackery nods to it. "That doesn't look like talking."

Under the veneer of calm, Jude's face is very pale. He shifts his grip on the knife, holding it half behind his back. "I want to know why you did it," he says. "Why kill Connor on Dylan's behalf?"

"I was the one who helped him catch that siren." Thackery's voice comes out quiet and slick as oil. He tilts his head and adds, "Your uncle and I agree on quite a few things. I did think, given your history, you'd share our point of view."

Jude exhales, ragged. "I don't," he says. "I don't understand anything that involves killing someone."

"Sometimes it's necessary," says Thackery. "We would've been found out. I daresay you wouldn't have fared well in that outcome either. You certainly wouldn't still be keeper." He taps the flat of his blade against his palm. "Though, as I ought to kill you, that doesn't much matter now."

My pulse races. Jude looks ashen, his skin tinged gray. He doesn't speak, but Thackery continues as if in answer. "It'd guarantee the continuation of the hunts. I'm sure you saw how many were indecisive at the meeting. If they find you bleeding out on the sand, they'll think you really were still under the siren's enchantment."

"Moira knows what you've done. If you kill me, she'll . . ."

Detective Thackery smiles. It reminds me of the smiles Dylan Osric gave: sharp and thin as a razor's edge. "She can't prove it," he says. "You don't have any proof at all, do you, Wick?"

Jude's grip tightens around his knife. He holds it out in front of him, cloudy light flashing on steel. He says, "I could kill you instead," and this time I hear a faint tremor between his words.

"Will you, now?"

Jude swallows. His eyes are wide, as if he can already see death rushing up to meet him. For a moment he remains like that, pale and still—before he brings his arm back, letting the knife fall to the sand beside him. "You know I won't."

"Yes." Thackery raises his own knife between them. I reach into my pocket, hand coming to rest on the now-warm metal of the revolver. "I know you're not a killer, Wick. You don't have the heart for it."

I step out from the crevice's shadow. Flipping the safety catch off, there is a small, sharp click in my ears. Jude and Thackery both turn at the sound.

"But I do," I say. And I point the barrel of the gun straight at Thackery's head.

CHAPTER THIRTY-FIVE

THREE THINGS HAPPEN in quick succession:

Jude looks at me, wide-eyed, and breathes, *"Moira."*

Thackery grabs him by the collar.

A blade is pressed up against Jude's throat.

I feel my heart beating as though it's about to tear free from my rib cage. My hand around the revolver is the only thing to steady me.

This isn't happening.

Thackery holds my gaze. His eyes are black as onyx and just as hard. "Careful with that, Miss Alexander," he says.

"Let him go." The words scrape my throat on their way out. "Let Jude go."

"Does anyone else know you're here?"

"The police," I tell him, not knowing if that's a lie. This is what Jude planned to do, and I pray to God he has. "I telephoned them before I came."

Thackery presses the knife close to Jude's skin. Jude lets out a small, gasped breath, and my thoughts narrow into a single stream of *stopstopstopstop*.

"You're lying," he says.

Steady now, Moira, whispers my father's voice.

My grip on the revolver doesn't waver. "Perhaps," I say. "Are you willing to take that chance?"

"You think I won't kill him?"

The truth is I know he will. The knife is a real and certain thing in his grasp, ready to slice Jude's neck in one motion. I can't risk firing off a shot at this distance, not with Thackery using Jude to shield himself.

Jude will be dead before the police arrive, and the last thing— the last thing I'll have said to him is this: *Just leave me alone, Jude Osric*.

I draw in a deep breath. "I think you will cut his throat and leave him for dead," I say. "But once you do, once you kill Jude Osric, I'll pull this trigger. I won't let you live a minute longer."

Because I am not Jude.

There exists inside me a blackheartedness that wants only for siren song and danger and blood. In this moment it's a very present part—an arrow that sights along the revolver to the space right between Thackery's eyes.

I'll kill him and take immense pleasure in doing so.

"Moira," says Jude. It's the first time he's spoken since Thackery grabbed him. He has to lean back from the knife at his throat. "Moira, don't."

Don't what? I want to ask. *Don't kill Thackery? Don't save your life?*

Before I have a chance, Thackery pushes the knife hard against Jude's neck.

A thin trail of blood snakes down toward his collar, and on impulse I gasp, "*Stop.*"

"Your promise of police intervention appears null, Miss Alexander."

Sweat slicks my palms. I want Thackery to drop his knife beside Jude's on the sand. I want to grab Jude and run, to curse him for endangering his own life, for playing a hand I told him not to.

"Dylan won't like you killing his nephew," I say in a rush. "He'll know it was you. You were working together."

"We're beyond that, I'm afraid."

I grit my teeth, fury igniting in my rib cage like a flame. "Why?" I snarl. "Men will be out there hunting sirens *tomorrow.*"

"I did try to warn you off, Miss Alexander." Thackery stares at me, his knife still pressed to Jude's skin. "You should've never gotten involved. People on this island go around thinking the sirens are a gift, as if we should thank them for taking our children and bloodying our waters." He shakes his head, eyes bright. "It's madness. Your father ought to have known better. We never should've enacted a ban against hunting them."

"You gave those cans to Russell—you let him poison those sirens."

"And where's your proof of that?"

My stomach churns. "Why do you truly want the sirens dead?"

It's obvious now, the way he speaks, that Thackery has known grief.

"That's none of your business." His knuckles whiten around the knife's hilt. "I've no need to justify myself to you."

In front of him Jude stills, his eyes darting to something behind me. I don't want to look over, don't want to shift my attention from Thackery, but they come into my line of sight soon enough.

Half a dozen policemen—all with pistols aimed in our direction.

Relief sinks into me like a stone.

Among them is Inspector Dale, and he looks at Thackery like he can't believe what he's seeing. "What is going on here?" he asks.

I turn back to where Thackery stands. There's a flash of mercurial resolve in his eyes, and I notice the slight shift in his grip on the hilt. Jude holds my gaze, pale-faced, his eyes black as pitch.

No.

Thackery's arm jerks, just as a sharp *crack* echoes through the air. I shut my eyes, thinking for one wild moment I've been shot, but a muffled stream of curses joins the ringing in my ears, and I look up.

I notice Inspector Dale first, walking to where Thackery is crouched, knife forgotten as his hand fists around his shoulder. Blood leaks out between his fingers, dark crimson, seeping through the fabric of his shirt. My eyes find Jude, bent over with his hands on his knees, shoulders shaking, and I let the revolver drop to the sand.

"Jude," I say, throwing my arms around him. "Oh God, I thought . . . I thought . . ." I stop, holding myself in check, and tilt his chin up.

A thin red line marks the skin next to his jugular. I can't stop looking at it.

He stares down at me. His pupils are blown wide, and I see my face reflected in their blackness. He lifts a trembling hand to my cheek.

"Moira."

Around us, the Dunmore Police are a clatter of noise: Pistols are tucked back into holsters; their boots kick up sand; questions and orders are passed from man to man.

I bring my attention back to Jude as he says, "Moira, I think I . . ." He sways a little on his feet. I place both hands on his shoulders to steady him.

"You've had a shock, Jude. You need—"

"No." He shakes his head. "No, I'm fine. Are you all right?"

I bury my face in the rough wool of his sweater, holding him close. "I'm sorry for earlier," I whisper. "I didn't mean . . ."

Jude laughs, a high-strung, broken sound. I pull away to see his expression.

"Thought I'd be the one apologizing," he says.

I tighten my arms around him and shut my eyes. "Yes, you can apologize too," I say. "Seeing as you did something so *senseless*."

"Worked, didn't it?"

I grin up at him. "You're ridiculous, Jude Osric."

Grinning back, he slurs his words together. "Shouldn't call me that."

"What should I call you, then?"

"Brilliant," says Jude, and he faints.

CHAPTER THIRTY-SIX

INSPECTOR DALE TAKES A SEAT at our kitchen table. It's late in the evening; past the lace curtains, the sky is already full dark. My mother fixes tea at the counter, her hands shaking slightly as she fills the kettle with water. I sit across from the inspector, lips pressed thin, my attention drawn to the notebook and fountain pen he sets out.

I tell him of Jude's plan to meet Thackery, my going to the lighthouse and finding it empty, of seeing Jude and Thackery on the beach. I tell him about Dylan Osric and the tortured siren, how the lives of Connor Sheahan and Nell Bracken were stolen in the hopes of keeping that secret.

He writes down my statement in a diligent manner, though he seems quite shaky and pale himself.

I think about Inspector Dale and Detective Thackery. I think of how people never really get the chance to know the entire story of someone else. And I realize that to know someone—truly know them—is to know their secrets.

Perhaps it explains why the sea takes secrets for a wish. They are the truest part of us.

Dale is also the one to tell me of Thackery's losses.

"His daughter," he says, voice quiet. "Lost his daughter just after the ban was introduced. He tried petitioning the Council to drop it, blamed them for a long while." He lowers his teacup, staring down at the tablecloth. "She was five years old."

"What will happen now?" I ask. "To the sirens?"

"I'll have a word with Mr. Earl first thing tomorrow," he says. "I make no promises, but I'm sure the Council will see reason now you've disproven two attacks."

My relief is near tangible, easing an invisible weight off my shoulders.

"Good," I say.

Once Dale picks up and takes his leave, my mother comes to sit in his place. She wraps her hands around one of mine, and our conversation is a soft, hushed thing, like a secret in itself.

"Why didn't you tell me what was happening, Moira?"

Shame heats my face, but I don't look away. "I didn't know how," I whisper, though that's only part of it. I didn't want her to know simply because I didn't care to share any of my goings-on with her.

The last time I let her hold my hand like this, we were at my father's bedside. We are closer now somehow, and she smiles even though her eyes shine with tears.

"You've done so much, Moira," she says. "Your father would be so proud."

We stay just like that, sitting at the table together, drinking tea. We talk and talk, making up for all the years we haven't— until evening becomes night proper.

I set my teacup down. "I was going to visit Jude."

My mother looks toward the window. "It's a little late for it now, dear."

"They're keeping him there overnight," I reply. "He ought to have some company."

"Well, here . . ." Getting up, she takes a few of the cakes she means to sell tomorrow and ties them neatly in cloth. "Bring him these."

I start on the path to Dunmore with a lantern in hand and my mother's cakes stuffed into my coat pocket.

After fainting on the beach, Jude was taken to the hospital. He was treated for shock, and having recently recovered from siren song, the doctors gave him additional care: salves and clean bandages and a tidier row of stitches since he'd torn the previous ones.

A nurse directs me to his room, and I smile upon seeing the light beneath his door. I turn the knob without bothering to knock and slip inside.

Jude is already sitting up in bed, head tipped back, staring at the ceiling. My heart does one slow roll in my chest before he turns toward me.

"Moira," he says, sounding so pleased that I break into a grin.

"Shouldn't you be asleep?" I ask.

A wicker chair is placed near the tiled wall, and I drag it to his bedside.

He leans against the bed rail. He wears a white undershirt, the short sleeves showing off his new line of stitches. A bandage covers the cut on his neck. Despite these things, he looks well—perhaps better than he has in days.

"Did you speak with the nurse?" His tone is conspiratorial.

"For a moment."

"You ought to tell her I don't need to be in here." He throws out an arm, gesturing at nothing in particular. "Keeping me overnight, I mean, it's quite unnecessary. I'm perfectly fine. Who is at the light?"

"Mr. Irving, I believe." Inspector Dale told me as much. Irving boarded the tender back when the police arrived to take Dylan Osric into custody.

Jude releases a sigh. "He and Daugherty are going to give me an earful tomorrow."

I pull the cloth package from my pocket, sliding it onto his nightstand. "My mother had me bring you cakes."

"Oh." He looks at the package. "Thank you. Tell her I'm much obliged."

"I shall." I reach over and take his hand atop the sheets. His skin feels warm next to mine. "Are you really all right?"

"Yes." He grins wide, terrifically bright. "Yes, actually. Moira—we did it."

"All thanks to Jude Osric's rash decisions," I say, which makes him laugh.

"I am sorry," he says, and I'm ready to scoff at the apology, when he continues. "There wasn't any other way. I didn't see—"

"We could've thought of something."

"Perhaps."

This time I do scoff. "You nearly got yourself *killed*, Jude."

"I know."

Night muffles the activities of the hospital. Everything seems incredibly still, and I find myself wondering if the world is still turning, if the island still exists outside these walls. And despite the fact that Jude is here, alive, I'll never be able to forget the sound he made when Thackery brought a knife to his throat, or the look in his eyes when we both thought he was going to die. I brush my thumb over the back of his hand.

"I rang him from the watch room," Jude whispers, "when I got back from Dunmore. Told him to meet me on the beach. I said I had proof—evidence that he killed Connor and Nell."

"Then what?"

"Then I sent a wire to Inspector Dale. I wrote you that note, grabbed a knife, and went. I didn't . . . I didn't realize . . . I thought perhaps I could reason with him." He takes a deep breath. "I guess it was quite senseless in hindsight."

"You're not going to contradict me at all, then?"

"No." He rubs the corner of his eye. "It was dangerous, I know. I saw a sliver of opportunity and I jumped at it. But, Moira, now that it's over—dear God, I'm just *relieved.*"

"Me too," I say in a whisper, and I feel silence close around us once more. Rain taps at the window glass. I try to recall the last time I slept, but it seems like years ago.

Softly, Jude says, "I'm glad you didn't shoot Thackery."

I look at him. It takes me a moment to think of something to say. "Well, I've never shot anyone. I didn't want to hit you by accident."

He holds my gaze, brown eyes wide and honest. "I'm glad you didn't," he says again, and there's an odd quality to his voice, a grave seriousness mixed in with the relief.

The words are a weight in the space between us, a balance,

anchoring me the way Jude Osric always has. A steady hand in the dark.

"Thank you," I whisper. I think perhaps we both know what I'm really thanking him for.

His hand grips mine, and we sit together in the small hospital room, on an island smeared in blood and secrets. It's an island filled with incomprehensible things, perfect in its imperfections—a flawed design that still holds despite the cracks.

And it is ours.

EPILOGUE

IN THE EAST OF TWILLENGYLE, the evening sky burns red. Night settles in sooner with the arrival of October, so a waxen moon joins the setting sun on the horizon. Jude steps out of the keeper's cottage, shutting the door behind him. He holds a lantern high.

"Whose bright idea was this again?" he asks.

"I think," I say, smiling, "it was yours."

"Ah."

We set off toward the path leading down to the beach. Jude is hatless, wearing his new oilskin jacket, and when he offers his arm, I press close to him. It still feels like a miracle that he's here at my side at all. We reach the bottom of the cliff and find a cleft in the rock.

Jude puts out his lantern light. He says, "You have iron on you?"

"Yes." I look at him, his dark eyes turned amber in the fading light. "Do you?"

"Yes."

I reach over, taking his hand. His palm is clammy and warm against mine. "We can go back, if you like," I tell him. "We don't need to do this."

Jude holds my gaze. "No," he says, voice steady. "I want to be here, Moira."

I grin back at him. We are close, hidden in this damp crevice of the cliff. Jude leans forward and kisses me. I grip the front of his jacket, my heartbeat fluttering.

"You know," he says, pulling back, "as of late, I feel almost as if I've lost my bearings. What are we to do now?"

"I will tell you," I say with a smile. And I lean close again, to whisper in his ear, as though I'm imparting the greatest of secrets. "You, Jude Osric, will keep the light. I will play my violin out on the cliff's edge. The sirens will remain safe beneath the waves."

He presses his face against the side of my neck. "That sounds agreeable," he says.

"I think so too."

Near the shore, a line of foam trails across the sand, as though the waves might swallow the island whole. My blood sings in my ears. I feel like I hold the world in the palm of my hand, vast and unfathomable, with every unknown waiting to be discovered. The two of us turn toward the horizon, and I survey the dip and flow of the ocean, waiting.

I hear Jude's sharp intake of breath and clasp his hand even tighter. We watch as one, two, three sirens emerge from the shallows, wild creatures stepping onto the beach like they know they belong there. My pulse hums with the cadence of island magic.

Jude and I stand in the shadows, out of sight, but the magic is part of us, too. It's in our breath and in our blood, woven into our hearts.

It's all I need in life.

ACKNOWLEDGMENTS

First, thank you to my agent, Kristy Hunter, for taking a chance on me. Thank you for your advice, your enthusiasm, and for being an incredible advocate. I so appreciate all that you do.

Thank you to my editor, Karen Wojtyla, and her assistant, Nicole Fiorica. It has been a privilege and a delight working with you both. Thank you for believing in this book.

Thank you to the amazing team at Simon & Schuster, including Justin Chanda, Sonia Chaghatzbanian, Tom Daly, Clare McGlade, Elizabeth Blake-Linn, Lili Feinberg, and Mackenzie Croft. Thank you also to Miranda Meeks for illustrating the beautiful cover.

Thank you to everyone who read and critiqued early drafts. To Shauna Gallo, especially—I'm so grateful for your advice and encouragement.

Diana Lavelle, Ariana Ellis, June Hur, Elora Cook, Kess Costales, Liselle Sambury, Fallon DeMornay, Deborah F. Savoy, Sarena and Sasha Nanua, Amélie Wen Zhao, Andrea Tang, Jessica Bibi Cooper—thank you so much for all your kindness and support along the way. It truly means the world to me.

Thank you to my family, for supporting my love of writing.

And finally, to my readers. Thank you for following Moira and Jude. I hope you enjoyed their story as much as I enjoyed telling it.

Turn the page for a sneak peek
at *Magic Dark and Strange*

WAKING THE DEAD WASN'T nearly so unpleasant as having to dig them up in the first place.

Catherine Daly paused her work to wipe the sweat from her brow. In the cool night air, her breath misted and the wind gusted at her back, tossing dead leaves up against the low cemetery wall. A fine enough night for digging, all in all. It had rained earlier in the day, softening the soil, and even without the lantern burning at the grave's edge, Catherine could see well by the quarter of moonlight.

She was used to the dark.

Up on the cemetery's hillside, she had a decent view of the cityscape below. Invercarn glowed with soft light, buildings lit by streetlamps, their facades elegant and imposing. The knolls and tree-lined paths of Rose Hill Cemetery promised only the best for those moneyed enough to be interred here. Not that they could much enjoy it once the coffin was nailed.

Unless, like tonight, certain services were called upon.

Catherine looked around at the sudden silence to find her colleague had elected to break when she had. Bridget leaned against her spade, the point sunk into the dirt.

"Keep digging," Catherine told her.

They had an audience after all. Catherine wanted him going back to Mr. Ainsworth with nothing but the coin he still owed and praise for their diligence. Thus far, he had watched them wordlessly, keeping back a few paces from the grave.

Geoffrey Watt.

He stood with his hands clasped behind his back, chin lifted. It was an attempt to maintain poise, perhaps, but by now Catherine had come to know when a client was nervous. He wasn't much older than she and Bridget—in his early twenties, at a guess—and had approached Ainsworth just last week.

His little sister had died of fever while he was away on business. He only wanted to say goodbye. Whatever time he was allowed, whatever the cost, he would pay it.

Catherine pitched another pile of dirt out of the grave. The well-to-do liked to bury their dead deep. There were resurrectionists in the city intent on digging up bodies to sell to medical students. Mortsafes were common implements in Rose Hill—the iron devices were cast over a number of graves on the hillside, set to guard the dead until the flesh became too rotted to be of use.

The robbers found their prizes more often in the public cemetery on the other side of the river. Rose Hill was private, guarded; Catherine was aware Watt must have paid off the watchmen to keep their distance.

The night wore on as she and Bridget continued to dig. They

passed six feet, then eight before Catherine's spade hit wood.

At the sound—a solid and unmistakable *thunk*—Bridget put aside her own spade and took up the crowbar. Catherine fetched her coat. Inside it was a piece of type. She rolled the metal between her fingers, looking down at the ground beneath her. Then—

"Only an hour?" he asked. It was a tone of voice Catherine had heard before. In it was a plea for more, but magic could offer only so much.

Watt was here to say farewell.

"Yes," said Catherine in answer. "Your sister cannot remain long in such a state of being. She has no place here, not anymore."

Watt inclined his head in a nod. He held his hat in his hands now, and his fair hair matched his wan complexion. Bridget loosened the last nail and moved aside the casket's lid. The girl inside was as fair as Watt, wearing a fine evening dress, surrounded by the pale lining of the casket. Catherine knelt at the foot of it, clutching her solitary piece of metal type.

It was a type piece that held an hour of her life. If she brought it to the lantern, she knew she'd find the stain across it. She'd pricked her palm earlier, marking the metal with blood. Now she set it on the casket's edge. Placing her hand atop it, she whispered, "Mary Watt."

Beyond the walls of dirt, the stars shone bright and dizzying. Catherine stood up, and the girl's eyes blinked open. For a moment, the two simply stared at each other. Mary was pale as a ghost, and much like one, she was still dead. An hour of Catherine's own ticking clock could give her only a semblance of life. It was quite clear—from her glazed eyes to her ashen cheeks—that she no longer belonged among the living. And when she spoke, her voice was thin and distant.

She asked, "Who are you?"

Catherine swallowed. Climbing out of the pit, she turned to Watt. "You have the hour, sir."

Watt made his way over to the grave where his sister lay. He was trembling. Once he was inside, the girl said, "Geoffrey."

Catherine met Bridget's gaze, and together they headed to the nearby cemetery wall, where they waited under the branches of an oak tree.

Catherine pulled on her coat and looked out at the city. By the time Watt had his hour and they filled in the grave, it would be near dawn. For now, shadows darkened the cobblestones, obscuring the places between the gas lamps and rolling carriages.

Bridget leaned against the stone ledge, arms crossed. In a quiet voice, she said, "Mr. Watt didn't need to hear you speak of his sister so unkindly."

Catherine gave her an assessing look. "I don't think telling him the truth is an unkindness. Mr. Ainsworth should be informing clients of such things."

"Perhaps," said Bridget, a touch uneasy. She didn't like speaking out against their employer, no matter how far they were from earshot. Her blond hair was coming loose from its pins, ruffled by the breeze. She had fair wrists, slender hands calloused from working jobs like this one, dirt under her fingernails. Catherine was equally pale-skinned and angular, her dark hair done up in a chignon.

Once Watt's hour came to an end, the two returned to the gravesite. Watt was embracing his sister, the girl limp in his arms. Catherine looked elsewhere as he lowered Mary back into the casket. When he climbed out of the grave, he clasped their hands in turn, seemingly unaware of the dirt staining his trouser knees. He pressed a silver coin into Catherine's palm, smiling despite the tears in his eyes. They were the same shade of blue as his sister's.

"For your troubles," he said. "Thank you."

Catherine cleared her throat. "Mr. Ainsworth will pay you a call tomorrow morning," she told him, "in regard to outstanding payment."

"Of course."

Watt lifted his hat to them, then left the cemetery without a backward glance.

When they were alone, they secured Mary's casket and took to heaping the dirt back in. Catherine touched the coin in her pocket. After this, they'd walk out of Rose Hill Cemetery, head over the bridge, and return to their room at the print shop. Gripping her spade, she sank the blade into the earth. She thought of Mary's pale eyes, her raspy voice. She thought of Geoffrey Watt clasping her hand, accentuating his thanks with silver. Soon he would blur alongside all the other clients in her mind.

Just another night's work.

WHEN CATHERINE HAD FIRST LOOKED upon the print shop, it was from her seat on her family's old cart. Her father sat beside her, holding on to the reins, his expression grim as he pulled the horses to a stop. It was early spring and late in the evening, cold enough to make Catherine's nose run. She wiped at it hastily with her sleeve. She didn't want Father to think she was crying. If she cried, he'd turn the cart straight around and head for home.

She would *not* cry.

"Well," said Father, sounding both entirely too lighthearted and quite near tears himself. "It seems a fine place."

"Yes." Catherine fought back the lump in her throat. "Very fine."

Indeed, it was. Four stories of neat, dark brick, lined with sash windows. There was a polished front door with a heavy bronze knocker—like something out of a story.

A fortnight ago, Father had written ahead and secured her a job here. Now, in the dim, watery streetlight, he told her, "You don't have to go."

She curled her hands together in her lap. Those were the words she'd said to her older brother the previous year, when he'd left to go work in the mines.

They'd had another year of poor harvest, and just two months back, a storm left their roof badly damaged.

Working at the city's newspaper, Catherine could make good money. Her family knew that as well as she did.

"I'll manage." Her voice came out high, trembling, and that wouldn't do. She said again, "I'll manage," and this time she spoke clear so as to make it true.

Father got down off the cart to tie up the horses. Catherine followed and reached up to stroke their necks.

"You must write," said Father. "And if you . . . if you wish to come home, for whatever reason, for *any* reason, Catherine—"

"I know." She suspected she wouldn't be seeing home again for some time. "I'll write."

He went around to retrieve her trunk from the back of the cart, and Catherine looked about the cobblestone street. Everything was rain-dark and slick; the smell of the river hung heavy in the air. It was so far from the green fields she knew, the clean, wet earth and the open sky. But it was home to her now.

She put her shoulders back, lifted her chin. Father appeared carrying her trunk, and she walked alongside him to knock on the door.

Two years had passed since then.

On the third floor of the print shop, Catherine sat at her desk in the room she shared with Bridget. Early-morning light shone over papers and inkpots through the leaded rectangles dividing the window glass. There wasn't time to go to bed after returning from the cemetery, and the piece of type she'd used to wake Mary Watt was still tucked in her coat. It was one of several Mr. Ainsworth had purchased from Stewart and Sons type foundry. A space, blank of any letter, crafted finely and made to be susceptible to magic.

She took up the letter she'd written to her family the night before and sealed it in an envelope, intent on bringing it to the post office later.

There were things she hadn't realized back when she'd started working here. The *Invercarn Chronicle* printed all sorts—local news and events, shipping news, a wide range of advertisements— but Catherine was often tasked with printing the obituaries. And for the first year, she hadn't worked any graveyard shifts. Since the recent establishment of the newspaper across town—the *Journal*—Mr. Ainsworth had introduced the farewell service as another means of profit. It wasn't something put into the advertisements, but word of mouth brought clients to the door.

Catherine stood up and attempted once more to scrub the grave dirt from her nails. Along with the desk and the washstand, there were two wrought-iron beds on either side of the room, two chests of drawers, two bedside tables spotted with dried candle wax. The wallpaper was peeling in parts where it met the ceiling, but altogether it was clean and dry, with a view of the street below. She pinned up her hair and smoothed her hands over her dress before making her way down to the print floor.

Light came in through the front windows, illuminating tall sheaves of paper and type cabinets, tins of ink and composing sticks. It lent a gilded quality to the room, as lovely as gold leaf, and gleamed across the iron hand presses. Printed sheets were hung to dry on racks along the ceiling. Work desks were piled with tidy stacks of paper, information to be typeset and printed. A few employees were already behind them, composing sticks in hand or scratching down notes with their dip pens.

Catherine took an ink-stained apron off a peg and slipped it on. She pulled free a type case from one of the cabinets, carrying it over to her desk. With the first of several death notices before her, she began composing type, adding letter after letter to the composing stick she held.

She said, "Good morning, Spencer," as her foreman walked by her desk.

He stopped. "Morning, Catherine. Last night went well, I take it?"

She nodded, holding back a yawn. Her shifts at the cemetery were infrequent enough she didn't much mind the sleeplessness that came part and parcel with the extra pay. Spencer folded his arms, his head tilted to the side. With his brown hair slicked back and the sleeves of his shirt rolled up, he looked neat and managerial despite his youth. He was twenty-two now, once a compositor himself, before Ainsworth promoted him. It was Spencer Carlyle who had answered the door when she had first arrived. She could still recall that younger version of him: the bright snap of ambition in his eyes.

He asked, "And are you well?"

Once, when Catherine was a child, she'd seen a man in town selling enchanted keys that could open any lock. She remembered how her grandmother had guided her away, telling her magic couldn't darn stockings or mend holes in the roof and it was best to attend to more practical things. Catherine's parents quite agreed. So did Catherine herself. Yet here she was, in the city, making use of it. At least it gave people a chance to say goodbye. Even so, her magic was faint and fleeting—she couldn't bring anyone back to life, after all. There were times she felt she ought to notice the absence of the hours she'd lost bringing back the dead, to be able to root around and find the hollows, like gaps from missing teeth.

She told Spencer, "Perfectly so," and cast her eyes back down to her work. He tapped his knuckles against the desk and left her to it.

The print floor was soon filled with mechanical clatter, the swish of paper, the squeak of ink rollers. Catherine conveyed the lines on her composing stick to a metal chase. There were blocks of wood, furniture pieces, made to hold the type in place. Once the news was typeset, she'd lock it up tight with a quoin key, before carrying the completed forme over to the press to be inked and printed.

From across the shop, the front door opened, the bell above it chiming as Jonathan Ainsworth stepped inside, a cold gust of city air following in his wake. Catherine set down her composing stick. His gray eyes alighted upon her as he removed his gloves. In his well-tailored day suit, he looked sharp as cut glass. "Follow me, please, Miss Daly."

Catherine folded her hands in front of her as she shadowed him up the stairs. The *Chronicle* was once a maze to her, the openness of the print floor at odds with the corridors and locked rooms of the upper floors. The staircase was steep and narrow, lit by gas lamps in brackets along the wall. The second floor was where they took meals, the third made up of rooms for lodging, while the fourth contained the newspaper's archives, as well as Ainsworth's office. It was a grand room positioned at the front of the building, with a fireplace and several armchairs, a large window overlooking the street. Through it, omnibuses and private carriages vied for space as they sped along, rattling to and fro on the narrow roads. They crossed the dark, winding stretch of the river by way of North Bridge, to where the copper-clad spires and peaked roofs of finer establishments prevailed.

Ainsworth slipped off his coat, placed it over the chair back, and took a seat behind his lacquered desk. He lived in that moneyed district across the river, and he'd likely one day have a fine monument built for himself in Rose Hill Cemetery. Only during working hours did he venture here, to the soot-black buildings and uneven cobbles of Old Town.

"Mr. Watt was pleased with your work last night," Ainsworth told her.

Catherine inclined her head. "I'm glad to hear it."

There were about a dozen employees at the print shop who could work the magic Ainsworth required for the farewell service. Without them, he wouldn't have business in the cemetery at all—unless, of course, he could manage the same sort of enchantment himself. Catherine had never asked him.

He ran a finger along the edge of his desk. It was covered with organized stacks of paper, journals, a bookkeeping ledger. He said, "I've another job for you, if you're interested in taking it."

Catherine raised her eyebrows. "What is it, sir?"

The clock on the fireplace mantel ticked steadily in the pause. Ainsworth opened his desk drawer, pulling out a sheet of paper. "Mr. Watt paid off his balance, but it wasn't coin he owed. He had information I've been after for quite some while." As Catherine watched, Ainsworth took up his pen and began to write. "There's an unmarked plot in the public cemetery—the grave of a coffin maker. A timepiece was buried with him. I'd like you to collect it."

Catherine swallowed. She knew what timepiece he was referring to. Most at the shop believed Ainsworth had been looking for it since starting up the farewell service. The device was rumored to bring the dead to life—not as ghostly likenesses of themselves, as her magic brought about, but truly living.

"You'll be paid for the retrieval, of course. And I want it done tonight." Setting his pen aside, he looked up.

Catherine already knew her answer.

"Certainly, sir," she said. "I'll see to it."

When he offered her the paper, she saw he'd written directions marking the grave's location. She folded it and tucked it into her apron pocket. "Will that be all?"

"Yes, Miss Daly, thank you."

She went back downstairs to resume her work, but at midday, she returned to her room on the third floor. She put Ainsworth's instructions away in her coat, located her bonnet and gloves, and fetched the letter she needed to post. The sky was clear blue beyond the window, like it was in her memories when she thought of her family home. It lightened her heart as she left the room and headed outside.